Murder at Bloodstone Bay

A Small-Town Cop Solves a Cold Case

Kathryn Danko

To Papa, who passed away in March 2024.
He never would have read this book; he hadn't picked up a novel since high school
but he would have been proud anyway.

Grazie!

Grazie means "thank you" in Italian.

Grazie to my readers! I cannot express enough how much I appreciate your support of this author. Writing a book is fun; publishing a book is scary. Will anyone read it? Will they like it? Will they suggest it to others? Many of you did that with my first book, _Murder at Capri Cottage._ And you're back! My sincere thanks.

Grazie to my team! My beta readers, those folks who cheer me on while offering critical comments for improvement: Karen Cremeans, Diana (Mama) Danko, Connie Dixon, Stacey Gumbert, Carol Hill, Tia Pfeiffer, and Barbara Wood. Your input is invaluable.

To my editor, Cindy Davis, I am so grateful I found you. I appreciate our partnership and your courage to tell me when I suck. Just kidding, but I am a much better writer with you in my corner! And Elizabeth Mackey, my cover designer, is a rock star.

My writing tribe keeps me going when I would rather hang out in my jammie pants with a Bloody Mary. _Grazie_ to Sally, Lou, Denise W and Denise R, Lou, plus the other talented, generous, and supportive women who drop into our session from time to time.

Last _grazie_ to Mama, who is my biggest fan and champion.

Chapter One

The two mayors ambushed her—not physically, of course—but mentally.

"You want me to do what?"

Her anxiety threatened to ooze onto her desk, spill onto the floor, and run past the town mascot, Bella the chicken.

"Find a missing person," Mayor Roberto Spinosi said for the second time.

"I believe all the residents in Celestino Village are accounted for," Delaney Becker answered, as she reined in her anxiety. Breathe in, breathe out. "Besides, you let me think this meeting was about the upcoming Seahorse Festival."

Mayor William Workman watched the verbal ping-pong and attempted to slow it down. "Shall we pause for coffee?" He gestured to the carafe and three mugs sitting on Becker's desk.

While Mayor Spinosi made a production of pouring and serving coffee, Becker mentally recounted her career as a Chief of Police: 500+ traffic stops, 300+ thefts, 100+ altercations at the senior community, usually involving a cane whack to the head over the last piece of peach pie. Speaking of peach pie, she was hungry. Where was she? Oh, 50+ lost or wandering animals, including a blind llama, numerous situations with drunk people, and one murder investigation.

One. And her solving it was a fluke. Dumb luck. A gift from her Fairy Godmother.

And no missing persons. Zero.

Mayor Spinosi added cream to Becker's coffee and set the mug in front of her. A short, portly man with unruly jet back hair, it was slicked back in the style popular in Italian mafia movies. At first blush, he could have played the lead mobster role: beady eyes in a face with dark stubble, gold chain around his neck, an untucked bowling shirt over tailored pants.

When he smiled, however, his face lit up like a gambler whose pony just won big. His face crinkled, and he had a dimple in his left cheek, with laugh lines around the corners of his mouth.

He showed his winning smile. "There you go, Chief. Sure to make you smile."

By comparison, Mayor William (not Bill or Billy) Workman was tall and lean with light brown hair and steel gray-blue eyes. He wore a tailored suit, navy pinstripe, with a light blue tie, white shirt, blue checkered socks, and Prada laced-up leather oxfords. Shoes and fingernails buffed. He rarely smiled, and when he did, he resembled a great white shark. An attorney by day, he trotted out the smile for cross-examinations; otherwise, he hid it behind his pleasant and proper demeanor.

Mayor Spinosi sat down. "As I was saying, word of you solving the cold case, you know, the prostitute who was murdered, reached William in Silver Hill, so that's why he's asked for help."

Becker wanted to roll her eyes, but held back. Everyone in a five-county area had heard of the case, her only murder investigation.,. The Eastern Shore of Maryland, a rural part of the state with tiny villages and towns, chicken farms, soybeans, corn and sea-side resort cities, had the last place ranking in the state for murders and serious crimes. A murder, even a cold case, was ginormous news on the Shore.

Mayor Spinosi took a sip of coffee and continued, "He's very impressed with our work."

Our work? She stifled a laugh. He wasn't even the mayor when she solved the murder case.

Becker nodded at William. "Thank you, but that doesn't mean I'm qualified to find a missing person. And we're so busy I can hardly keep up with my chief duties." She gestured around her office. Her desk was a paper scrapyard, heaps piled here and there, the filing cabinets, and, before she cleaned up this morning, on the chairs and floor.

"And Mayor Spinosi, with all due respect to your role as my supervisor, I'm not sure you could convince the town council and tax payers of Celestino Village for funds to solve a crime outside of city limits."

"I thought you might say that." His dimple winked at her. "First, the woman was last seen in our village, not Silver Hill."

"Okay," Becker said, "that muddies the waters a bit, but as you both know, the Maryland State Police are better equipped to handle a missing person, regardless of where the person disappeared. This sounds like a case for the Criminal Investigation Bureau. I have the number."

She fumbled with her phone as Bella the chicken jumped on her lap. Becker absentmindedly stroked the bird's unruly feathers, which curled and twisted in all directions.

"Ah," Mayor Workman said, a hint of condensation in his voice. "The town mascot. Very unusual, to say the least."

"She has several million followers online," Mayor Spinosi said. "Our merchants have seen a 10% increase in sales during our 'Pic with a Chick' day, held monthly. Seems everyone wants a photograph with a fluffy white bird."

"Clever," Mayor Workman said, an indulgent half-smile on his face.

"As I was saying, the number for the CIB is—" Becker said.

"That won't be necessary, Chief. We want you, not MSP."

Becker's face was on fire. "Why? I've never investigated a missing person. One solved cold case murder doesn't make me an expert on violent crimes."

"We believe you understand the local...issues. And you know the missing woman."

She should ask for the disappeared woman's name, but Becker was intent on stopping this train wreck. "I can't believe the town council would approve our handling of a crime from a neighboring city, regardless of the place the individual went missing."

Mayor Spinosi looked smug. "Yesterday, the town council approved the funding in a special executive session. We collectively feel you are the right person to lead the effort in this multi-jurisdictional case." He paused, looking self-satisfied at his use of a seven-syllable word. "It will be good for both Celestino Village and Silver Hill if we clear the case."

Well shit. Becker rubbed her brow. "We're understaffed now. I have an officer off on short-term medical leave, and another on vacation for the next three weeks, visiting her family in Puerto Rico."

"We want you to do this." Mayor Spinosi's eyes flashed.

Becker's eyes flashed back, and she took a breath. Quickly, she thought of another tactic. "With all due respect to both of you, there's a reason you picked me. I'm assuming part of it is my ability to manage people and processes. Correct?" She had no idea where she was going with this, but it felt like she was headed in the right direction, and they both nodded in agreement. "Frankly, I don't feel comfortable jumping into this case before I chart out a course." She didn't know how to chart out anything, but they didn't know it. "So, I'll need a week or two to do that. Is that fair?"

Partial defeat on their faces, they simultaneously deflated: Mayor Spinosi's body like a wet loaf of bread in a chair, and Mayor Workman's rigid posture curving a bit, matching the downward arc of his lips.

Mayor Workman said, "It's fair. A week it is." His lips broke into his famous shark smile, and his eyes bore into hers, saying, *I know you're buying time. Good luck! I'm going to win.*

She smiled back, her competitive spirit already plotting how to get out of this damn mess. "Yes, that is sufficient."

"Before we leave, would it be beneficial to know a bit about the missing woman so you can consider how to solve the case?" Mayor Workman asked.

He's good, Becker thought. She reluctantly said, "Yes, Mr. Mayor."

"A young woman went missing in 2017 after a tumultuous youth comprised of acting out inappropriately, surrounding herself with the underbelly of the human race, and imbibing alcohol at establishments known for fist-fights and fentanyl."

Becker stifled a smile at his command of the English language, the formalization of every statement and expression. Who used terms like "underbelly of the human race"?

Then she realized who he was talking about. "Mayor Workman, are you referring to Michelle?"

She met his eyes, filled with sadness and longing, the shark's smile long gone. "Yes, Chief, I want you to investigate the disappearance of my daughter."

Chapter Two

Becker sat on her deck and took a sip of Brunello di Montalcino, her favorite wine. She had paid too much for it and had been saving it for something special, but the meeting with the mayors had rattled her. She tried to forget the request to find Michelle Workman as she swirled the robust red wine around in her mouth, the deliciousness like a ballerina in motion.

Thoughts of William Workman kept returning. She recalled the pain in his eyes when he spoke about his missing daughter. Although she didn't have children of her own, she could sort of relate. Her beloved companion, Kevin, was her best friend, and she loved him madly; contemplating life without him made her beyond sad. Her eyes teared up as she patted his fur, sticking up here and there, and even though he was "just a dog", he probably loved her better than any other soul on the planet.

And she couldn't imagine a world without her "adopted" brother, Fernando. Friends since they were wee kids. He loved her with a protectiveness that humbled her. And he was so proud of her, he would be president of her fan club, if she had one.

The longer she thought about it, the more she understood losing a daughter was beyond her emotional comprehension. Becker felt a sympathy pang in her chest, then pushed it aside. She needed to spend less time empathizing for William and more time figuring out how to get out of the case.

Thankfully, the phone rang, rescuing her from her musings.

A whisper came through her speaker. It sounded like her mama. "Can't believe it...Nonna...surprise."

"Mama, is that you? Are you talking about those Nonni biscotti cookies again? Are they on sale at a good price?"

No answer. A garbled voice, then the line went dead. She called her mama back.

"Heller, this is Rosa Becker's house. Whaddaya want?"

A smile broke across Becker's face. Big and squishy. "Nonna? Is that you?" Kevin picked up on the joy in her voice and let out a woof and a fart.

"Yepper. Del, put down that wineglass and come say 'heller' to me." Her grandmother was one of only two people on the earth that shortened her name. And the only person who could rattle her mama. "I just rolled into town a few minutes ago. The RV is parked out front and your mother is having a cow—no, having a bull. They're bigger, right? Anyways, the RV is leaking oil so there's a black puddle underneath Big Betty...not that I think that's what she's mad about. It's prolly the rainbow paint. I'm not gay, mind you, but why should they get a rainbow? We straight people have nothing. Well, maybe we have the color gray. You been to Walmart lately? That's the color of choice for heteros."

Becker stifled a laugh. "I'll be right over."

"I can come get ya. No skin off my bum."

"I'll walk. Wouldn't want Big Betty to leak oil all over the streets of Celestino Village."

***

The RV was a rolling psychedelic rainbow, with "Honk If You're In The Mood" painted on the driver's side in twelve-inch-high letters. A converted school bus, it had patches of rust around the wheel wells, and it stank like diesel oil, fast-food hamburgers, and spaghetti sauce. It took up most of the city block and completely ate up the view of Mama's house and gardens. Becker walked around the side of the bus near the loading door, and Big Betty started playing *Let My Love Open the Door* by Peter Townsend.

A car rumbled to a stop on the street. She peeked around the hood to see her boyfriend, Mack Brown, standing there, taking in Big Betty. He was in some sort of trance, eyes huge and round, and when she walked around the vehicle, he startled.

He got out of the car and gave her a sweet kiss. "Hello, beautiful. What the heck is this?"

"It's Nonna's ride. She just came into town."

"Your stories about her don't do her justice."

Becker eyed the RV. "Obviously."

"I'm glad I got to see you, but I have to run. I'll call you later."

He gave her another kiss that made her tingly all over as he whispered, "I miss you, Del."

As his truck drove away, she shook off the wooziness and then walked through the garden and in to the back door. Mama sat at the table, a large glass of amber liquid in front of her. Becker took a sip of the amaretto, then raised her eyebrows at her mama, who usually enjoyed the cocktail out of a small jelly jar. Mama sat rigidly, like she was afraid to move, and her bright eyes darted around the kitchen, taking in the utter chaos; it seemed all the contents of the cabinets were on the countertops. Bowls, baking ingredients, utensils, flour, measuring cups, pots, and pans surrounded Nonna. She was rolling out dough for ravioli as she shook her ample butt to *Fly me to the Moon,* crooned by Frank Sinatra. The irony was not lost on Becker.

"Hi Nonna!"

She whirled around with a knife in her hand and lunged at Becker, who yipped and sidestepped just in time. Nonna looked at the knife like it had magically appeared in her hand. "Oh, *mio piccolo sole*, my little sunshine, I didn't mean to kill you. If I did, that there knife would be in your gut to the hilt. I just wanna hug. Wait, that's about the same thing for you, yes?"

Becker, a non-hugger, smiled. "I'll make an exception for you!"

Her grandmother set the knife on the counter and hugged Becker, picking her up and whirling her around in the tight kitchen, accidentally brushing a bag of flour off the counter. It hit the floor with a huge 'poof'. The white stuff wafted up like fog on a dance floor. She and Nonna giggled. Mama groaned. And something growled.

Nonna was a head taller than Becker, and twice as wide. Becker shared her unruly black-brown hair and fierceness, but Nonna's bright blue eyes and beak nose were her own. She was wearing a tight red t-shirt that read *Italian Grandma* but translated as 'Italian Grand' because her big boobs hid some of the letters. She had on a pair of red striped pants, maybe pajama or maybe lounging, with extra fabric that hung in pleats. Did they sell clothes made of excess circus tent material these days?

Nonna put her down and pinched her cheeks. "You look hot, as the young people say, but too skinny. We need to fatten you up. It's important to have a little reserve if you get pregnant. I hope you are seeing someone because I need a grandchild. I'm not going to be alive forever, you know. Lester can only fit the bill for so long."

Becker looked at the floor. A gray bird with stripes gave her the side-eye. "Lester?"

"Lester the Lover," the bird answered.

"He's an African Gray parrot. I won him in a Texas Hold'em play-off at a campground in Ohio. The dipshit I was playing against went all in and lost, and I got Lester." Nonna made the sign of the cross. "Bless me and Lester, but I've wanted to let him fly out the window almost every day. He can be good company, but he's like Erma Crestfield. Do you remember her, Rosa?" Mama nodded. "Erma never shuts up. She's on husband number..." Nonna looked at Mama, who held up her hand. "Five. The woman probably sucks in bed, not in a good way, and jabbers the whole time."

Becker laughed. No wonder why her mama had an oversized glass of amaretto. Her house already had a zoo-like atmosphere, circus tent pants and all, and her grandmother had only been there a few hours.

Becker poured a glass of wine, a pinot grigio, and kissed her mama on the cheek near her pinched lips. She sat down. "What brings you to town, Nonna?"

Nonna had resumed her dough-cutting and gestured wildly with the knife. "So, six months ago I'm in, ah, I think Idaho or Iowa, not sure. They look about the same, and Big Betty breaks down. A nice young Italian guy, I have his name for you to call because he's definite husband material, tows me to his garage. A nice garage, by the way, with four clean, well-lit bays. I would imagine his house is clean since his business is. Probably picks up his underwear and puts dirty dishes in the dishwasher after he eats. Oh, and the waiting area has Fig Newtons. I love a Fig Newton." She scratched her face, leaving a flour smudge. "Anyways, I decided two things as I was munchin' on the Newtons. One, I needed to paint Betty something different from shit brown, and two, I missed my family and wanted to come home."

"Why did it take you six months to get here?"

Her grandma blushed. "I met someone."

Lester the parrot squawked, "Kiss, kiss, kiss mee!"

Mama looked like she was going to faint.

Nonna said, "I don't wanna talk about it. Let's talk about you! Are you dating anyone?"

Becker rolled her eyes. "Yes, Nonna."

"A good Italian boy?"

"He's a great guy, a marine biologist, who also owns an art gallery. He also has an adorable daughter named Bea."

"Does this whale hunter have a name?"

"Yes. Mack Brown." Becker changed topics so Nonna wouldn't hound her over dinner. "How's the ravioli coming? I'm hungry."

An hour later, they sat down to dinner enjoying the pillowy pasta stuffed with spinach and feta cheese, while Lester the parrot repeated, "Feed me, feed me, feed me," a hundred times. Becker rubbed her brow. At least Kevin, hoping for a morsel, just stared at you during dinner, and kept his gob closed.

"Mama, how was class today at Celestino Village? What did you make?"

Nonna had pushed three raviolis into her mouth. She looked like a hamster with her cheeks puffed out. "Huh?"

Mama sat up straight and smiled. "I teach cooking classes at the retirement village. We perfected meatballs today."

Nonna swallowed, but still had remnants of food in her mouth when she said, "Retirement village? Any hot guys?"

"I thought you were seeing someone."

Nonna wiped her mouth, smearing tomato sauce on her chin. "We're not exclusive. He's a big teddy bear, but there's room in my life for other animals, if you know what I mean."

Not for the first time, Becker wondered how her Mama was so genteel and sweet, understated and mannerly, when her grandmother was clearly not.

"Del, as much as I want to be close to you and Rosa, I need a place to park Big Betty. I'm guessing your officers will notice her at the curb and give me a ticket or something. I saw two campgrounds on the internet." Nonna pulled a brand-new iPhone from an expensive designer bag. Becker raised her eyebrows. Nonna was on a retiree's budget. Huh. "Let's see, there's Sea Salt Oceanside, and the Spotted Dick Resort. Who names their business Spotted Dick?"

"The guy who owns it is British. He thought it would be cute to name it Spotted Dick after a pudding in the UK. Unfortunately, a few years back, a bunch of campers contracted some sort of communicable disease and it brought a whole new meaning to the name. I understand it's a fun place if a bit run down and seedy. Sea Salt Oceanside is the better choice. Clean. Family-oriented."

Nonna nodded. "Spotted Dick's it is."

Chapter Three

Becker's weekends off were sporadic, so she made the best of them, doing what made her happy. She gravitated toward stress-free pursuits like tending her mama's garden, going to the beach, or browsing antique shops. Today, Becker drove to Silver Hill with Kevin as her co-pilot, his head out the window, ears and tongue flapping in the wind. She was curious about Michelle Workman's hometown, even if she was still working on ways to get out of the investigation.

Celestino Village, fanciful and romantic, was founded by Italians. The buildings were ornate, with dentil molding and gargoyles. It even featured a fake Rialto Bridge, a scaled-down replica of the one in Venice, Italy. By comparison, Silver Hill, organized and practical, was laid out in a typical grid pattern, the downtown area near the river, and mansions ringing the commerce district. The English settled it as a port for trade with America before the War of Independence, and in Becker's opinion, lacked the soulfulness and energy of her hometown.

Silver Hill had a souvenir shop, bakery, specialty olive oil store, an old firehouse turned into a funky clothing and jewelry establishment, and a diner called Sunny Side Up where Becker ate a mouthwatering mushroom and brie quiche for breakfast. It was a warm fall day, so she sat at an outside table, Kevin lying underneath, hoping for scraps.

Nonna called. "I'm loving the Dick. My next-door neighbor is a retired blaster from the mining industry. He's teaching me how to make a small bomb."

"NONNA! Please do not make a bomb!"

A woman seated at the next table gasped, scrambled to her feet, and scurried down the sidewalk, her half-eaten western omelet forgotten. She looked over her shoulder at least five times until she rounded a corner and Becker lost sight of her.

Becker lowered her voice. "I'll be by later today to say hello. In the meantime, teach Lester the parrot how to say 'No explosives in or near Big Betty'."

As she finished breakfast and contemplated her day, she felt eyes on her, turned her head, and nodded at a man standing a few feet away. He had a buzz-cut, graying at the temples, and piercing blue eyes. Law enforcement, Becker thought. He walked over and Kevin growled. He was a big man, tall and meaty, with a scowl that took up his entire face.

"Sheriff Paul Atkins, Ma'am. And you are?"

Becker stood up, feeling like a dwarf next to him. She stuck out her hand, and he ignored it. "Chief of Police Delaney Becker, of Celestino Village."

"Thought so. What are you doing in my town?" His scowl turned menacing, so she scowled back. So much for pleasantries and a warm welcome; two could play this game.

"Sightseeing. Is there a problem with that?"

"When you threaten the locals with bomb-making, it is."

Becker's face was hot. "I didn't threaten anybody."

"I don't appreciate you being here, and I sure as hell don't approve of you nosing around in our business. This investigation thing is bullshit. I told William the same thing."

The guy was blunt as a sledgehammer and she reacted before she remembered she would not take the damned case. She matched his tone with, "I didn't ask to investigate Michelle's disappearance. I would have turned it down. My mayor, and yours as well, ordered me to do so. So, if you have any issues, take it up with Mayor Workman. Are we done here?"

He opened his mouth to say something but was interrupted by a woman behind him. "Oh Paul, a word about plans for the Seahorse Festival?"

Sheriff Atkins stood aside as a curvy brunette sidled up to him, patting his arm. Becker stared, confusion fogging her brain. Why was she supposed to be searching for Michelle when the woman was standing right here?

"Mooney, not now. I'll come by tomorrow when I'm on duty."

Mooney? Not Michelle?

"Oh hi, I'm Monica Workman, but everyone calls me Mooney." Ah, Becker thought, Michelle's older sister. Mooney bent down to scratch Kevin's head. "What a good boy! And a handsome one at that!" She stuck out her hand for Becker to shake.

"Hello, Mooney. I'm Delaney Becker. My side-kick is Kevin."

"I recognize your name. You're the woman who is going to find Michelle. I can feel it. The tarot card reading I did for myself this morning confirmed my intuition. Why don't you come to my place? We can have some tea and get to know each other? I can read your palm if you'd like and I can talk with Kevin to see how he's feeling today. I can tell he's a little gassy."

"Um..." Becker was at a loss for words.

"Oh, I'm guessing you haven't met a psychic like me. Let's start slow with tea." She grabbed Becker's arm, pulling her away from Sheriff Atkins. "Bye, Paul. I look forward to seeing you tomorrow."

They reluctantly trailed her down the street. Mooney walked fast with a gentle step that made her almost appear to be floating, her gauzy dress swirling around her legs. They followed her into a doorway under an *Apothecary and Amulets* sign. Becker smelled sage, lavender, other herbs, having a hard time differentiating them from Mooney's perfume. Patchouli, Becker thought, as she looked around the space. Stones were scattered on tables and cabinets: amethyst, quartz, obsidian, citrine, many she had never seen before. Colorful scarves and textiles hung from the walls; a vintage damask couch filled with bohemian pillows sat at the back of the space. Mooney gestured her to it while she bustled about making tea, humming Phantom of the Opera.

"Delaney, I hope you like chamomile tea. It can be soothing. Based on yours and Paul's body language, you could use some calming right now."

"Mooney, I'm glad to meet you. I appreciative you saved me from having to punch Sheriff Atkins in the nose, but I have bad news. I will not be investigating Michelle's disappearance."

"We'll see. For now, let's just sit for a minute and visit."

Becker rubbed her brow. She moved pillows aside, dropping on the couch while Kevin made a circle then plopped at her feet. "Please call me Becker. And thank you for the tea."

"Okay, Becker it is. Don't let Paul bother you. He's like a territorial bull elephant, but he has a soft side."

"I believe you." Becker wanted to tell Mooney what an ass Paul was, but she bit her tongue. Professionalism and all of that.

"No, you don't; it doesn't take a psychic to read the doubt in your eyes." Mooney gave her a conspiratorial smile. "Enough about Mr. Unfriendly. Tell me about you!"

Becker didn't talk about herself. She was usually the one asking questions, rarely sharing her personal life. Where to start?

"I can tell I've made you uncomfortable." Mooney poured tea from an electric tea pot into pottery mugs, hand thrown on a potter's wheel. Becker spied a shelf of them; a bright orange and yellow one caught her eye. She wanted to buy it and take it home. Mooney surprised Becker by getting off the couch and walking over to the exact piece she was drooling over. She picked it up, a dreamy smile on her lips, then handed it to Becker. "A gift."

Becker protested, but Mooney waved her off. "I made the mug, and it chose you. It also connects us, and will help you find Michelle."

Becker wanted to tell her she would not look for Michelle, nor did she believe a piece of pottery could identify a human to hang out with...but instead she said, "Thank you, Mooney. It's beautiful."

Mooney pulled a homemade dog biscuit from her dress pocket, gave it to Kevin, and sat down. "I'm happy you're happy — Where was I? Oh, I was asking about you but you squirmed in your seat so I'll go first. I grew up here and went to college at Hood, expecting to continue to law school and become an attorney like my father. I was taking a pre-law class when Michelle went missing. Not only did I find the course to be utterly...uninspiring, but my chakras became unbalanced. Do you know what that feels like? "Becker hadn't a clue, so she remained silent. "Anyway, I realized I was pursuing a career to make my parents happy. Once I faced that, I settled on a business degree. When I graduated, I worked in merchandizing in New York. I hated my job, and big city life negatively affected my aura." She took a sip of her tea. "I've always loved nature; as a kid, I charted the moon phases and celebrated the full moon, thus the nickname Mooney. So, thirteen months ago, I left the concrete jungle and came back home."

"You like the country."

"Yes. Rural America speaks to me. It's where I belong. I felt it was a good place to open my shop, despite some of my family member's opinions on the subject. Speaking of which, have you met Mimi yet?"

Becker blinked at the change in topic, her brain scrambling to keep up with Mooney's bunny-trail communication style. She finally said, "No, but I've heard stories."

"Well, I'm sure she'll tell you all about my bizarre choice of careers when you interview her. She was mortified when I opened this shop.

She told me, and I quote: 'First Michelle disappears, and then you become a psychic. God help me, but I have no idea why I deserve such madness from my family'."

They both shook their heads. Mooney did not seem the least bit bothered talking about her high-society mother, so Becker said, "I understand your mother is very protective of the family."

Mooney pursed her lips. "No, she's protective of her identity, her reputation, and how she is perceived in town. If you don't mind, can we save our discussion about Her Highness for another day? I'm having a wonderful time with you and don't want to ruin it."

Becker nodded.

"Okay, your turn."

Becker talked about her childhood in Celestino Village, losing her father at an early age, and the rift between her and her sister. She shared memories of the police academy, and her rise to the Chief role in Celestino Village. She told Mooney about her Mama, Nonna, and her boyfriend, Mack Brown.

"You're an artist?"

Becker stared at her. "What makes you say that?"

"You use words that are vivid. Visual. I just assumed you paint or sketch or doodle in margins."

"I dabble." Becker was a painter, a secret hobby that started as a way for her to manage her anxiety. Later, it developed into a thriving business; her beach scene watercolors were in homes across the globe; her savings account was flush because of it. She still kept it hidden, though, concerned her talents as an artist could tarnish her reputation as a tough small-town cop.

Mooney gave her a knowing smile. "Uh-huh. I'll stop prying."

The bell over the door tinkled and Mooney yelled out, "Welcome to A&A! If you need help, please ask!"

Becker looked at her phone; she had spent over an hour with Mooney. "I didn't realize I've been here for so long. You have a business to run."

"I would rather talk to you, Becker! But you're right." They stood up. "I want to give you something else before you leave." She picked up two stones from the counter, then handed them to Becker. "The orange one, carnelian, is for Kevin. It's good for digestion. Put it in his bed." Becker stifled a groan. Kevin let out a soft woof, and Mooney winked at her.

"The bloodstone is for you, for courage and strength. You have plenty of both, even though you doubt yourself. But it can't hurt to have it in your pocket while you look for my sister."

Chapter Four

S omeone was watching her. Becker glanced up from her book without moving her head. Since the rumors in town started circulating about her investigating Michelle Workman's disappearance, which she would not do, she had felt eyes on her on at least four occasions. She covertly scanned the nondescript parking lot beyond the pots of herbs and flowers on her deck. Her eyes wandered past the pavement, to the cemetery, to a mound of dirt with dying and dead flower bouquets piled up like sorrowful memories. Becker said a silent prayer for the newly deceased hoping all the hype about heaven was true.

She continued to scan the horizon and came up empty. Maybe her visit with Mooney and hearing of "feeling people" was rubbing off on her, she mused.

She was startled by at the knock on her door. "Come in!" Becker yelled, setting down the murder mystery novel, one of six or seven this month. Becker devoured books almost as fast as she ate Mama's lasagna. She had an innate ability to identify the murderer in the initial pages of any book. If only I had the same talent in real life, she thought.

It had been a busy week. She was looking forward to the weekend to recharge and relax. She had held off Mayor Spinosi by conveniently being out of the office when he scheduled a visit, and she ignored many voice mail messages. She'd have to deal with the mayors soon, but this afternoon was for sharing cop stories and camaraderie with her best friend, Keisha Carter. And this evening was for visiting with her steady boyfriend, Mack Brown.

Keisha came in. "Girl? Where are you?"

"Back deck! Grab some wine for us and come on out!" Kevin's butt wriggled in excitement. Keisha always brought a toy or gift for the mutt.

Keisha stepped onto the deck with a glass of wine in each hand, and a toy under her right elbow. She wore a loose t-shirt—the outline of her shoulder holster and Sig Sauer noticeable beneath the top—raggedy jeans, and a pair of black combat boots. Her afro was trimmed close to her head, and she wore no makeup or jewelry. Becker loved her no-nonsense style; she was a natural beauty but hid behind an androgynous persona.

She gave Becker a big smile as she handed over a glass of wine. Becker took a sip, tasting tart cherries and herbs. She smiled back at Keisha. "Hey, second-best cop in the state."

Keisha laughed at the running joke. "First," she said. "You're second." She took out a fuzzy hedgehog toy from under her arm and a drinking straw from her back pocket then set them both on the floor. Kevin chose the straw first, ran to the living room, added it to a pile on the floor in the corner next to the bookshelf. Other dogs hunted ducks or truffles; her canine had an obsession with straws, frequently presenting them to Bella the chicken, who also hoarded the damn things.

Kevin walked back to Keisha to take the toy, his tail wagging. Becker said, "You love dogs. I can't believe you've been to animal control a dozen times and haven't found a best friend."

"I know. The staff over there are super and the animals are well cared for, but I hate going, seeing all the dogs in kennels, their eyes full of hope of going home with someone. I hate leaving without a furry friend."

"So, what's stopping you?"

Keisha fiddled with her wineglass. "Great use of Interrogation 101, Becker. Get to the core in one question."

Becker shrugged, took a sip of wine, and stayed silent.

After a moment, Keisha looked up from her glass. "We work such long hours..."

"That's an excuse. There are many options for doggy day care. You have me and Mama, and I'm sure Molly could help from time to time. Then there is the 'Bark and Bone' just outside of town. Kevin stays there a few times a month getting the zoomies with the other dogs."

"I'll think about it, Becker...really." Keisha touched the basil plant next to her chair, releasing the spicy fragrance. "On to other subjects. How does it feel to be Ms. Newspaper Celebrity for a day?"

Becker stared at her. "What are you talking about?"

"Only that you and Michelle Workman will be household names, if you both aren't already."

"Excuse me?" Becker leaned forward so suddenly that Keisha flattened her body against the chair.

"Whoa, Becker. Don't shoot the messenger."

"How do you know about Michelle Workman?"

"The mayors put out a joint press release. Look it up on the Celestino Village Press website."

Muttering curse words, Becker scrolled on her phone, found the article and started reading.

Chief of Police Delaney Becker Tapped to find Missing Woman
Mayor Roberto Spinosi, of Celestino Village, and Mayor
William Workman, of Silver Hill, announced today an investigation into the disappearance of Michelle Workman, daughter of Mayor Workman, who went missing in 2017.
"Chief Becker is uniquely qualified to find Michelle because of her local knowledge, her positive relationship with the

Maryland State Police, and her ability to solve cold cases, like the recent Casino Prostitute Case," Mayor Spinosi said.

Mayor Workman added, "I have the utmost trust and confidence Chief Becker will locate my daughter and bring her home."

The two mayors work closely during the year on many initiatives, including the annual Seahorse Festival. This is the first time the two towns are working jointly on a matter of law enforcement.

If anyone has information about Michelle or related to the investigation, please contact Chief Delaney Becker.

Becker scowled at her phone before slamming it on the table, fury rising from her belly. She rubbed her brow, then patted Kevin on the head as he chewed on the fuzzy hedgehog, as she tried to get her anger under control.

Her voice was staccato. "This makes me furious. Neither the mayors nor a reporter at the Press contacted me. It pisses me off the mayors made it public without my knowledge. I haven't even agreed to do it yet! We just met last week, for God's sake. And the article makes me out to be some sort of miracle worker with missing people. It's utter bullshit."

They sat in silence, Becker fuming. Kevin put his paw on her leg and made a soft woof.

"I'm going to call Mayor Spinosi now and resign."

Keisha wisely kept her mouth shut leaving her thoughts unspoken.

"I mean, I won't be bullied into an investigation I'm not qualified to do, and am not interested in doing." Becker's foot tapped to an internal anxiety beat. "It's ludicrous for me to even be involved; I've never investigated a missing person in my life."

Keisha said, "Perhaps not, but you can do it. You figured out the Casino Prostitute Case. Tap into that, Becker."

Becker whirled on her friend and banged her fist on the arm of her chair. "Dumb luck."

"That's not true," Keisha said softly, "and you know it. I was with you every step of the way. We worked hard. If you want to attribute your success to dumb luck, have at it. My success was because of solid police work."

Keisha's voice quivered; Becker mentally kicked herself. The last thing she wanted to do was upset her best friend. Becker nodded, her foot-taps slowing down. "You're right. I apologize." She sighed. "Thank you for the vote of confidence, Keisha."

They each took a sip of wine. After a few moments, Keisha said, "Tell me you will not quit."

Becker felt the anger well again, but she channeled it. "Hell no. I'm not letting them win."

"That's my fierce friend."

Becker blew out a breath. "You'll help?"

"You know it."

"I have little to go on. I read my file, a paltry five pages, that's like starting from scratch."

Keisha smiled at her. "Would not take the case, but still reviewed your file?"

Becker shrugged, giving her a small smile in return. "Curiosity... Let's see. The youngest daughter of four, all girls, family very gentrified and protective of their standing in the community. Wealthy and proper. Michelle, not so much. She was an individualist who didn't fit in, and didn't want to." Becker paused, thinking of the time Michelle set up a stand in front of the house to sell Gatorade because 'lemonade sucked'. "Over the years, the rift got bigger as she moved further away from her family's expectations."

Becker set down her wineglass and rubbed her face. "The family dynamic at the time she disappeared was contentious, brought on by a bogus arrest for prostitution. I have no proof, mind you, but I would bet her parents, probably her father, fabricated the whole thing as an attempt to reel Michelle in. But it backfired."

"Geez, if your intuition is correct, that is sad as hell. What type of father would purposely have his daughter arrested?"

They sat in silence for a minute.

"How will you approach it?" Keisha asked.

"I'll bully the mayors into letting me hire Molly Zimmer, for starters."

Molly was a forensic scientist, recently moved to Celestino Village from Pennsylvania, where she worked with the Philadelphia Police Department.

"Tit for tat, since they bullied me into taking this case with their news article." They smiled at each other, knowing Becker wouldn't do it, professionalism and all of that. "I need backup so hopefully I can get Guido Tucci to agree to an Assistant Chief role. I'll need coverage because I'll be spending a bunch of time in Silver Hill, and won't get much support from the sheriff down there. He's already told me to 'get off his lawn'. I'd call him an ass, but that would be too kind."

"Huh. You'd think he would be at least cordial. After all, Mayor Workman is his boss and the father of the missing girl. Seems like political suicide to be a butt-head."

"Agreed. I have no clue as to why he was so confrontational. Perhaps it's an ego thing? I guess I'd be miffed if Mayor Spinosi brought some-one in around me...but I'd also get over it pretty quickly."

"What can I do?" Keisha asked.

"Take the case as lead investigator?" Becker joked.

Keisha told her no, but she'd be willing to go to Silver Hill for a few days. "I've got some vacation to burn. Want me to do some reconnaissance?"

"Sure. I am interested in people she hung out with, maybe starting in high school? Yearbooks, articles about her, that sort of thing. Stay under the radar so we don't upset the sheriff more than we have to."

***

Becker wandered into the *Grand Girasole*, Mack Brown's art gallery, at dusk. The indoor space was magical, with illuminated art pieces around the room, creating a soft yellow glow. Becker headed towards the patio in the back, where she found Mack resting on an L-shaped outdoor couch under a pergola strung with twinkling lights. A carafe of coffee and a bottle of her favorite Italian Cream sat on a table in front of him.

He turned around and gave her a dimpled smile. "Del! I'm so glad we could steal a few minutes together. Our schedules have been crazy lately." He patted the spot next to him then kissed her cheek. She watched him pour her coffee, taking in his wavy black hair, toned muscles, and strong jawline. What a handsome man.

"What?" he asked, when he caught her staring.

"Oh nothing, just glad to be here. It's been a rough day."

"Speaking of which, when were you going to tell me about the missing person investigation?"

Her frustration amped up ten notches at the question. Mack was one of only a handful of men she had dated in her thirty years. She was a novice at this "sharing-my-life" thing. Progress had been slow; she let him down before but was doing better. She was a private person by nature and opening up to him, or anyone for that matter, was difficult.

"I'm as surprised as you are." She told him about the meeting with the mayors, her reluctance, and the unexpected news article. "Needless to say, I'm not happy about it, but I can't find a way to wriggle out."

"I know how busy you are, so don't take this the wrong way, but I can't imagine a more honorable thing than to find a missing person, someone's child. If we ever lost Bea, I would want someone like you on the case. You're persistent and driven. And you have exceptional leadership skills. And you're detail-minded and thorough. And...a great kisser."

She laughed covering his hand with hers. "I feel like I'm out of practice in the kissing department."

He raised an eyebrow and leaned in. "How long do you have? We can hone those skills now."

"Shush," she said, as their lips met.

Chapter Five

S potted Dick Resort was worse than Becker remembered. The place smelled like marijuana. The people looked like a rag-tag cast from a walking dead movie. Not all of them, of course, including Nonna. She resembled a pumpkin today with her orange top, short tangerine skirt, and little green pillbox hat on her head.

Big Betty took up a space. A new Beemer was behind it, eating up another campground spot. Next to the shiny car sat a shinier grill, a just out-of-the box patio set, and two hand-crafted Adirondack chairs in front of a clean, unused fire pit. A pile of logs sat nearby. Becker marveled at the stuff, and Nonna's ability to pay for it. She either maxed out her credit cards or found a wealthy suitor. Or both.

Nonna was cooking hamburgers on the grill. She waved to Becker with a spatula. Lester the parrot's squawks came through the window, pieces of *Mary had a Little Lamb*, followed by *Twinkle, Twinkle, Little Star*. She wondered how grilled parrot tasted, medium rare, then told herself to stop it. Apparently, he was an agreeable companion to Nonna.

Lester yelled to her, "Cop! Cop! You're under arrest!" Becker tried not to feel self-conscious as an older guy in a white wife-beater shirt from campsite 12 looked at her. Note to self: next time, ditch the police uniform and come in ratty jeans and a t-shirt to blend in better.

She pecked Nonna on the cheek. "How are you settling in? Are you sure you don't want to go to Oceanside? A friend told me the grounds are pretty. The bingo games on Thursday pay out well."

"Heaven's no. I'm in love with Dick's. The 'Dickies', as they call themselves, are a hoot. I'm going to put in my application to be a Dickie, since I'm stayin' for a while."

"What do you have to do to become a Dickie?"

"I'm not sure. I think I have to smoke marijuana and cluck like a chicken." Becker felt her eyes go as round as an owl's. She opened her mouth to speak, but only a squeak came out. Nonna smiled at her. "Just kidding, Del. You pay $50 to have your name listed in the camp directory."

They ate burned burgers with tasty pickles from the neighbor, the bomb maker. Nonna pointed out his campsite with a fork, her mouth full of potato salad.

"So, tell me about your missing person's case. I'm a good listener. You'd be surprised I'm an even better detective. When I was in Idaho, or Iowa, no, it was Minnesota, I'm sure of it, I helped the sheriff locate a stolen macaw named Blue. He had been gone for five days. The owner was sure he flew the coop."

"How did you find Blue?"

"He came in the window to visit with Lester."

"Great investigative work, Nonna." Becker took a bite of her hamburger, trying to miss the charred meat. "My case involves Michelle Workman. A while back, I was looking for a murderer—"

"The prostitute thing. Your mama told me all about it."

"Yes. Michelle's name came up during the investigation because she went missing under suspicious circumstances. She had also recently been arrested for solicitation. So, I considered her for a minute, realized she wasn't my dead prostitute, and moved on. Now her father, the mayor of Silver Hill, wants me to find her."

Nonna leaned forward, eyes like laser beams. "Do you think she's pushing up daisies?"

Becker reached for her iced tea and took a sip. "Not sure yet. She was quirky and individualistic, but didn't seem to have any enemies. She was likable, if weird."

"Like me."

"Exactly." Becker smiled at her grandmother. "Unlike you, though, she was the youngest of four girls: Meghan, Marissa, Monica, and Michelle. Her last name is Workman, but as a kid she called herself Michelle Workwoman, and thumbed her nose at her wealthy family by playing the trombone, for example, instead of something refined like the violin or piano. She'd play it in front of her house, walking up and down the sidewalk."

Nonna laughed. "Yep, sounds like somethin' I'd do. I took up the accordion on account of I could make it sound like it was passing gas."

Becker chuckled. "Michelle could also tinker under the hood of a car or truck; she was an expert with Volvo station wagons. My favorite story about her is: she snuck into a bachelor party when she was sixteen and played roulette like a pro, winning $192 until the groom-to-be kicked her out. She reminds me of you and Bea."

"Who is Bea?"

"My twelve-year-old friend. She's bold and brave, and persistent. Took her two years and 300 signatures from her neighbors and friends to get the town council to approve her backyard chicken flock."

"I need to meet her. Maybe she can be my mini-me. I've always wanted one."

Good grief.

***

Becker left Nonna's for home. She was sure eyes were on her as she exited the campground, and she subtly checked the rear-view mirror, shaking off an unexpected chill. Stop it! Don't wear your uniform next time to draw attention.

Nonna's questions about Michelle prompted Becker to pull out her thin file on Michelle Workman when she got home. She settled down on her couch next to Kevin to read. Michelle's police record was slim; she had a few speeding tickets over the years. Beyond that, she had an unblemished record until she was arrested on a solicitation charge. She scanned the transcript of an interview she conducted years ago with the Silver Hill officer who had arrested Michelle at Dave's Dive for prostitution. It was in May 2017, a few months before Michelle went missing. Becker recalled the officer was a youthful recruit with impeccably polished shoes, acne on his chin, and soulful blue eyes. He had the unfortunate name of Peter Peters.

"What can you tell me about that night?"

"The sheriff asked me to visit the bar and look for suspicious activity...ah, of the prostitution type."

"Had you been there before canvassing for hookers?"

"No, Ma'am. I'd never been there, period. My mom wouldn't let me go when I was in high school. When I started in the academy, I didn't think it would be...ah, right to visit."

Officer Peter Peters looked like he was still high school aged, God bless him and his high-sheen shoes. "Okay," Becker said. "Then what?"

"When I first went in, I saw the mayor's daughter, Michelle, talking to the bartender."

"The man she solicited?"

"No, Ma'am, it was Edward Landon. From what I could overhear, they were just friends. The guy she solicited came in later."

Becker wanted to scratch her eyes out. Why mention the bartender? She swallowed her frustration. "Describe the guy."

"Um…he gave off surfer-dude vibes. White, scruffy blond hair. On the lean side, maybe six feet tall."

"What else?"

"It didn't seem like they just met."

"What do you mean?"

"You know how you can tell when people are friends or dating? Like, she was hanging on his arm. She patted his head where his hair was sticking up. They were…comfortable? You know, jabbering about the weather and the Shorebirds game."

"Did you hear her ask for money in exchange for sex?"

Becker recalled he'd turned pink at the question.

"Sort of. She asked him if he had money and if he did, she'd show him a good time."

"And you arrested her for a 'sort of' proposition?"

Peter Peters shrugged as his face turned tomato in color. He didn't answer the question, so she concluded the interview.

Becker flipped over the paper noticing her scribbles: AGG, short for *agguato*, or "ambush" in Italian. It was obvious to Becker the arrest was flimsy and forced. After reading the short transcript, she agreed with her former self: Officer Peters had no real evidence, no transaction occurred, and no one was caught with their pants down, so to speak. Had the case gone to trial, it was likely the charges would have been dropped. Michelle wasn't a prostitute; she was set up by someone who wanted it to appear that way.

Who ambushed Michelle? Why? Maybe Sheriff Atkins was behind it, although she couldn't think of a reason why he would want her arrested. Could Mommy or Daddy Workman have orchestrated the charge via the sheriff to rein in her behavior? If that was the case, Becker thought, it clearly failed. The arrest led to increasing ugliness within the family, frequent calls to the police during screaming matches, and many nights Michelle didn't come home, including six months later when the twenty-year-old disappeared.

There was a knock at her door, startling her. She looked through the peephole. Molly Zimmer gave off a ray of sunshine vibe. Literally. Dressed from head to toe in hues of yellow. A large woman, with ample curves and hips, she wore a caftan with diagonal stripes in mustard, amber and saffron, and a chunky necklace and earrings the color of lemons. She was wearing shoes, a sometime thing, and they were yellow, too.

Molly's best friend, Franklin, rode on her head, grooming her hair, tucking strands of it into her chartreuse hair band. Franklin was a sugar glider, a nocturnal marsupial related to kangaroos. He was six inches long with a six-inch bushy tail, weighed about five ounces, and had over-sized liquid brown eyes in a face that looked like an opossum, only cuter. He usually was in Molly's bra, where he slept away most of the day.

She opened the door. When Franklin saw Becker, he started chattering as he reached for her arm.

"Franklin missed you," Molly said.

Becker had long ago accepted that either Molly and Franklin truly communicated, or the woman was delusional and believed she was conversing with a sugar glider. Regardless, Molly was a beloved colleague, a friend, smart and kind, so Becker ignored the eccentricity.

Franklin crawled up to Becker's shoulder. She kissed his head. "I missed you, too, Franklin." She turned to Molly. "And you. This is a pleasant surprise. I'm glad you stopped by. There's something I want to talk to you about."

Molly recently moved to the village. She volunteered at the police department, answering phones, handling paperwork, and performing research. Although she wasn't using her skills as a forensic scientist,

Becker wanted to kiss Molly every time she walked into the police station for handing the day-to-day administrative duties she despised.

Molly gave Becker a hug, and Becker let her. She wasn't a hugger by nature. "We've been busy."

"I'll say. I haven't seen you in, what, a month?"

Molly nodded. "That's about right. I've been in Philly getting the townhouse ready to sell, painting every wall the color of a cloudy gray day. I hate it."

"But buyers will love it."

"That's what my realtor says. Personally, I liked the orange and purple better, but I want to sell it sooner rather than later, so I picked drab." Molly gave her a slight smile. "Frankly, I need the money. My 'hobby flower job', as mother calls it, is barely paying the bills. She wants me to quit and find something more appropriate. Apparently, the residents at Celestino Village look down on her because her college-educated daughter is wasting her time creating and delivering floral arrangements."

"But working at the flower shop makes you happy."

"It does. Fernando is a great mentor and boss, he compensates me fairly, and, because he's a good guy, he charges me a fraction of what he would charge anyone else for the apartment above the shop. So, I'm doing okay for now. Love for my job aside, it's nonsense to leave any position without a new one."

"I have a solution, I think." Becker gestured to the couch. "Sit. Franklin and I will grab us a glass of iced tea." Becker walked to the kitchen, found a half-full bag of mini-marshmallows, and gave one to a purring Franklin. She poured two glasses of tea. Returning to the living room, she handed one to Molly. They sipped.

Without preamble, Becker said, "I'd like you to work part-time for the police department. I've gotten approval to pay you a salary."

Molly and Franklin stared at her. "Really?"

Becker said, "Really. I'm not sure how long it will be for, but it would help you pay the bills and help me with investigating a cold case." She took a few minutes to tell Molly about the request from the mayors to investigate Michelle Workman's disappearance.

"This won't be easy," Becker said. "I'm guessing it will be high profile; both mayors like the attention a story like this brings, even though it's a sad tale. We'll be interviewing pillars of the community, family members, friends, business associates, and others familiar with Michelle and the facts surrounding her disappearance. It will be...touchy, I guess is the right word. For example, Mayor Workman asked me to leave his wife out of the investigation. Mimi can be prickly. Difficult." Becker paused, scratched Franklin's head, and handed him back to Molly, who promptly put him in her bra. "I told him no go if we didn't have full access to anyone we needed to talk with, including family.

"It's going to be hard on the family, no doubt."

"Hard for us, too. I met the sheriff, and it didn't go well. The best we can hope for is he leaves us alone. God knows he's not going to be helpful. Did I mention he's in the running for the Asshole of the Year Award?"

Molly asked, "Are you trying to hire me or scare me off?"

Becker chuckled. "I could hire Franklin and you'd have to show up."

"Chief, we come as a package deal, and we accept your offer of employment."

Franklin chirped.

Chapter Six

Early the next morning, she called Mayor Roberto Spinosi; after pleasantries, in her most professional voice, she said, "Roberto, I need to voice my concern over the article in the *Celestino Press*."

"What are you disturbed about? We told the truth; it was a good story."

"Perhaps I should have accepted the job first?"

Dead silence, then a soft, "Oh."

Becker got mad again. "You've put me in a difficult position, Mr. Mayor. The workload of the police department is beyond manageable. I'm trying to limit overtime, per your request. I have an officer on medical leave, and one in Puerto Rico visiting a sick relative. Who do you want me to tap to help with the investigation?"

He stuttered and stammered a non-reply, then blamed Mayor Workman for grandstanding and talking him into the newspaper announcement.

"I'm at a loss for the next steps." She held her breath, hoping he would come to the same conclusion she already had.

"How about Molly Zimmer? Can you hire her?"

Becker smiled into the phone. "Yes, yes, I can."

"Splendid."

They disconnected. She was punching in the phone number of the president of her concerned citizens' group when her mama called.

"Delaney? It's Mama. I was wondering if you could come over for a cup of coffee and a chat."

"Is it Nonna?"

"No, Nonna is fine, if you define 'fine' as driving up to the house in a shiny new black BMW. Her bus—"

"Big Betty, you mean."

Mama sighed. "I hate to encourage her when she's naming inanimate objects. But yes, Big Betty is too wide for some streets in the village. Apparently, she clipped a phone pole and broke a mirror. I asked her where the Beemer came from, named Wilbur, by the way, and she told me 'None ya'."

Becker thought of the new campground equipment at Spotted Dick's. Did Nonna came into some money? "I'll look into it when I have a minute. I'm busy right now with the Workman case."

"Well, that's what I want to talk to you about. I know a bit about the family. It might help."

Interesting, Becker thought. "How about I come by for lunch?"

"I would love it! I have enough time to make my famous pasta fagoli! Goodbye, Cara." Becker didn't have time to answer. Mama had hung up and was likely already reaching for a can of beans.

She finished her calls, checked her emails, talked to a few of her officers, and cleaned her apartment. An orderly person by nature, it didn't take long to wipe down the countertops in her compact kitchen, scrub the sink in the tiny bathroom, and tidy up her bedroom. As she put the nautical-inspired blue and green hued pillows on the bed, she tripped over Kevin's dog mattress in the corner, a blue fluffy thing he never used. As many times as she shooed him off of her queen bed, he found his way back; she awoke most mornings with his body squished next to hers.

She watered the plants on the deck. Halfway through she noticed the olive plant wasn't in its usual spot. Did she move it?

Kevin pawed at her leg, startling her. She had been putzing around for nearly two hours.

She threw on a blue t-shirt with *I'm Italian, I Don't Need a Recipe* on it, a pair of ratty jeans, with blue Converse high tops. After she put on Kevin's leash, they walked to Mama's house, taking a little longer than normal so Kevin could smell every telephone pole, fire hydrant, and bush. He peed on a few.

It was a beautiful fall day with a clear blue sky. The leaves hadn't turned yet; Mama's summer flowers were still vibrant. Becker smelled the scent of lavender when she brushed against the leaves, noticing the newly planted mums next to the cottage fence. Mama had a fresh pitcher of lemonade and two glasses sitting on the table on her patio.

Kevin pulled Becker into the house. Mama was at the stove, stirring the pasta and bean soup. She stopped long enough to give Becker a kiss on her cheek.

"How fun this is! Lunch with my daughter and...grand-dog!"

Becker laughed. She told Kevin to sit, manners still being an iffy thing for him. Becker was proud of him when he plopped his butt down, tail wagging, for the chewy bone she fished out of a glass jar on the counter. He took it from her, located a sunbeam on the floor, and laid down in it to make quick work of the bone, white wiry hair sticking up this way and that. He farted. The dog could have been a cow for the amount of methane gas he produced; Mooney's stone didn't seem to be working.

"Oh, Kevin," Mama said. "Do you have to do that in the house?"

Kevin ignored her.

"How has your week been, Mama?"

"*Bene*, good. This week we made my famous gnocchi in tomato sauce at the cooking class." Becker smiled indulgently at her mama. All of her dishes started with the word 'famous'. "It was *delicioso*, of course. I used Yukon gold potatoes; they are so nutty and creamy. I baked them. True Italians bake, not boil. And the tomato sauce was so flavorful."

"Mama, you're making me hungry."

"Me too. Anyway, the rest of the story is about my gnocchi: one student asked me for private lessons! Can you believe it?"

Kevin barked at the excitement in Mama's voice. "Kevin and I both believe it! You are a gifted chef, and now a talented instructor. I'm so proud of you! Did you say 'yes' to her?"

Mama looked sheepish. "I said yes to...him." Becker raised her eyebrows. She gave Mama the side eye. "Wait, wait, wait. Delaney, this is business. No hanky-panky where business is concerned."

"Okay, Mama."

"Oh look, the pasta fagoli is ready! And the crusty bread is warm. Let's eat."

Mama had purposely changed the subject; Becker let her.

They made small-talk over lunch on the patio. Afterward, as Becker carried the dirty plates to the kitchen, despite Mama's protests, she asked, "You mentioned on the phone you know the Workman family?"

Mama went to the "liquor cabinet" where a lonely bottle of amaretto sat next to a bottle of wine, a half dozen fancy wineglasses, and pint jelly jars. Mama wasn't a big drinker; she liked the idea of having a special place for booze more than the booze itself. She took the square amaretto bottle with two small glass jelly jars from the shelf, pouring the amber liquor into the glasses.

They sat sipping the almond-flavored liquor. Mama said, "Let's see, where to start. I met Mimi at a football game between Celestino High School and Silver Hill Academy. We sat next to each other on the bleachers." Mama hesitated for a moment. "I hate to talk bad of people, but it was obvious she was scanning the crowd as we were talking, hoping to be seen with someone more important than me: Rosa Becker the nobody. Then she learned my ancestors founded Celestino Village, and I became more interesting."

"She was a social climber from way back."

"Yes, I'm glad you said it so I didn't have to. After the game, we stayed in touch with an occasional call or meet-up at school events, that sort of thing. I was a loner in high school, shy, really, so any friend was better than none. She was likeable enough, But when she met William, it all changed. She traded me for him; the Workmans were like royalty in Silver Hill." She shrugged her shoulders. "I saw them together once, at the Seahorse Festival. Mimi had a new air about her; she was more standoffish, almost rude. They looked good together, though."

"Did you ever meet any of her daughters? I'm primarily interested in Michelle."

Mama stared at what little was left of her amaretto. A few minutes later, she said, "I can't say I met any of them...but I saw Mimi and the girls at the beach once. The littlest one, who I assume was Michelle, was maybe four or five years old. She was playing in the surf, covered in sand. She picked up a big piece of seaweed and put it on her head. From where I sat, I could see Mimi's face get red. She jumped up and grabbed Michelle, yanked the seaweed off, pulling Michelle's hair. Mimi dragged her by one arm to the blanket, leaving a red handprint on Michelle's skin. The poor child cried on the blanket for a half hour or more. The saddest part?" Becker nodded as her Mama teared up. "Kids cry really loudly, sometimes to be dramatic and sometimes because of big ouches. Michelle was sobbing without making a sound."

***

Belly full from lunch, anticipating a nap, she almost missed the muddy footprints on her stairs. Much too big for her shoe size.

The door to her apartment hung open, pry marks around the lock. Wood splintered in the frame.

Her breath hitched; her pulse quickened as she grabbed for her non-existent gun. Shit!

She backed slowly and quietly down the stairs, senses on high alert. Were those footsteps? A robbery in progress?

Fear caught in her throat; her mouth went dry. Something tugged at her arm and she jumped. She had forgotten about Kevin, who was pulling on his leash.

She continued to back down the steps until she was on the sidewalk in front of her apartment. She drew out her phone, hands shaking, almost dropping it. Three tries later, she punched in the correct numbers.

Her voice wobbled. "Guido, 10-13 at my place. Emergency. Bring me a gun. No injuries. No 911 assist."

"On my way."

Less than three minutes later, Guido Tucci's police car flew around the corner without lights on or a siren blaring. Smart, Becker thought, he's not sure of the situation, so it's better to come in unannounced. He jumped out of the car, stood next to her, gave her a once-over from head to toe, and whispered, "Chief, are you okay?"

She kept her voice low. "Yes. Damaged door. Hanging open. Perp may still be inside. I backed out quickly."

He wordlessly handed her a Sig Sauer. She checked it, tied Kevin to a pole, told him to stay quiet, which he actually did, and gestured to Guido to follow her up the stairs. They crept without a sound, guns drawn. At the landing, Becker pointed left and tapped Guido's chest. He gave her a slight nod. Becker would go right.

They rushed through the door, Becker's heart beating fast. She hurried to the bathroom, then bedroom, sweeping her gun in an arc. She yelled, "Clear!"

Guido yelled back, "Clear!"

Her breath caught as she walked through the doorway into the living room. KEEP OUT OF SILVER HILL was spray painted in red above her window. The paint had dripped onto her window blinds and down the wall, like trickled blood from a scene in a low budget horror movie.

Her heart jumped around in her chest thumping in her ears as she took in the gruesome-looking paint. Guido came from behind her and put a hand on her shoulder; Becker jumped. "Take a few deep breaths, Chief. I'll go get Kevin. Can you walk through again, inspect things?"

She nodded, slid Guido's gun into the waistband of her jeans, then retraced her steps. In the kitchen, her Tuscan print was hanging slightly askew. In the bathroom, her hairbrush was crooked on the counter, and in the bedroom, an imprint on the comforter made bile rise in her throat. You will not throw up, she told herself. It's better to channel the fear. Get mad.

When Guido returned with Kevin, he grabbed a few glasses of water. They sat on the couch as the dog sniffed around the apartment. Becker's adrenaline drained and fatigue settled in. "I'm beyond pissed off at not having my gun. I know better."

"We all make mistakes, Chief."

"Easy for you to say. You always carry yours."

He looked at her, concern in his eyes, and remained silent.

She took a breath. "I'm sorry, the last thing I want to do is pick a fight with a friend and colleague, especially one that comes running so fast. Thank you, Guido." The sip of water cooled her throat and temper. "I can't believe someone has been in here, in my home. My safe place. And he had the nerve to move my stuff. He sat on my bed." She shuddered. "It grosses me out."

Guido looked over at the graffiti. "He's cocky, that's for sure."

"Or she. I'm not sure; the footprints were bigger than mine, probably man-sized, but it could be a woman with larger feet. I'm sure if we called the state police in, they wouldn't find anything." Becker rubbed her face, talking fast. "Anyone who watches TV these days would know to wear gloves. Besides, I'd be playing into the perp's ego. I don't want to go there. Plus, they would want to file a report, leading to a full-blown investigation. The press will get hold of it..."

Guido put a hand on her shoulder, interrupting her. "Slow down, Chief. You don't have to decide this minute. How about I take a picture of the damage to the door and your wall, let you think about it? I'll also get a photograph of the footprints, take measurements. I can call my buddy Stan, who owns a security company, get him to call you."

An hour later Guido left, after securing the door with a 2x4 nailed to the frame temporarily. Fighting exhaustion, Becker propped a chair against the knob, grabbed all the blankets and sheets from the bed, minus the comforter, then threw them in front of the broken door. She laid down next to Kevin on the floor, Glock within reach.

She drifted off to sleep thinking *I didn't want the case, but I'll be damned if I let someone scare me away.*

Chapter Seven

Becker's comforter was already at the dry cleaners and the blood red STAY OUT OF SILVER HILL was gone, courtesy of Sherwin-Williams paint. After a trip to the hardware store, she had pitched the blinds and put-up new ones, then deep cleaned the apartment. She'd thrown her hairbrush in the trash, replaced it with her spare, and was dusting the bookcase when she found an envelope stuck between *The Book Thief* and a music box, a gift from Fern for her graduation from the police academy.

She didn't put the envelope there; she had a basket on the kitchen counter for mail. Dread lodged in her belly, and goosebumps broke out on her arms. She backed away from the bookcase like it was a wild Siberian tiger.

Where did the envelope come from? Who put it there? Why? Did it have to do with the break-in and nasty graffiti on her wall? Of course, it had to. When did the perp put it there? Was it there yesterday? Or did he come back today while she was gone? She shivered, disrupting her erratic thoughts. Becker, get a grip. The envelope can't hurt you. It was probably left yesterday: you didn't see it. Breathe.

She walked to her police car parked in the lot behind her apartment, to grab a pair of latex gloves. She was calmer when she plucked the envelope from the bookcase and tore it open.

Dear Chief Becker,

Stop looking for Michelle Workman. She's alive and healthy, and living with me, a long way from Silver Hill. I rescued her from Ladybank Manor because her mother tried to kill her. She hated Michelle's guts.

You are putting her and yourself in danger by investigating her disappearance. Please don't make me do anything else to get your attention. Please don't make me hurt you.

Sincerely,

Her loving husband

Becker dropped the piece of paper on the table then paced in her tiny living room, back and forth, back and forth. She was debating her next steps when her phone buzzed. It was Officer Guido Tucci. *Are you good today?*

She texted back: *Not really. Just found a menacing note from the perp. He must have planted it yesterday.*

After a volley of texts between them, Guido convinced her to report the crime. Blood-red graffiti was one thing, a letter that threatened body harm was another.

She picked up her phone to call Keisha when an incoming text from Fern popped up. *Visit later? The wine is chilled!*

Fernando Rossi, her "adopted" brother, was a positive and kind soul. Time spent with him buoyed her spirits. She needed him today, texting back: *Yep! See you around 4:00.*

She called Keisha. "Can I speak with Corporal Carter of the Maryland State Police? Not my friend Keisha."

"You sound off, Becker. What's up?

Becker said, "I am off. Some asshole broke into my apartment. I need to file an official report."

"Geez, I'm sorry...when did this happen?"

Becker told her briefly about the break-in and letter.

"I'm actually on duty today, and am about three minutes from your place. Can I come by?"

A half-hour later, Keisha finished her crime scene work She had snapped many pictures, took testimony from Guido, and interviewed Becker with a matter-of-fact approach. It calmed Becker. When she left with the bagged envelope and letter, Becker's shoulders were no longer sagging. Her burden was lighter.

Later, after a chubby guy named Bob installed a new door and security system Becker led Kevin to *Flowers by Fernando*, the florist shop Fern owned. He sat at a table outside, surrounded by mums and asters. She felt a pang of love for him; after her papa died, he took her under his wing as his baby sister. He asserted he would look after her, and, true to his word, he had been her champion and protector, especially in high school. After her sister hightailed it out of town with the calculus teacher, Fern deftly helped her get over the embarrassment. The shame.

He waved as she came into view, and then gave her a bear hug, smooshing her face in his chest. Fern was over six feet tall with "cornflower blue" eyes (so-called by a previous girlfriend, Becker still teased him about it) and a medium build. If he skipped yoga classes too many times, his belly pooched out. Today he looked lean, with a contented look on his face.

"Fern, *mio fratello*, how are you?"

"Great! Sit for a spell. I'll get you a glass of dry Riesling and you can tell me how things are in your world."

Becker lowered into a bistro chair on the sidewalk in front of the shop. Dozens of mums surrounded her, their spectacular colors reminding her of a box of Skittles. She smelled the sweet alyssum, a honey-like fragrance, and the mint in pots interspersed with the chrysanthemums. Fern came out of the shop carrying a glass of wine in each hand, set hers on the table smiled at her.

"You look frazzled. Is it the because of the article in the *Celestino Press*? Finding Michelle Workman?"

Becker was not ready to talk about the blood-red graffiti so she told him a slight fib, feeling bad about it. "Yes, my energy is sapped although this damned investigation isn't even started." Becker rubbed her brow. "Sorry, Fern, that sounded sharp. What I meant to say is the mayors made that joint announcement to bully me into the case, and I'm already weary of it." And, she added silently, "I'm afraid of the potential danger."

Fern was an attentive listener; Becker told him about the last few days, including her dislike of Sheriff Atkins. Her admiration for Mooney. Her recollection of Michelle Workman.

"I'm familiar with some of those names."

"You mean me? Or Mayor Spinosi?" Becker gave him the side eye.

"Smartass. Of course, I know both of you. Years ago, I was a gym rat for a while, before yoga—"

Becker interrupted him, "I miss Jorja." The owner of the *Flying Fish, a yoga studio in town,* was Fernando's girlfriend and Becker's landlord.

"She's doing well. We need to get together soon." He grinned, his eyes filled with happiness and contentment. "Anyway, your buddy, Paul Atkins, was also a gym rat." Becker shot him a withering look. "We lifted weights together, acting as each other's spotter. As you would imagine, he's quite the hulk; what I could bench press, he could easily pick up with his hand."

"And knowing how arrogant he is, he probably rubbed your face in it."

"Yep. But I didn't want a best friend, only a partner for safety, so I ignored the jabs. He's not a bad guy if you keep on the right side of his ego."

"You're too easygoing, Fern. Why should you have to be on the right side of his, um...anything? What an idiot." Becker's body language shifted, as if ready for a fistfight. "And nobody disrespects my brother!"

His face softened; his eyes warmed. Oh no. She knew what was coming next: his "I'm proud of my sister speech".

"There's my fierce little sister! I'm supposed to be your protector, not the other way around, but I love how your caramel eyes flash when you get riled up. Your back goes all stiff. Your biceps get all quivery."

"Yes, yes, I know. And how my black curly hair shines, and how I look professional in my uniform." She sighed. "I love your compliments. Thank you, Fern, but not now."

"All right. Back to Paul Atkins. You'll probably need him; try to appeal to his over-sized ego to help you. You could probably exploit the 'damsel in distress' thing."

Becker gave him a tight nod, face still hard.

Fernando changed the subject. "The other person I, um, am familiar with is Meghan Workman. We dated a few times after high school."

"Hmm. Keeping secrets from your sister? I don't remember you being an item back then."

"We weren't. We dated, just a few times. She didn't hit your radar because, well...she wasn't for me. It was a short-lived relationship. She was beautiful, cultured and intelligent, but when you dug down beneath the surface, she was a narcissist. What really turned me off was the way she treated Michelle when she was nine or ten years old." Fernando took a sip of his wine. "Michelle was so...different from the rest of the family. She collected rocks, feathers, Indian artifacts, that sort of thing, from the marsh behind her house, something Meghan and the family barely tolerated."

"She was quirky. Odd. Independent."

Fernando nodded. "Very much so. I remember one time I was at their big house in Silver Hill when Michelle brought a baby muskrat home. That's when I saw Meghan's ugly underbelly. She berated the poor kid, slapped her for being so 'revolting', and dumped the new-born kit in the trash. Right then and there, I was done."

"You're too kind for someone like that."

Fern swirled the wine in his glass, nodding. "Honestly, muskrats are disease-carrying rodents, and personally, I'm not a fan, but I couldn't leave Michelle there in tears. So, I fished the baby out of the trash, handed the little thing to her and we trudged into the marsh to put the damned muskrat back where it belonged."

Chapter Eight

B ecker's new resolve had her researching Michelle's case the next day. She typed "Ladybank Manor", the name of the Workman home, into the search bar on her computer. Almost immediately, an image popped up, of a gorgeous Victorian mansion. She clicked on a button, opening a page about the family history.

Originally from England, the Workman surname referred to laborers on farms and in manufacturing plants, a so-called "work man". However, William's descendants were textile tradesmen who rubbed elbows with several royal families in the 1500s. Later ancestors were merchants; part of William's family tree included a ship builder who became an owner of a small fleet of vessels. His ships carried goods to Australia until the exportation of convicts became more profitable.

William's kin emigrated to the US at the turn of the century, and settled on the Eastern Shore of Maryland, in the Silver Hill area, continuing in the ship trade. Warren, William's father, established a bank in the late 1880s, building Ladybank Manor a few years later. He added the titles of "mayor" and "father" soon after. William was the youngest of three children.

Becker looked up from her computer glancing out the window. It was a dreary fall day; the sky was spitting rain. Kevin and Bella were cozy in their basket. Becker contemplated more coffee as she eyed her lunch panini, sitting on her desk. Eleven a.m. seemed too early. Her phone rang. It was Keisha Carter.

"Chief, an update on the break-in investigation. Not surprisingly, there were no prints on the letter."

"Wow, quick results."

"I know a guy." Keisha chuckled. "Just kidding. We fast-tracked it for a law enforcement colleague."

"Thanks, Keisha. I'm not surprised the MSP came up empty with the prints. Everyone watches those detective shows and knows how to get away with a B&E, even Kevin."

Keisha chuckled. She asked, "Speaking of entering...did you get a new door? Security system?"

"Yes, and yes. I accidentally set the damned alarm off last night playing with it."

"It happens. Those things are pretty sophisticated. At least you've learned what not to do."

Becker said, "It goes right into the state police dispatch office; I've got to be more careful so the cavalry won't show up. It would help if I read the instructions."

***

A while later, the sound of multiple shuffling feet, like a bunch of tipsy line dancers at an Italian wedding, stopped outside of Becker's office door. Her visitors wouldn't be leaving any time soon, if her guess was correct. She looked at her half-eaten panini. So much for lunch.

In her doorway stood her "Gruppo", a rag-tag bunch of wannabe detectives, seventy- and eighty-year-old retirees who considered themselves responsible for Becker's success in solving the Casino Prostitute Case. Becker had to admit they had been helpful, and, as a bonus, provided comic relief, but she was elbow-deep in preparing for her court visit later today. She didn't have time for a social call.

They crowded into her cramped office, the men chivalrous by giving the chairs to Arima Patel, the only woman, and Cephas Jones, the oldest of the group. Joey *Smiling Joey* Vito and Johnny Hudson stood. When they had arranged chairs and bodies, Joey gave her his signature open mouth smile, showing most of his thirty-two teeth. "Hey, Chief!"

"Hi Joey, how are things on your street?"

Becker's officers had visited the neighborhood several times in the past few weeks for noise violation complaints. A certain single young woman, good-looking, had moved into a house two doors down from Joey's. Whenever Claire was gardening or sunbathing, potential suitors drove by honking the horn. After every honk, a grumpy neighbor called in to the police station, making more noise than the cars. Becker was proud of her officers for responding so quickly, until she met the beautiful co-ed and figured out the cops weren't enforcing the law, they were visiting Claire.

"Quiet. Old lady Winters is on vacation so there's nobody to complain about car horns."

Becker smiled at him. He was wearing a vintage-looking two-tone bowling shirt, pink and black, with black linen pants, big gold rings on both hands, with chains around his neck, an ornate cross hanging from one of them. His sparse black hair was slicked back; he carried himself like an aging mobster. Which he was.

"Good. Arima, Johnny, what's happening in the Gardens?"

Arima spoke, her soft voice reminding Becker of a mourning doves' coo. "We love your mama's cooking classes. She's asked me to help her prepare a few Middle Eastern dishes to give us a break from all the pasta with tomato sauce." Arima's face turned red. "I mean, there's nothing wrong with Italian food, no disrespect intended, but some participants have acid reflux, and, well..."

Becker interrupted her to save her further embarrassment. "No offense taken, Arima, I think it's wonderful you're going to teach classes with Mama—"

Johnny Hudson stepped on Becker's words, and she politely let him. "We need a pie baking class."

A retired forensic accountant, Johnny was as awkward as a blue-footed booby. His IQ was off the charts; he could do with numbers what Fred Astaire did with his feet when he danced. The man was brilliant, an analytical genius. With humans, however, he could barely hold a conversation. She thought his two-step was probably awkward, too.

"The powers-to-be at the Gardens decided to hold pie night twice a month instead of once a week. Yesterday there was an altercation between two of the residents for the last remaining slice. They were wielding their canes like swords when one of them smashed the iced tea urn. Poor sight, or so he said, which I think is a bald-faced lie. Anyway, the manager had to come out and break up the ruckus. She gave each of the men half a piece. The guy who broke the urn, soaked in iced tea, started arguing again over the bigger slice."

The room erupted in laughter.

Becker addressed the last person in the room. "Cephas Jones, you're new to the Gruppo. How did they rope you in?"

Cephas Jones, a beloved resident of Celestino Village, was a stately African-American gentleman who wore designer suits, volunteered tirelessly for the good of the town, and insisted you call him by both his first and last names. It was an endearing quirk of his, like the herbs tucked into the buttonhole of his suit. Today he wore rosemary.

"Joey talked me into it. Some of the Gruppo members are on vacation, so I decided to fill in." His smile dimmed, face serious. "I understand you need our help."

She looked around the room, at the eyes filled with excitement gazing back at her. It was obvious the Gruppo was collectively bored; the chance to be amateur sleuths trumped listening to random honking horns, learning how to bake Mama's famous ziti, or watching fights over rhubarb pie.

"I'm guessing you are here to assist with the missing person's case?"

"Exactly, Chief. We'd like to support you in any way we can. Finding Michelle will be a big, how do you say it, 'feather in our cap'," Joey said as he looked toward the basket occupied by Kevin and his fluffy chicken friend, "Sorry, Miss Bella."

"I just started the investigation and at this point," Becker said, "there's nothing for you all to do."

Joey's face fell. The other members looked just as despondent. Becker's big heart, usually tucked away, pumped compassion through her body. "Wait...on second thought..."

The Gruppo leaned forward, anticipation pulling them toward her like a fish on a hook.

There was a commotion outside of her door. A squawk, then, "Mouse! Mouse in the house!" Franklin chattered like a pair of wind-up toy teeth.

Nonna, wearing a green and brown camouflage jumpsuit, made a grand entrance into the small office. Lester perched on her shoulder. The members of the Gruppo gaped at Becker's grandmother, except for Joey. He had a huge smile on his face.

"Heller, Del, and all of you old people. This looks like a party! Where's the food? Wine? Spirits?"

Becker smiled indulgently. "Nonna, we're not allowed to drink alcohol at the police station."

"That's unfortunate. You're the boss. Can't you change the rules?" Nonna looked around the room, eyes lighting on Johnny Hudson.

"Aren't you a tall drink of water? I could slurp you up." Poor Johnny turned a shade of purple.

Becker introduced everyone in the room to Nonna. Joey Vito kissed her hand, while she giggled.

Nonna said, "I'd like to be part of your Gruppo. I dressed for the occasion, you know, to go undercover." She set Lester down on a filing cabinet then hiked her ample butt onto a corner of Becker's desk. The "You got This" sign flew to the floor.

This can't turn out well, Becker thought. A group of 70-something's and her grandmother, "solving" a crime. She didn't have much choice; the word "no" was not part of Nonna's vocabulary. She sighed, picked up her growing file on Michelle's disappearance, telling them bits and pieces of her fledgling investigation. She was also buying time to make up something the Gruppo could do.

She said, "Since we are at the beginning, gathering information is important. For now, I'd like you all to talk to your friends and family about what they remember when Michelle disappeared. Maybe they heard gossip through the grapevine at the time, or something that could be of value."

Becker congratulated herself on the idea that would keep the Gruppo busy, out of her way, and perhaps gain information at the same time. "Be discreet. The powers to be in Silver Hill aren't happy we are involved in this investigation."

"Can we wear badges? It will go with my navy-blue muumuu," Nonna said.

Becker's right eye started ticking.

Johnny said, "I asked the same question a while back. It went nowhere."

Becker rubbed her eye. "No badges. You're in an advisory capacity, you're not detectives, so please don't get yourselves into any trouble."

As they said their goodbyes, Becker asked herself: *What could the Gruppo possibly do to mess up her investigation?*

Chapter Nine

A yellow potted mum greeted her on her doorstep when she came home from work. The note read: *Looking forward to tonight. Love, Mack.*

She carried the plant in the apartment, plucked out the note, and put it in a bowl with dozens of others. Her boyfriend, besides being a giving lover, was a thoughtful man. He frequently brought her gifts, little tokens like a book, a shell, or a piece of sparkly crystal from his gallery, the Grand Girasole; he kept Flowers by Fernando in business with frequent deliveries.

He had come into her life through her friend, Bea, showing up to be near the young girl after a twelve-year absence, ready to be in her day-to-day life. Bea and her family made it easy for him to slide into his new role, giving Bea two father figures along with her two rabbits (Salt and Pepper), twenty-six chickens, and a koi named Underpants.

Becker took a quick shower in her shoebox of a bathroom changing into a pair of stretchy jeans and a sweatshirt with a Flying Fish logo. She fed Kevin, checked her emails, grabbed a bottle of chianti, then crawled into her vintage truck with her sidekick. Her phone buzzed in her pocket, showing the number for the police station.

"Chief Becker, can I help you?"

"Hey, Chief, it's Molly. I have some interesting news I'd like to share with you tomorrow about the criminal background checks you've asked me to do. Will you have time?"

Becker searched her brain for tomorrow's schedule. "We've got the Crime Steppers meeting, but otherwise, I'm in the office. We'll talk then."

She arrived at Mack's place within minutes, a stone's throw from the village and her Mama's house. His rancher sat on five acres at the end of a long driveway, with pastures on either side. In the back was a barn he used to store a small tractor, tools, other things men collect, and Bea's chicken flock.

As she parked her truck, one chicken, a rooster named Robbie, came over for his greeting. The dog slinked away, afraid of the little bird with a huge crow. Just then, he let out a "cock-a-doodle-do". Kevin ran for the doggy door on the screened front porch. Becker laughed.

Mack met her at the door with a sizzling kiss and hug. She looked at him with blurry eyes. "And hello to you, too."

He said, "I've missed you, Del. When are you moving in so I can see you every day?"

She took a step back.

He chuckled. "Oops, that sounded better in my head than out of my mouth."

Becker walked into the kitchen. It smelled of mushrooms and herbs. She admired the vase of sunflowers on the counter, and bent to say hello to Meno, who purred loudly in response. Kevin was already curled in his basket, ignoring the cat.

Bea was at the kitchen island doing homework, her head bent low to her book, lips moving as she read. She looked up. "Hey, Becker! Dad made your favorite, *boscaiola*. I'm doing homework, although I don't know what history has to do with being a poultry veterinarian. Some of these subjects are useless, don't you think?"

Bea was a chicken expert, studying breeds, learning husbandry practices, unlike other young girls her age who studied makeup application and how to take selfies with puffed-out lips.

"I disagree, Bea. Any subject that makes you think bigger will be useful for your goal of being a vet For example, studying history can be helpful to understand our relationship with birds through the ages."

The young girl nodded, red hair bouncing in her face. Her green eyes were serious as she listened to Becker. "Okay, I can accept that. How about Phys Ed?"

Becker shook her head. "You have me there. How are the new chicks doing?"

As Bea scratched Kevin's head, she launched into a one-sided discussion about the birds, telling Becker some of their names (Sandy, Sophie, Piper, Rudy and Popeye), their health, the average temperature under the heat lamp, and the amount of food and water they consumed daily. Becker listened intently, not because the information was all that interesting, but because Bea's excitement was infectious.

When the girl took a breath, Mack interjected, "Okay, Bea, let's clear the island for dinner. Del, can you help me plate the pasta? And grab the open bottle of Nebbiolo."

Becker gave him the side-eye. "Look at you, drinking a red wine besides cabernet sauvignon!"

Mack smiled, showing his dimples. "Fern and I have been experimenting. It's not a hardship, as you can imagine. We want to introduce some new varietals during the Seahorse Festival. Fern says he sees an up-tick that weekend in traffic from people that attend the event."

Becker poured the wine into glasses and took a sip. "Mmm, it's robust and earthy. A hint of thyme? And definitely dried fruit. Strawberries?"

"Del, if you ever decide to leave law enforcement, you could be a sommelier."

They sat down to dinner. The boscaiola was mouthwatering, a dish of pasta, mushrooms, and bacon in a light creamy tomato sauce. Becker and Mack sipped their wine while Bea talked about Sammy, her brother. "He was carrying a small log the other day. It was too big for him. He accidentally hit his privates. He called them his 'family Jews'. I'm not sure if it was his speech impediment or whether he thought it was the right name. I tried to get him to say 'jewels', but he pretended not to hear me."

As Mack cleaned the plates, Bea said, "Becker, Dad told me about the missing girl you're looking for. Was she my age?"

"No, she was older than you by a few years."

"Do you think she's dead?"

Becker put her arm around the young girl, a protective reaction. She loved Bea like a daughter and wished she could fib her way around the answer.

"She has been gone for over six years. Unfortunately, the longer a person is missing, the more likely she's not alive. But I am hopeful we will find her safe and sound."

Bea's eyes were serious as she looked at Becker while petting Kevin's head, the dog still hovering for scraps. "Why did she leave?"

"I'm not sure yet. It appears she was having a tough time with her family. She was...quirky and didn't fit in. There were some arguments at home. She might have run away."

"If she ran away, where would she go?"

Becker made eye contact with Bea; the seriousness on her face made Becker sad. "Bea, that's a brilliant question. I don't have the answer yet."

"Maybe she had a friend who took her in. Or maybe she had a secret place all of her own. You know, somewhere she could hide from her family."

"Perhaps.

"Someone could have taken her."

"Yes, kidnapping is a possibility."

"You've got a lot of work to do, Becker. I hope you find her."

Mack said, "Bea, I hate to interrupt, but would you check on the chickens? Make sure they are in their pen? It's getting dark out and you know Beep-Beep sometimes forgets to go in."

Bea put on her boots then headed to the barn. Mack sat down next to Becker, brow furrowed, jaw tight. "What's with the new door on your apartment?"

Becker mentally kicked herself for not telling him. Shit. "I had it replaced... I need to apologize. I'm sorry I forgot to tell you. Um, someone broke in to my apartment." She watched the concern on his face grow deeper as she told him the story.

Mack rubbed his mouth and then let out a heavy sigh. "I'm aware your job is dangerous and I can't do anything about that...but I wish you would let me in from time to time."

She grabbed his hand. "Oh Mack, I let you in more than you will ever know. I've been closer to you than any other boyfriend I've ever had."

He nodded; Becker could tell her words didn't hit their mark.

"I promise to do better. Being the lone ranger gets old for me, but I've been taking care of myself for so long it's become a habit."

He nodded again then kissed her forehead. "Okay, I'll hang around while you get rid of that habit."

Bea came in. Shortly after, Becker and Mack said their goodbyes. He gave her a long hug and whispered in her ear, "I don't have Bea this weekend. You wanna have a sleep-over?"

"Sure. Pajamas optional?"

She thought about his smoldering eyes the entire way home.

Chapter Ten

"**C**hief! Do you have a minute?"

Joey *Smiling Joey* Vito yelled at her from a block away. He jaywalked across the road, beaming his signature smile at her.

"Hey, Kevin, a perfect day for a walk and a poop, eh?" He smiled at the dog, too. "Chief, I have a problem."

"I'm all ears."

"My cousin is coming into town."

"That's a problem?"

"His name is Angelo *The Angel* Zullo."

Becker vaguely recalled tales of *The Angel*, a notorious mobster known for his love of women, wine, and winning (or losing) at the poker table. He was a former heavyweight boxer-turned-body guard for the mob bosses in Chicago. He reputedly had a short-temper and a penchant for beating people up, with or without provocation.

"Well, shit."

"I agree." Joey wasn't smiling. "I tried to, whadda-ya-callit, dissuade him from visiting, but you can't tell him nothing. I don't need him mad at me, if you know what I mean."

"I do. What do you want me to do about it?"

Joey rubbed his belly, protruding under his Hawaiian themed bowling shirt. "I dunno. Maybe you can scare him a little?"

Becker held back a laugh. Her short, 5'2" frame was supposed to be intimidating to a guy who was as big as a Sasquatch, minus some of the hair? "Okay, Joey, I'll talk with him when he gets here. Text me and I'll come by in my uniform, looking as fierce as I can."

She and Kevin meandered around town, enjoying the quiet before the merchants opened up for the day. They walked around the circle, over the fake scaled-down version of the Rialto Bridge, and stopped next to the fountain, adorned with cherubs. A few bubbles floated on the water, remnants of dumped detergent, probably a from high school prank.

Around the circle were shops for souvenirs, gourmet cheeses, flowers, antiques, and Mack's art gallery. There was also a bed-and-breakfast, a diner, an Italian restaurant, and the yoga studio Becker lived above. She loved the architecture of the town and envisioned her great-great-grandfather, hammer in-hand, constructing the buildings to bring the town to life over 100 years ago.

Becker walked Kevin back to her place. After a hurried shower, she dropped the dog off at the police station, green straw in his mouth, before the Crime Steppers Meeting. She walked across the street to the Pasta Palazzo, a two-story white building with columns and a large porch surrounded by urns of herbs and flowers. She smelled lavender as she said hello to a few of her officers; Mama Becker stood in front of the door.

"Cara, it's been ages since I saw you! Have you changed your hairstyle? Are you growing it out?"

"I was just at your place last Sunday for dinner."

"Yes, I remember. But that was over a week ago! Hair grows fast. When are you visiting again? I have a new Tuscan lasagna recipe to try, but it's too much for one person. A mother needs time with her daughter and you are always so busy."

Becker suppressed a sigh at her mama's attempt to use Catholic guilt to make Becker feel bad, then let it go. Mama was one of the kindest people she had ever met, and it was out of love she wanted more of Becker's attention. "Mama, I need to be Chief of Police now. Can we go to dinner tomorrow night? The restaurant you like in Ocean City? My treat."

Mama's face broke into a big smile. "Oh, I would love to! Except, can you come to the house instead? I really want to make the soon-to-be famous Tuscan lasagna for my cooking class. I need a taste tester first."

"Are you kidding? A home cooked meal beats going out any day. I'll bring wine."

Becker slowly worked her way through the room, nodding or waving to a handful of her officers, said hello to Fern, and stopped at a table where Molly and Johnny Hudson were sitting. "Hi, Molly. Johnny. Franklin."

Molly said, "Franklin isn't here. He was under the weather this morning so I left him at home to rest."

Becker said, "Poor little guy. I hope he's okay."

"How do you know when Franklin is sick?" Johnny asked.

"He tells me." Molly turned red. "I mean, I can 'read' his eyes and body; even his fur looks different when he is off. Ah, here's Roman, good morning!"

Roman Costa was the owner of Pasta Palazzo, a dapper Italian gentleman in his seventies who referred to himself in the third person. Like his good friend Cephas Jones, he wore expensive suits—Armani being his favorite—with pressed shirts, colorful ties, and a sprig of basil in his buttonhole. His hair was gray with white strands, and it sat at the top of his head like a meringue pie, arranged artfully with a little swirl. Crime Steppers' meeting day was his favorite day of the month; he sold mimosas as fast as his bartender could mix them.

He set down steaming mugs of coffee in front of Molly and Johnny. "And for you, Chief? Roman can bring you a Bloody Mary?" His eyes twinkled as he smiled at her.

"Roman, I'm working!"

"Bah, you Americans…"

Becker made her way to the front table with the Crime Steppers officers and sat at the end next to Cephas Jones, who was filling in for the absent president. "Morning, Chief. Ready to get this show started?"

Becker nodded at Cephas, who called the meeting to order, dispensed with the secretary's and treasurer's reports, then told the newcomers why the group had such a strange name. "Back in the day, a few older residents put up signs and incorrectly spelled 'Stoppers' with an E. Crime Steppers stuck." He then turned the floor over to Becker for the crime report.

"We've had three incidences of graffiti in the last two weeks." Technically, Becker thought, there were four, but hers was unrelated. "The drawings are very crude. We are sure it's the same man or woman since the artist signs his or her work with a star. If you have any information, please let me know or call the Celestino Police Department."

An older woman with what looked like a gray beehive on her head raised her hand. Becker nodded at her.

"What is the guy drawing?"

Before Becker could answer, someone said, "A cockroach." Another voice said, "No, a grasshopper." A third said, "A squirrel."

"Let's get a betting pool going," Joey Vito said, "and when Chief finds the perp, we can ask him what the graffiti is. Whoever is closest wins the money."

Becker hid a smile. "Everyone, listen up! We're not sure what the drawings represent. And I'm not sanctioning gambling. Let's move on to the second issue I have to discuss. The number of wellness checks my officers are making has risen dramatically." Becker pulled out her phone and scrolled to the information. "In six months, we've had over sixty calls for help. In case you aren't familiar with the term, a 'wellness check' is a request for us to verify a person's safety. Usually, it's our older residents, but sometimes it's looking in on kids. Once, it was for a hamster."

Someone yelled from the back of the room. "Was he okay?"

"Elvira," Becker said, "the female hamster, was fine. Folks, we need you to step up and help your neighbors. We're looking for volunteers to assist with these types of checks."

Johnny Hudson waved his hand. Once Becker's nemesis, he was now just a pain in her side, mostly during these meetings. His questions were legendary in their ridiculousness.

"Chief, what kind of training will we receive to check in on rodents?"

Someone next to Johnny groaned.

Becker said, "Johnny, you won't be assigned rodent duty. We'll leave that for the county animal control folks. Children's services handle wellness visits on kids. So that leaves adults; our office will provide classes on fall protection, how to determine if someone has had a stroke, that sort of thing. It's mandatory for volunteers. There's a form on the front table for sign-ups."

Becker rushed to the last topic to pre-empt anyone from asking another asinine question. "The only other business item I have, before turning the meeting over to Cephas Jones again, is our investigation of Michelle Workman's disappearance." Becker had no actual news to impart, but if she didn't mention it, the Crime Steppers would make up their own stories. "Mayors Spinosi and Workman have requested we look into it, and we're in the early stages of the investigation. Cephas Jones, back to you."

"Thanks, Chief." He looked out into the audience, fifty or some people eating eggs, sausage biscuits, and copious amounts of coffee. One table held an empty bottle of red wine. "Can you believe the Seahorse Festival is in a month? For those of you who are new to the Crime Steppers, we help with three events a year: the Celestino Celebration in the summer, is our biggest. Next is the Seahorse Festival in the fall, which is a joint effort between us and the town of Silver Hill. That's coming up, so I've created a sheet for volunteers. It's sitting on the back table, so be sure to scribble your name down to help with trash, parking, or manning our booth." He glanced at his notes. "Oh, the last event of year is our spring Shop and Sip, a day for shopping in town with wine from La Dolce Vita, a nearby winery."

Someone off to the side of the room yelled, "That one I'll sign up for!"

Chapter Eleven

B ecker stood in the parking lot between a garage and *Dave's Dive*, the place where Michelle was arrested for prostitution. True to its name, it was an unkempt dump.

A car pulled up behind her. Mooney crawled out. She reached back in the vehicle to pull out two to-go cups. She walked over to Becker, holding out one. "Chief! I felt you come into town from my shop!"

Becker was at a loss for words, which happened a lot around Mooney.

"I brought you a coffee with that sweet Italian Cream you like."

"Um... Thank you. Do you mind me asking, how do you feel people?"

Mooney giggled. "I wish I could tell you I was hit on the head as a child and became psychic because of the bump, but my story isn't as interesting. I guess I was eleven when I first heard a...whisper. No, that's not a good word." She paused, eyes to the sky. "Murmur. That's it. A murmur, like when someone is talking really low and there are actual words coming out of their mouth, but the words are all garbled. Does that make sense?"

Becker was at a loss again. It made no sense. She nodded anyway.

"Unfortunately, it only happens with a select few people. You, for instance, and Kevin, because of your bond. My Aunt Millie. A random guy I met on the beach one day last summer." Mooney sipped her coffee. "My sister Michelle."

"If you can 'feel' those select people, why can't you find Michelle?"

"The murmurs only happen when someone is close by."

Becker asked, "How close?"

"A couple of miles, I guess. When Michelle went missing, I drove around town to some of her favorite places to listen for her." She shook her head, sadness in her eyes. "I came here."

"Why?"

Mooney gestured to the garage with her cup. "That's Gus Fornash's garage. She learned how to work on cars there, and when things got bad at home, you could usually find her here hiding under the hood of a car."

A sign, swaying in the breeze by one hook, read FOR_ASH GARAGE. The building had two grimy, dusty glass garage doors. An old Volvo, rusted and missing an engine, sat on blocks next to the building beside a trash dumpster, old milk crates from a small town in Virginia, cardboard boxes from car parts distributors, and empty bags of Kittypuss cat litter. The place looked desolate, almost deserted, waiting to crumble onto the pavement...except for two new bright green bowls on the ground, and a small three-legged tabby cat drinking water from one of them.

"She could wrench, especially Volvo engines."

Mooney said, "Yes. She was a natural."

Becker turned toward Dave's Dive. "Michelle spent time there, too."

"How hard is it to paint the building, clean the windows, throw that gigantic pile of empty beer cans in the trash? And clean up the cigarette butts?" Mooney asked.

"About as hard as replacing some of the metal signs on the front of the building, including the one with the bullet hole in it." Becker glanced at her smart watch. "Mooney, I'm glad I bumped into you, but I have to run to court. Did you come by just to say hello, or for a reason?"

"Both." She smiled. "Hello again. And, the reason I stopped by is to ask if we can we hold our upcoming interview in my shop instead of the Silver Hill police station. By explanation, I am an empath, and when I go in there, sadness, frustration, and shame come into me. It's hard for me to think. Afterwards, it's hard for me to shake off the residue, so to speak."

"Um."

Mooney patted Becker's arm. "I knew you would understand."

***

Becker pulled her car into the lot next to the courthouse, a Victorian brick building built in 1894. The windows were arched, painted white, the entrance under a roof with four columns. Above the porch was a tower with a clock, capped with a six-sided dome roof. She felt the importance of the place as she entered the building and moved toward Judge Green's courtroom.

She turned a corner in the hallway; Sheriff Paul Atkins barreled towards her. Great. Too late to run in the other direction, so she might as well use the time to her advantage. "Morning, Sheriff. Glad I ran into you. I—"

"Wish I could say the same, Chief Becker." His stance was aggressive, feet wide apart, one hand on his gun. "Why are you back in my town?"

Becker narrowed her eyes. She imagined sparks coming out of them, lighting the sheriff on fire. eyes flashed. "Sheriff, last time I checked, the city isn't named Atkinsville. So cut the shit, okay? I've already tried to make nice by explaining I am involved in Michelle's case by order, not choice. I need you to help or stay the hell out of my way. Which will it be?"

Sheriff Atkins stared at her, mute. Becker's impatience (and temper, if she was honest about it) flared. "I understand down here it takes longer for people to comprehend a question and formulate an answer as compared to, for example, up north in Celestino Village. I can wait for your brain to process my simple question."

The tips of his ears turned pink. "Becker, don't be such a—" He stopped mid-sentence, then looked over her shoulder. His face transformed into one of congeniality and cooperation. "Whatever we can do to support you... Oh, hello, Judge Green."

Becker turned around to greet the judge. A short, wiry man in his sixties, Harold Green dominated any space with his erect posture and commanding voice. He was a fair magistrate, as long as he didn't smell a liar or bully.

If Sheriff Atkins wanted to look like a hero to His Honor, she would let him. "Sheriff Atkins, thank you for your generous offer to use your interview room at the station," she said, with a smile in her voice. "The Workman family will be much more comfortable here than in Celestino Village's police station."

"What a splendid idea, Chief," Judge Green said, cupping his hand on her shoulder. "I applaud you both for cooperating on this case. Some law enforcement professionals would find it easy to posture, working at cross purposes instead of for the common good."

Becker hid a grin; Sheriff Atkins' ears had turned a bright red. She was sure she would pay for this later, but for now it was fun and she was getting her way. "You don't say, Judge. Well, I'm grateful for Sheriff Atkins' help. And Sheriff, does next week work for you and Officer Peter Peters to interview with me?"

Sheriff Atkins said, "He goes by 'Pete', by the way. Peter Peters is awkward, don't you think?" Neither Becker nor the judge smiled. "He'll be available."

"And you?"

His voice was sharp and short. "What do you need with me?" He looked at the frown on Judge Green's face and softened his voice. "If you don't mind me asking, Ma'am."

"You were the sheriff when Michelle went missing. I want to get your insights about events leading up to the disappearance, and your recollection of what happened afterwards."

Sheriff Atkins nodded. "Of course."

Judge Green smiled at both of them. "Chief Becker, we're needed in court."

As they walked away, leaving Sheriff Atkins standing in the middle of the hallway, Becker glanced over her shoulder. He looked like a cheetah waiting to pounce on a rabbit, all tense and coiled. He brought up his hand and pointed his index finger at her, thumb in the air, like a pistol. She read his lips: "Bam."

She smiled keeping pace with Judge Green, following him into the courtroom. It was a beautiful space; dark mahogany wood on the walls, benches, and witness box; it surrounded the jury area and wrapped around the judge's bench. It reminded Becker of a library in a stately 1880s home where men smoked cigars, drank bourbon, debating the issues of the day.

Becker had expected several cases for the afternoon. The court dismissed the first and her next two were no-shows. She had a hit-and-run case; the driver jumped a curb and plowed down six prized rose bushes. Judge Green made the driver pay court fees, buy new plants, and put them into the ground herself.

Her fifth case was for public indecency. Becker testified the defendant was walking down the road wearing only a shirt, carrying his shorts and underwear. "Your Honor, the defendant wouldn't comply with repeated requests to put his clothes on, so I had to arrest him."

"Sir, what do you have to say about your public indecency charge?"

"Um...your Honor..." Everyone leaned forward. He was a low talker.

"You'll have to speak up. I can't hear you, nor can the court recorder." The judge smiled at the plump woman to his right, sitting at the stenotype machine.

"Um...sir, I was having a horrible day. I'm not guilty by reason of poison ivy. I was embarrassed to tell Chief Becker but...I came in contact with it earlier in the day. I'm highly allergic. I was walking home as fast as I could but I was having to itch myself, front and back, and it was easier to do it without, um, undergarments on." He sheepishly added, "I'm very sorry, your Honor. I had to go to the hospital that same day and they made me stay overnight. I had it real bad."

Judge Green sighed. "I feel for you. You obviously suffered enough. Not guilty. Case dismissed, please pay the court costs on your way out."

Both the judge and Becker rubbed their brows. *You can't make this shit up*, she thought.

Chapter Twelve

M olly interrupted her musings about Angelo *The Angel* Zullo, Joey's cousin, which were taking a rather unprofessional turn. She had Mack, for goodness' sakes. She didn't need a mafia bad boy in her life; she needed to keep him in check while he visited Celestino Village. Geez.

Becker clicked off her screen as Molly sat in a chair across the desk, getting another glimpse of Angelo on the monitor. It was a picture taken at a recent fund-raising event. He was tall and meaty, but not fat, with wavy black hair, brown eyes, and an infectious smile. His hair brushed the collar of his designer suit; a Rolex peeked out from under his shirt sleeve on his left wrist, a diamond winked from his ear. He looked charming, yet dangerous.

"Chief?"

Becker's brain had a big blank space where her thoughts usually resided. "Oh, yes, um, is Franklin better?"

Franklin scurried out of Molly's dress, across the desk, to Becker's shoulder. She stroked the soft fur on his head with her index finger, then reached in a drawer for a sugar glider treat. Franklin munched on it contentedly.

"Yes, but he still has the sniffles. Today's the first time he's been out in a few days. I had to bring him with me; he was getting cabin fever. We're both glad to be here." She pulled out her notebook, getting down to business. "I just started my criminal and background checks on the family, so nothing to report on yet. You mentioned yesterday you might have others to add to the list. Who would you like me to include?"

"Please add Sheriff Paul Atkins, and Officer Peter Peters." Molly raised her eyebrows at the comical name. Becker shuffled some papers, looking for additional notes. "Um, Gus Fornash."

"And Gus is?"

"He's the garage owner at the place next to Dave's Dive. His name came up as a...friend? Mentor? I'm not sure of the exact nature of their relationship, but he and Michelle spent time together working on vehicles."

She scribbled on her pad and looked at Becker.

"Oh, last, Edward Landon."

"Did you say Edward Landon?"

"Yes, L-A-N-D-O-N. He was the bartender at Dave's Dive, working the day Michelle allegedly propositioned the 'surfer dude'. I am hoping he can identify the blond who was talking to Michelle."

Molly looked shell-shocked. "Edward Landon is who I wanted to talk to you about today." She glanced at the notebook she had carried in with her. "He went missing three months before Michelle did."

Becker stared at her. "Tell me more, please."

"I always start an investigation by looking at the big picture, and then analyzing smaller, incremental pieces. It gives me context. With this case, I started with missing persons in the state of Maryland for the last ten years, statistics about who disappeared, for how long, circumstances of the disappearance, any trends...that sort of thing. Then I narrowed my search to Celestino Village, Silver Hill and a few small cities on this side of the Chesapeake Bay Bridge. I did comparisons between the state and local results, ran some statistical probabilities. Edward's disappearance came up as an anomaly." Molly flipped a page and continued, "I'll explain the anomaly in a minute. Other items of interest...he was the same age as Michelle when he went missing, he was in the same high school class, and they lived a half-mile away from each other by car."

Becker had a puzzled look on her face. "Does it take longer by truck?"

Molly laughed. "My bad, I didn't express myself very well. The Landon property is across the marsh from the Workman property. They share backyards, so to speak. It's less than a quarter mile, assuming you can trudge through the muck that far. I printed you a map." Molly gave the piece of paper to Becker. "The marsh between the houses is part of a bigger wetland called the Grimmy Swamp, and it eventually leads to Bloodstone Bay."

Becker scanned the map. "It always amazes me that almost 20% of the Eastern Shore of Maryland is wetlands, marshes, and swamps." She looked up at Molly. "Thank you. Great work."

"Not done yet. Two things. First, I mentioned an anomaly, which is this: two people missing in such a short time in a small community doesn't fit with the state and local statistics."

"One too many."

"Exactly, Chief." Molly rummaged through her paperwork. "The last item I'd like to discuss is Edward's missing person's report. I printed it out. I accidentally left it on the copier; let me run and get it."

Becker smelled fresh brewed coffee. "Take your time. I need a jolt of caffeine." She let Franklin jump from her shoulder to Molly's and then walked to the far corner of the police station to the "break room" where a couple of pea-green cabinets covered with an orange Formica countertop sat flanked by a ratty refrigerator. The 'fridge was a relic, donated by Miss Mabel, a relic herself, and the town's oldest resident. It occasionally made death spiral noises; it clanked and hissed at random, making Kevin bark and Bella squawk. Becker didn't care. The ancient appliance kept her Italian Cream cold.

The front door opened. Kevin ran in, his leash and Bella trailing behind. One of her officers stood in the doorway. He gave her a quick wave, then backed out shutting the door. Kevin wriggled around Becker, stayed still long enough for her to remove his leash and scruff his ears. He ambled over to his basket, pushed Bella aside with his nose, and plopped his butt near hers.

On the way back to her office, Becker's phone buzzed. A message from Keisha. *I've got some prelim info, meet tonight at my place, 7:00?* Becker sent back a thumbs-up emoji.

Molly was sipping some green goop that smelled like tacos.

"What are you drinking?"

"A concoction of cilantro, licorice root, lots of garlic."

Becker shook her head. "That sounds disgusting."

"It is. I'm afraid of getting sick from Franklin, so it's 'Mean Green' as a preventative measure."

Becker picked up Edward Landon's missing person's report from her desk and started to read. Forty-eight hours after he disappeared, his mother, Edwina, filed the report. According to her statement, he didn't come home from bartending at Dave's the previous day, and didn't send her a text, something he routinely did so she wouldn't worry.

He had been wearing a bright blue shirt with ocean birds on the front, khaki shorts, and Converse sneakers, the same bright blue color as his shirt. He had worked the early shift, cleaned the place, and set up the bar for later that evening. The bartender, who took over at 3 p.m., was smoking a cigarette on the front porch and waved to Edward as he walked toward home.

Molly pushed another piece of paper across the desk. "Here's the flier they posted online and around town."

The picture of Edward appeared to be at his high school graduation, some three years before he disappeared. He was a gawky-looking kid:

long face, small ears, frizzy reddish-brown hair that curled at his nape. He wore braces; his smile was tight, almost forced. Becker thought he might have been trying to hide his dental work, or perhaps he didn't want his picture taken, period. That might explain the use of the older photograph for the flier, versus a more recent version.

Becker noticed the contact person was Sheriff Atkins, and not the Maryland State Police, who was better manned and equipped for such work. Becker wondered if the sheriff had been grandstanding, or if the family specifically requested him as the point guard for the investigation. It was curious and something she would look into.

"Can you call Edwina Landon and ask if I can visit with her tomorrow? And if not tomorrow, find out when she's available. My Spidey Sense is kicking in; there's something about these two young people missing within ninety days of each other, in a tiny little town. Not only is it an anomaly, according to your analysis, but it smells bad."

After Molly left, Becker resumed her research on Angelo Zullo. He was born in Chicago in a neighborhood formerly known as "Little Sicily" to first generation Italian-American parents. His father, Vinnie *Siggie* Zullo, got his nickname from chain-smoking cigarettes. When Angelo was a teenager, his father died, not from cancer, as his nickname would suggest, but from a gunshot wound to the chest. Vinnie was cutting grass one moment, dead on the lawn the next, a victim of a drive-by shooting. The nondescript sedan, a shotgun hanging out the rear window, looked remarkably similar to a car owned by Vinnie's best friend.

When the cops arrived later and asked his mama about the shooting, she said she was in the house, cooking dinner. Angelo knew it was a lie. She had been at the dining room window when the fateful shots rang out. From his favorite tree in the front yard, twenty feet from his now-deceased father, he saw the pain and grief on her face.

The same cop who interviewed his mama put his laser-sharp blue eyes on the young boy. Angelo told him the same thing. "I didn't see nothin'."

The cop, an Irish-American, was a frequent visitor to Little Sicily. He smelled a cover-up immediately, but let the Italians work it out on their own. They always did.

Angelo's silence with the cops and his identification of Vinnie's killer, dispatched by the mob three weeks later, earned him financial help for his boxing career: dirty money paid for the best coaches and trainers, leading to *The Angel's* heavyweight ranking in the Top 10. Years later, he retired from the ring with a pocket full of money and a promise to protect members of the mafia.

The national criminal databases cited many references to *The Angel* using his fists to rough-up or beat-up people, a few arrests for assault and battery, and a bunch of cases dismissed because of a lack of cooperation from victims or witnesses. He'd never been arrested or charged with manslaughter, murder, or any other capital crime.

Or maybe he just didn't get caught?

Chapter Thirteen

"Hey, Becker! I was worried. You're never late." Keisha stood in the doorway of her apartment, gesturing Becker in.

She handed Keisha a bottle of Old Vine Zinfandel along with a paper bag containing goat cheese, Havarti, sharp cheddar, and a box of gourmet crackers. "Couldn't be helped. I had to teach a seventeen-year-old kid how to change a tire. His car was on the side of the road and his nose was in his cell phone, watching videos, since he was clueless about what to do next."

Keisha laughed. "You can't do that too many times before you're called 'nice'. It's going to ruin your reputation as a tough cop."

Becker growled at her as she walked into the apartment, a tiny first floor unit a few blocks off the boardwalk in Ocean City, Maryland. The living room, just inside the front door, held a loveseat and matching chair, tucked into a corner with a reading light. To the back of the unit, on the right, was a galley kitchen, wide enough for one person, including a compact nook with a round table that doubled as Keisha's office space. If you looked out the window in the dining room, cricking your neck just so, you could see a tiny patch of blue water past the boardwalk, between the tattoo parlor and used bookstore.

The bedroom was as tight; a queen-sized bed dominated the room, leaving enough floor space to walk sideways to the elevator-sized closet. The bathroom had a puny sink, which reminded Becker of the ones found on small fishing boats.

The only thing remarkable about the apartment was Keisha's collection of *sabai* grass bowls. Bought over the years, she had grouped them according to color and pattern, the vibrant colors catching Becker's eye. She admired one with gray, orange, and neon pink swirls. "Your collection is growing. They're beautiful."

"Thank you," Keisha said. "But I'm going to slow down. I think they make my apartment feel smaller."

"I don't think it's the baskets. No disrespect... Why not move?" Becker bumped into the table as she closed the door.

"I love being so close to the beach. Unless it's really ugly out, I run every morning, two miles toward Rehoboth, two back toward Assateague. I also spend many nights sitting on the beach with a glass of wine, off season, of course, looking at the ocean." Keisha opened the bag Becker brought, peering in. "Give me a minute to uncork the wine to put the cheese and crackers on a plate."

"I can help," Becker said.

Keisha shook her head. "Kitchen is too small." She picked up a Silver Hill High School yearbook from the table and handed it to Becker. "I got a small bounty while I was on 'vacation' in Silver Hill. Here, this should keep you busy. References or pictures of Michelle are marked with Post-it notes."

As she settled into the comfy chair, Becker opened the book, published the year Michelle graduated. She leafed through the first few pages to get a sense of the high school itself, the teachers, events, clubs, sports, the "in" kids, the "not-so-in" kids. It reminded her of Celestino High: a small but quality institution in a rural town.

The first picture Keisha tagged was of Michelle in woodworking class. She had her head bowed over a lathe, working on what appeared to be a table or chair leg. Her eyes were intent behind her safety glasses, and she had a half-smile on her face.

The next picture was Michelle's graduation photo. She wore a plain white t-shirt under pink bib overalls, the pant legs tucked into mud-caked, dark green muck boots. She was leaning against a bald cypress tree, unsmiling; the photographer captured a flying osprey in the marsh behind her, over her left shoulder. It was organic and earthy, and utterly unlike any other graduating picture in the yearbook.

The last photo of Michelle included Edward Landon, both of them in their band uniforms. She held a trombone; he held a trumpet. They were looking at each other, not the camera. Both were laughing.

Keisha came into the living room and set a tray of cheese and crackers on the couch. She returned with two glasses of wine handing Becker one. "Find anything of interest?"

Becker put her nose in the glass, smelled blackberry and strawberry aromas, then took a sip of the fruity wine. "Actually, I did."

Becker flipped to Michelle and Edward's band picture. "Not to jump to conclusions, but I find it odd there were two disappearances in a small town within ninety days of each other; my guess is they're related. They were neighbors. This photograph proves they were probably friends."

They were quiet for a moment. Becker snagged a piece of goat cheese, laid it on a cracker and popped it into her mouth. The cheese was tart yet buttery at the same time.

"How about I report on other things I discovered about Michelle?" Keisha picked up a small notepad from the table. "For being as 'colorful' as Michelle was before she disappeared, there's nothing on social media and very little online. She kept a low profile. I found a few articles on *Celestino Press's* website; Silver Hill doesn't have its own newspaper."

She passed a few pieces of paper to Becker. "I made copies so it's easier to review. Toward the back of the stack are articles about her disappearance. You can look at them later. There are three I want to discuss tonight. The first is about her working at Gus Fornash's garage. It was when she was still in high school."

The newspaper picture showed a young Michelle next to a man ten years older than her. He had a red bandanna tied around head, his untamed, shoulder-length brown hair sticking out from beneath. He wore a green Grateful Dead t-shirt over a pair of ratty blue jeans. He had his arm draped around Michelle's shoulders, as a brother (lover?) would. They were both smiling at the camera.

She scanned the article quickly; it described Michelle as an ace under the hoods of cars and an expert at small engine repair. Gus quoted, "Michelle is pretty near the best wrencher I've known. She can even build an engine from scrap, using whatever she finds in the shop."

Becker looked up from the article. "I visited Gus's garage, which is next to the bar where Michelle allegedly solicited a guy. It was closed, but I will go back and snoop around."

Keisha said, "Hmm... The second article is about a group called the 'Marsh Keepers', which was formed in the 1950s to protect the marshes and swamps in Maryland, primarily here on the Eastern Shore. You can read about their good deeds later. For now, look at the photograph and names underneath."

Becker recognized several faces from the photo. The first person she identified was Sheriff Paul Atkins, which surprised her; he didn't feel like the type to volunteer for a cause, let alone the environment. She picked out Michelle, standing in the back; on one side of her was Edward Landon, and on the other was a man named Hamilton Parsons. If anyone had the looks of a surfer dude, it was Hamilton.

Becker looked up and met Keisha's eyes. "We may have found our surfer, the one Michelle allegedly propositioned for sex in exchange for money."

"I thought the same thing," Keisha said.

"Okay, here's the last article." Becker scanned the story, a fluff piece about seniors at Celestino High School and Silver Hill High School, their plans for after graduation. Michelle Workman quoted, "I want to be a free spirit and backpack across Europe, and spend some time in England, looking for other Workmans like me."

"Maybe she ran away, after all," Becker said. "Anything else?"

Keisha pulled out her phone and looked at her screen. "Not much. I've requested a copy of Michelle's file, including the missing person's report, and any notes related to the search. So far, nothing."

Becker frowned and rubbed her brow.

"Becker, it's only been a few days. I'm not concerned yet. The staff at the Silver Hill Police Department is little. Like yours, they don't have a full-time administrative assistant that pulls records. If I don't get paperwork in another day or two, I'll call you to bring in the big guns."

Becker nodded and Keisha continued, "I got a hold of the state police file, which was slim. Michelle went missing on a Friday. William and Mimi Workman reported it the following Thursday. Six days...The Friday she disappeared, she went to Sunny Side Up, the diner in Silver Hill, and picked up an egg and bacon sandwich. Around 10:00a.m., she stopped at a gas station just outside of Celestino Village. In your jurisdiction, Becker. Later, a traffic camera spotted her car going south." Keisha paused, scrolling on her phone. "It was the last time anyone saw her."

"That's curious," Becker said. "Why would she grab breakfast in Silver Hill, drive north to fuel up near Celestino Village, then drive back south, past Silver Hill?"

Keisha took a sip of her wine. "No idea. One of the many questions we have to answer, Becker...how about you? Anything to report?"

"Not really. The Gruppo, who now includes Nonna, is 'helping' with the investigation. I couldn't tell them no when they dropped into my office." Just then, her phone buzzed. "Speaking of which..."

Nonna's voice came through the speakerphone. "I want to report a crime."

***

"You realize this wasn't a crime but a misunderstanding, correct?" Becker asked.

Nonna's crossed her arms under her large breasts. It reminded Becker of a busty woman wearing a German Octoberfest dress.

"The man urinated in Big Betty. I don't like anyone using my toilet but me and maybe a few family members like your mother, maybe Fern, although I don't know him very well, maybe your friend Mack..."

"Nonna. He's ninety years old and lost his glasses. He thought he was in his own camper."

"Don't believe it. He has a Grand Lodge Park model. Those things retail for $65,000. I bet he's got granite countertops and high-end fixtures. Probably a jetted tub. He had to see that my toilet is not the same quality as his toilet."

Lester the parrot screeched, "No peeing in the pool!"

Becker lowered her voice. "Nonna, you're upset. I'm sorry. Let me clean the toilet for you and I'll talk to Mr. Lee tomorrow."

"You mean Mr. Pee." Nonna grunted.

Chapter Fourteen

L adybank Manor, the Workman mansion, was on the way to Edwina Landon's place. Becker stopped the police car in front of the wraparound front porch, tastefully decorated with pumpkins, cornstalks, and gourds on straw bales. Mums and asters filled the window boxes. It looked professionally arranged, almost clinical, like a featured property on one of those home and garden TV shows. It was that lovely.

The marsh was behind the Workman property, stretching to beyond Bloodstone. She wondered if some days the area smelled faintly of sulfur, the aroma of marsh gas, and if it was repugnant to Mimi. Becker never minded the rotten-egg scent, but she also didn't live next to it 24/7.

As she drove around a bend in the road, the Landon house came into view, modest compared to the Workman estate. It was a two-story Victorian with a turret on one side, painted gold with ruby trim.

She parked her cruiser in the circle driveway and got out. Edwina met her at the door. She looked like an older, female version of her missing son. "Chief Becker, so nice to meet you. Come in!"

Edwina led her to a small sitting room off the front hallway filled with antiques, a gramophone that appeared to be the real thing, not a reproduction, and a cozy fireplace with a marble mantel. Vintage cabbage rose wallpaper completed the Victorian feel of the room. Becker noticed several tiffany lamps as they made small talk for a few minutes.

"I'm so glad you are looking for Edward."

Becker's breath hitched. "Ma'am, I don't mean to get our conversation off on the wrong foot, but I'm actually looking for Michelle Workman."

Edwina's smile didn't falter. "I realize she's your key priority. I'm hoping you'll learn something about Edward during the investigation."

Becker relaxed, smiling in return. "I hope so too, Mrs. Landon. Tell me about Edward. I've seen his picture but know little about him. Start anywhere."

"Please, call me Edwina." She poured each of them a glass of sweet tea. "Edward is actually my sister's son, my nephew. I adopted him as a baby with her blessing. She had a drug addiction and, um, couldn't care for him. She died when he was a toddler."

"I'm sorry."

"Me too. It was sad to lose her, but having Edward wa— I mean is, the joy of my life. I never married, never expected to have children, and then Edward was dropped into my lap, thank the Good Lord." She took a sip of her tea. "He was a wonderful baby, quiet, sweet natured, never cried. I know I'm making him sound perfect. He was. He grew into a sensitive boy, if a little awkward. My son was...shy, deeply introverted. He had few friends and spent a lot of time by himself, outdoors mostly, collecting rocks, feathers, leaves, driftwood, that sort of thing."

"He sounds like an interesting boy."

"Yes, Beyond interesting. He was profoundly curious, particularly with nature. Got straight As in science. Many of his teachers over the years told me he was kind to other kids, even if they weren't kind back."

"How did he and Michelle meet?"

"When he was...ten, I started taking him to the library. I was afraid of computers, which is silly. I eventually got over it, but back then we used the encyclopedia to identify the feathers he found. He met Michelle while they were reaching for the same book. She accidentally knocked him down. He was a small child, but had a growth spurt in high school, making him one of the tallest in his class."

"So, he and Michelle became friends?"

"Very much so. They both had this...fascination? I think that's an appropriate word, with swamps and marshes. As they grew older, they spent a lot of time wandering around Grimmy Swamp with Edward's dog, Buster. He died last year."

"He seemed to have a happy childhood?"

"Oh yes. I'm sure it was tough to grow up without a father figure in the house." She looked out the window, eyes unfocused. "Over the years he had mentors, male teachers, or other members of the community who looked out for him. He's a genuinely contented person. He graduated high school with good grades, yet he didn't apply to any college; I've often thought it was because of Michelle. He would have left her behind with that...awful—I'm sorry to use that word, family of hers." She wiped condensation from her glass with her thumb. "It's not godly to talk about others, so I'll stop there. Let's see. Oh, after high school he had several jobs: he worked at a beef farm, he tutored kids in math, he was a bartender. He was 'finding himself' and where he belonged, you know?"

Becker nodded. She did the same thing before becoming a cop.

"The bartender's job surprised me. He was never very social. And he picked that ghastly Dave's Diner when he could have worked someplace nicer."

Becker didn't have the heart to correct her that the place was appropriately named "Dave's Dive". She asked, "Can you tell me about the time leading up to his disappearance?"

Edwina fiddled with her watch. "About six months before he disappeared, I noticed a change in him. It didn't seem like much, but looking back, it may have been significant. He was...moody? Maybe a better way to say it is he was short-tempered, not that he got angry and showed it, more...impatient. There was several nights his bed wasn't slept in. I asked him about it and he said he was staying at a friend's house, but wouldn't give me a name. I dropped it. After all, he was twenty years old."

Edwina looked at Becker, eyes misty. "A mother never stops worrying. Whether her child is two or twenty, it's the same."

A lump sat in Becker's throat. Her mama's love was unconditional. She reached out and squeezed Edwina's hand.

"And then he didn't come home."

"Even on those nights he was elsewhere, he sent me a text, a word or two like 'I love you', or 'See you tomorrow'. After two days of no texts, I contacted the sheriff and filled out a report."

Edwina was a wilting like a flower in a vase without water. Becker didn't want to push further, so she said, "I'm sure I'll have more questions but for now I'd like to see Edward's room, if you'll let me?"

"Of course. I haven't moved anything, except to dust."

At the top of the stairs, the bedroom was to the right. The turret Becker saw from the outside was part of his room, with views of the swamp, road, and side yard. She watched two cardinals fly by, chased by a blackbird. It was like being in a tree house.

She turned her attention to the sparsely furnished room: a queen bed, two end tables, a small dresser, a chair piled with books, a telescope. A huge built-in bookcase was on one wall. She walked over to it, drawn in by the hundreds of rocks and dozens of feathers that were displayed. She noticed a shelf full of nature-themed photographs Studying several, she made a mental note of the subjects: a bald cypress tree, an Assateague pony, marsh grass a heron, an abandoned pier, an old boat.

"He took his camera with him when he scouted the wetlands, or with the Marsh Grass Society, or whatever it's called. Grimmy Swamp was his favorite place to take photographs, but he also shot pictures in Bloodstone Bay, Katy Bay, and Driftwood Swamp."

"These are beautiful photographs," Becker said. "I appreciate you showing them to me."

Edwina walked Becker to her car, and as Becker was pulling out of the driveway, her phone rang. She answered it on speakerphone.

"Chief Becker, this is Meghan Workman." The voice was tight and staccato.

"Yes, Meghan, what can I do for you?"

"We have an interview scheduled for later this week. However, I have a Garden Club meeting and have to cancel our appointment. We'll reschedule soon, probably within the next two weeks. I'll call you when I have my calendar in front of me."

Becker thought: Attending a meeting about plants is more important than finding your missing sister? Hmm. "Meghan, I'm afraid that won't do. I've told your father I will conduct interviews this week. How does your schedule look today? I can meet at your convenience."

"Um, I'm rather busy."

"You name the time. I am available whenever."

Meghan blew out a breath, loud enough for Becker to hear. "Fine," she said, her tone resigned, "I guess today will have to work. Why don't you come to my house in an hour?"

Becker said again, "I'm afraid that won't do, either. I'm conducting interviews at the Silver Hill Police Station." Meghan pushed back, so Becker flipped on her siren, drowning out Meghan's protests. "I'm sorry, I can't hear you. I have a traffic stop. See you then."

Becker hung up, satisfied to have the upper hand.

Chapter Fifteen

M eghan's crinkled nose was in the air as she glided into the police station. Becker watched her check in with the desk officer, then perch on a bench, expensive pocketbook on her lap, hands enclosed in baby pink designer leather gloves. Rail thin, she wore a cream-colored jacket and skirt, with a pink shirt that matched her gloves. She had on a pearl necklace, bracelet and earrings. Based on the way she carried herself and the vibes she gave off, Meghan appeared to be a mini-version of her prim, proper, socialite mother, Mimi.

I'll let her sit for a minute, Becker thought, as she thumbed through her notes on the Workman family.

Meghan was the oldest daughter, seven years older than Michelle. An academic achiever, Meghan graduated from high school as valedictorian, president of the high school class, and lead in the high school play. She attended Harvard as a liberal arts major, graduated with honors, returned to Silver Hill to marry a prominent attorney in the area, became a full-time mother. She occasionally dabbled in interior design, mostly for friends and family. Like her mother, she also had four daughters: Caroline, Constance, Christina, and Clarissa.

No police record. Not even for illegal parking or speeding.

After a quick trip to the restroom to put a bit of water on her unruly black-brown hair and pinch her cheeks for a little of color, Becker walked to the front of the station. "Meghan, hello, I'm Chief of Police Delaney Becker."

Meghan stood regally on a pair of modest pumps, pink, of course, and gave her fingers to Becker, palm side down. Becker wasn't sure whether to kiss her hand or shake it, so she gave it a squeeze and dropped it. "This way, please."

They settled into the windowless interview room, a claustrophobic space no bigger than eight feet by eight feet, painted an institutional green that glowed from the fluorescent light. Meghan left on her coat and gloves, despite the sauna-like heat. Becker shrugged off her light-weight jacket, wishing she could shed more clothes; it had to be over eighty degrees in the cramped room.

"Thanks for coming in."

Meghan looked at her as a scientist would a lab specimen. "You didn't give me much choice."

"Well, I'm glad you are here, regardless of the circumstances. Your father asked me to handle Michelle's investigation with some urgency. I am attempting to do just that."

"I'm sure it's important for you to follow Father's orders."

"I think it's more important that we find Michelle, don't you?"

Meghan's nose pinched, but she stayed silent.

"How about we start by you telling me about Michelle, growing up with her, your relationship, that sort of thing?"

"This is...distasteful, sitting in this disgusting little room. It's also a waste of my time. I talked to various police officers years ago. Don't you people keep records? It seems awfully irresponsible, not to mention inefficient for the taxpayers."

Becker told herself to stay calm. She mustered up her most indulgent smile. "I've reviewed Michelle's file, but you would do me a great favor by filling in some holes, so to speak."

"Fine," she said. "As you are well aware, Michelle was seven years younger than me; it's not like we were twins."

"Was? You think Michelle is dead? Otherwise, you would have said 'is', I believe."

"Yes, I think someone murdered her. She was such a troublemaker, doing what she wanted to do when she wanted to do it. She was a blight on the family name."

"She embarrassed you?"

"Absolutely. Michelle tried to ruin everything Mommy worked for, our reputation in the community, our standing as the first family."

"You didn't like her."

"I never said that."

"Well, listening to you now and hearing stories about how you slapped her around when she was a child leads me to believe there was no love lost between the two of you."

Meghan stared at Becker as silence filled the room. After a few moments, Meghan's face transformed; her face softened, her lips curled into a plastic smile, her eyes showed warmth, filling with fake tears, the furrow in her brow disappeared. It gave Becker the creeps.

When Meghan spoke, her voice changed to a sing-song, let's-get-along tone. "Oh, I loved her. She was my baby sister, after all. When she was little, I dressed her up like a doll and drove her around town in her baby buggy. Mommy has one of those old vintage wicker ones; I think it belonged to my great-great aunt Melba."

"And when she got older? What was your relationship like then?"

Meghan kept the mask of pleasantry firmly in place. "She was so...different from the rest of the family. But we thought she was delightful."

"Yet you hit her and were verbally abusive."

She gave Becker another smile that didn't reach her eyes. "Sometimes a child needs discipline, but it expressed my love, not abuse."

Becker mentally shook her head at the statement. An expression of love? Excuse me? "Do you hit your own children?"

"Goodness, no. They are angels."

This was going nowhere. "Your relationship with Michelle was...pleasant. How did she get along with your other siblings? Your mother? Father?"

"She and Mooney were best buddies. Mommy tolerated her silliness and Father was indulgent."

"And your other sister, Marissa?"

"Marissa gets along with everyone."

Becker said, "Yet she left for college. Never came back, from what I understand."

"Some birds fly out of the nest early to find their own place."

Becker changed topics, "Tell me about the day Michelle went missing."

Meghan's face turned red and her eyes darted around the room. "I don't remember the day. I remember the search afterwards."

"You weren't there when your sister disappeared?"

Meghan looked at the floor. "Yes, but I can't recall what happened. I was...distraught."

Becker's eyebrows shot up. What? "What made you distraught?"

"Just the whole situation."

"Can you elaborate?"

"Have you ever lost a sister, Chief?"

Becker would not touch that question, even though her relationship with Alyssa was estranged for years. "Let's focus on you, Meghan. Were you still distraught during the search?"

"No, I took part in looking for her. Sheriff Atkins organized several parties to scour Silver Hill. He had helicopters in the air over the forests, swamps, really, most of the county; I think he even told them to circle your town. We looked for four days and found nothing."

"Four days seems like a short time."

Meghan narrowed her eyes as a sly grin appeared on her face. "How many searches have you been involved with, Chief Becker?"

Becker ignored the question. "You mentioned you thought Michelle was murdered? Who do you think could have done it?"

Meghan's gloves were off. Literally. The pink ones were still on her hands, although the temperature had risen in the room. "Don't you think it's your job to find out?"

"I could use your help, of course."

"She hung out at that garage run by Mr. Fornash. He seems squirrelly, if you ask me. Another person to consider is her friend, Edward Landon. He was very odd."

"Edward went missing before Michelle. How would that work?"

Meghan sighed, long and loud. "I'm not sure. Again, your job. Are we almost done here? My calendar is very full this time of year."

Becker said, "One last question, Meghan. Could someone in your family have killed her?"

Meghan's good girl face slid back into view. "Of course not. We have a reputation to protect. Nobody in the family would sully our good standing by murdering someone."

***

Becker mulled over her interview with Meghan on the way back to Celestino Village. Not much to grasp at except the strong dislike (maybe hate?) for her sister. She walked into the police station with a slight headache.

Molly jumped out of her chair, breathless. Her face was pale, her eyes were darting around the room, her hair was sticking up, as if she had been teasing it. "Oh Becker, I'm so glad you're back. We can't find Kevin."

Becker's mind went blank. "What do you mean, you can't find him?"

"I went across the street for a carry-out coffee from the Shanty, and when I came back, he was gone. I wasn't gone that long. I mean, it was only a few minutes. I'm sure I locked the door. At least I thought I locked it. I always do, I…"

Becker touched Molly's shoulder as she swallowed past the panic in her throat, threatening to choke her. "Slow down, it's okay. Sometimes I leave and don't lock the door." Tears rolled down Molly's face. Franklin scurried to her shoulder then patted her hair.

"Take a breath with me." They both inhaled and exhaled for several moments. Sadness settled in Becker's chest, like the pneumonia she had when she was a child, threatening to cut off her oxygen, making her feel hopeless, vulnerable. She willed her face not to crumple. *I will not cry. He's going to be fine.* "Let's start from the beginning. When did you leave to get coffee?"

"Around 3:00p.m."

"Did you see anyone near the station?"

"No."

"How about on your way to the Shanty?"

"No. Wait, yes, a few tourists, women dressed in red. Maybe four of them. Probably a bachelorette group; one was wearing a tiara."

The door to the station opened; they both jumped. Guido Tucci walked in with a smile and ice cream cones; he stopped in his tracks. "What's wrong?"

"Kevin's missing."

He dumped the cones in the wastepaper basket. "What can I do?"

"Go look for a group of women dressed in red. Ask if they saw Kevin outside of the station."

He kissed the top of Molly's head. "On it."

"Can you also canvas the merchants?" Becker asked. "See if he was seen wandering around town?" It was a long shot; he wasn't a runner.

He occasionally was off the leash at the beach or park but stayed glued to Becker's side.

"Will do, Chief. While I'm gone, consider putting out an ABP on our private channel so our officers can keep an eye out for him."

Becker agreed and a few minutes later, picked up the headset to tell her patrol officers to be on the lookout for the beloved mutt. She took in a big breath pushing aside thoughts of him injured on the side of the road, or hurt at someone's hands.

A half-hour went by. Guido returned with nothing of note from the women in red. "One of the older ladies, Mabel, said she thought she saw Kevin with a middle-aged man." He took out his phone, scrolling for his notes. "Mid-forties, white, chubby—her word, not mine—wearing sunglasses. Baseball hat, brown hair. Or blond. Not sure." He sighed. "Chief, she wasn't clear about the type of dog, and was fuzzy about whether they got in a car, truck, or kept walking. I'm sorry."

Another hour passed by. She kept it together, barely. Thoughts about the adorable mutt made her want to cry, so instead she made coffee, drew a map of the town and areas previously searched, refused a ham sandwich from Mack, called Guido multiple times, and gave Bella the chicken a hug.

Cops filtered in. Filtered out. Filtered in again. Brewed coffee wafted; the cops and volunteers drank the place dry.

After three hours, Becker hid in the police's bathroom station, tears running down her face.

At the five-hour mark, she prayed to Saint Anthony, patron saint of lost things.

She hoped he was listening.

Chapter Sixteen

Becker and Mack drove around town until it got too dark to find a wayward dog. They headed back to his place, sad and tired.

Neither of them slept; they were up at dawn. Exhausted, they were pouring coffee in to-go cups when her phone buzzed with an incoming text. *Look in the mailbox. You're lucky this time.*

Her hands shook, and she dropped the phone. She ran to the window, her mind a jumble, scanning the front of the house. No one there. She grabbed her Glock as she flew out the door. She ran up the driveway, gravel biting into her bare feet. She had forgotten her socks and shoes.

She saw a white patch in the weeds near the mailbox. Kevin?

He was tied to the mailbox, the rope wound so tight he was choking. She kneeled on the ground, Glock digging into her back, to quickly uncoil the rope. He jumped on her shoulders, knocking her down. She laugh-cried and let him lick her face as she sank her fingers in his dirty, matted fur. No injuries or broken bones she could tell. He was fine. Fine!

She put her head in the scruff of his neck as Mack crouched beside her. He reached out to hug Kevin at the same time Kevin jumped on him. They both fell into the tall weeds. Poison ivy flashed in Becker's mind; she smiled. Who cares? Her baby was home.

As they all got up, Becker almost hit her head on the open mailbox. She retrieved the letter inside, grabbing it with the edge of her shirt.

Becker couldn't take her eyes off of Kevin as they trudged back to the house.

Once inside, she gave the dog another once-over through teary eyes, feeling his head, back, neck, legs, paws, even his teeth. She wasn't sure what she was looking for but it felt good to run her fingers in his coat, reminding herself he was fine. Mack set down a bowl of water; Kevin slurped and slurped, splashing liquid on the floor and wall.

"He looks okay, Mack, except for the mud and dirt."

"He's got to be tired if he's been tied to that damn pole all night." Mack gave her a side hug and she let him.

"He's probably hungry." They fed him, gave him a bath, and settled him into his dog bed, where he promptly fell asleep.

Mack asked, "What does the note say?"

She had forgotten about the letter. Dread filled her chest in anticipation of another missive from the person who broke into her apartment. She drew the envelope from her pocket with a kitchen glove, took out the piece of paper and set it on the counter. They read it.

Dear Chief Becker,

I told you rather kindly to leave Michelle and me alone and you ignored me. I'm asking again: please leave us alone. We're safe for now, but you are going to ruin it.

Next time, Kevin won't be alive when you find him.

Sincerely,

Michelle's loving husband.

Becker's face got hot. It felt like the top of her head was going to blow to Mars. "That son of a bitch! Not one, but two threatening letters! He's picked the wrong dog and person to mess with." She paced the room, rubbing her brow. "Loving husband, my ass. What sort of man would hurt an animal? No, don't answer that. He's sick. I'm going to spend every waking hour hunting him down. Damn him!"

Mack was quiet. The silence stretched from several seconds to a minute. "What do you mean by two letters?"

She covered her face with her hands to regain composure, then poured another round of coffee. "I found the first letter the day after the graffiti, tucked into my bookcase."

"You told me about the break-in and graffiti, but you didn't tell me about the letter. Do I have that right?" His posture became more rigid, his hands squeezing his coffee cup.

"It wasn't on purpose, I swear."

His voice was soft, but sharp. "Del, do you think we're building something serious together? Like a picket-fence-and-kids kind of serious?"

Wow, that was out of nowhere. She stuttered, "I do."

"Can you explain to me how that would work when one person in our relationship isn't open with the other?"

Becker was tired and irritated. "Mack, I want to have this conversation with you, but please, not right now." She rubbed her brow again; a headache bloomed near her left temple.

His eyes were sad. "Okay."

She put her hands on both sides of his face. "No, I mean it. I'm not avoiding the topic, just delaying our discussion. I'm sorry."

He nodded, weary from the events of the past twenty-four hours. "Let's take a nap. We're both exhausted."

Kevin woke up, followed them into the bedroom, curled himself into a ball at the end of the bed, snoring immediately. Becker drifted off with a smile on her face.

***

She dropped off Kevin at Mama's the next morning. He did his best to make her feel guilty with his sad eyes and doggy cries. She stayed resolute. Until she found the evil letter-writer, she would shuttle Kevin to various houses to keep him safe. She also moved Bella to Bea's chicken coop for the short-term. She didn't want to obsess about the fur and feathers in her life.

As Becker drove to the police station, her phone rang.

"Chief Becker?" The voice was familiar, and full of fear.

"Yes, can I help you?"

"It's Mooney. Can you come to Silver Hill? Someone's damaged my store. I need you."

"Sheriff Atkins is in a better position to help." Becker didn't want to piss the guy off any more than she had to, and truth be told, she wanted to find Kevin's kidnapper and wring his neck, not hold Mooney's hand in Silver Hill. "Do you need me to call him?"

"No, he'll show up, too. But whoever did...this...it's related to Michelle's disappearance. He left a note." Becker's gut clenched. "I'm on my way." She flipped on her flashing lights and made it to *Apothecary and Amulets*, Mooney's store, in twenty minutes.

Bullet holes pocked the front window; the glass on the door was shattered. People milled around, curious and concerned about the carnage to the historic building. Three police cars blocked the street, blue and white lights reflecting off of the fractured window.

Mooney met her on the sidewalk, standing next to a tall, buff, thirty-something with a dark tan and a winning smile. He looked familiar; she couldn't place him. Becker saw the worry lines on Mooney's face, the tight smile, the dried tear-tracks. Her protectiveness of such a sweet soul kicked in. She grabbed her hand. "Mooney, tell me what happened."

Mooney blew her nose. "Oh Becker. I got a call from the owner of the Sunny Side Up just before dawn. She drove by the shop and saw the glass sparkling on the sidewalk around the street lamp. I came and found...this. According to Sheriff Atkins, someone used a gun with a silencer to cause the damage. There was a letter on the sidewalk addressed to me." She sniffed. "I can't believe this happened. My shop is a safe haven, a peaceful place for friendly souls to gather. And now someone...evil...has ruined it. I'll need a bushel basket of sage to cleanse the ugly from my space."

Becker gave her a reassuring smile. Mr. Thirty-Something said, "I'll help you, Mooney. It's what Michelle would want."

Becker stuck out her hand. "I don't think we've met. I'm Chief Delaney Becker, of Celestino Village. I'm helping with the investigation into Michelle's disappearance."

"I read about you and want to thank you in advance for all you are doing to find her. I miss her very much. I'm Hamilton Parsons, her boyfriend."

Hamilton Parsons was the "surfer dude" she recognized from Michelle's yearbook. Was he the person Peter Peters identified as the man Michelle propositioned at Dave's Dive? Officer Peters said they seemed friendly...but why arrest her for approaching her own boyfriend? If not Hamilton, who was the man in the bar? And the use of the term "boyfriend" was interesting. Becker reined in her thoughts.

"Good to meet you, Hamilton. I'm sorry it's under these circumstances. We'll talk soon about Michelle. For now, I want to focus on the break-in." She turned back to Mooney. "Let's go inside and check on the damage and your letter."

Their shoes crunched on the glass in front of the door and just over the threshold. A few pieces of pottery in back were in pieces, hit by stray bullets. The damage was less than Becker assumed it would be; this was clearly a warning, intended to scare. Mooney's pinched face showed a direct hit.

A detective from the Maryland State Police waved at her as he scribbled in a notebook and took pictures. Sheriff Atkins stood nearby, back rigid, eyes flat, staring at her. "Really? Don't you have your own crimes to solve, Chief Becker? Come to Silver Hill for excitement?"

Mooney's eyes flashed with anger. "Paul, not now. I asked Becker to come down. I needed her. This..." She winced, "horrible mess is related to Michelle's disappearance. Mayor Workman would want her here. Can you please go away?"

He lowered his voice, eyes flashing back. "No, Mooney, I can't go away. But I'll play nice only because I have to."

"Where's the letter? I want Becker to see it."

He gestured to a nearby countertop, and they all walked over.

Dear Ms. Workman,

You were closer to Michelle than just about anyone, so I am asking you to please help me stop this investigation. Michelle is alive and well and I am taking care of her. You're putting her in danger by letting Chief Becker look for her.

Sincerely,

Her loving husband.

PS I'm sorry about the damage but I needed to get your attention.

"Wow, he was busy yesterday," Becker muttered aloud, immediately regretting it.

Sheriff Atkins asked, "What are you talking about?"

"Someone kidnapped Kevin yesterday, the same person who did this." Becker looked at Mooney just as her eyes rolled to the back of her head. She caught her as she fainted. "Chief Atkins, help me get her to the couch?"

A few minutes later, with the help of rosemary oil, suggested by a red-faced cop, who was a customer, Mooney came to. Becker sat next to her on the couch, hoping the worry on her face wasn't showing. Sheriff Atkins hovered next to them.

"Mooney," Becker said gently, "Kevin is fine. I found him tied to my mailbox, tired, dirty and hungry, but unharmed."

Mooney slowly sat up. "Who would kidnap such a sweet soul? This man is wicked. Awful, awful aura." She wobbled to her feet. "We need some St. John's Wort tea to protect us from this evil." She poured three cups of the hot brew and handed them out.

"Becker, I just remembered something. You said the person who took Kevin did this. How do you know?"

"He left a note, very similar to yours, telling me I was putting Michelle in danger and to stop the investigation. He signed it the same way as *her loving husband*."

Sheriff Atkins spoke up, startling them both. "Maybe it's the truth, and she is safe. You should let this go."

She stood up, narrowing her eyes at him. She hoped she looked as fierce as Fern said she did when she was in uniform. "I shouldn't even dignify that with a reply, but I will. First, you realize your reasoning is flawed, don't you? If Michelle is safe, why not show us? If we're putting her in danger, why not ask for our help? We are law enforcement." She gave him a withering look. "Or at least one of us is."

Sheriff Atkins opened his mouth to speak; she cut him off, this time shouting, "I'm not done yet. 'Loving husbands' do not kidnap dogs or shoot up buildings. This guy is looney-tunes. He's a coward. And he's scared. He's afraid we're going to ferret him out and make him pay for what he's done with or to Michelle." He opened his mouth again. "I'm still not done yet. He's also underestimated me. I'm going to find his sorry ass."

She turned on her heel and walked toward the door. One detective clapped. Mooney yelled, "You go, girl!"

She glanced over her shoulder. Sheriff Atkins stood rigidly, almost at attention, his eyes filled with malice and hatred.

Chapter Seventeen

B ecker woke up pissed off, angry air coming out of her ears, because of yesterday's run-in with Sheriff Atkins. She ate breakfast pissed off. It got worse after a call this morning from Mayor Spinosi. After forced pleasantries (she could tell he was rushing to get to something important) he had *ordered* her to interview Mimi at Ladybank Manor, instead of the Silver Hill police station. After she told him she thought it was a bunch of bullshit, he told her it wasn't up for debate. Period.

She used the drive-time to Silver Hill to practice her deep breathing exercises. By the time she arrived, irritation had replaced anger. Now, she was perched on a small chair in the parlor room, almost to the point of toppling over, and fiddling with her recording device. She worked at staying calm, breath in, breath out, while she waited for the Queen of the Workman mansion to arrive.

Becker scanned the room, eyes landing on expensive antiques and art. In one corner, a sizable collection of vintage watches sat on lighted shelves, diamond faces glittering. A black baby-grand piano was angled in the other corner. She wondered who likely played classical pieces from Beethoven or Mozart. Her guess was Mimi. Or Meghan.

Mimi swept into the room ten minutes later, wearing a classic tweed Chanel suit, skirt just above the knees, a pair of Jimmy Choo shoes, and about a million dollars' worth of sparkling jewelry, mostly diamonds.

Her expensive perfume smelled of roses, a trace of jasmine. It made Becker sneeze.

"Officer, welcome to my humble home." She stuck out her hand.

"Good morning, Mimi." Becker shook her hand, sneezed again.

"You can call me Mrs. Workman."

"Fair enough. And you can call me Chief Becker."

Mimi wore an imperial half-smile, condescension traveling from her eyes to her curled lips. She delicately sat down on a settee across from Becker, arranging her body like a store-window mannequin. Her gaze landed just beyond Becker's left shoulder. Becker fought the urge to look behind herself. Perhaps the woman was near-sighted, or maybe she was playing some sort of game Becker wouldn't be joining. "Mrs. Workman, I'm ready to get started if you are."

"I'll be ready in just a minute." As if on cue, the doorbell rang. Mimi stood up, regal and poised, murmured, "Excuse me," and left the room.

A man's voice drifted from the hallway; she assumed it was Mayor Workman. Her anger returned. She stared at the watches. *Get a grip. You can politely ask him to leave.*

Sheriff Paul Atkins stood in the doorway, his cold blue eyes assessing her, his tailored blue suit impeccable, his inflated ego flying around the room, threatening to dive bomb Becker. Her gut clenched; she wanted to punch the smirk off of his face and replace it with a bloody lip. She took a deep breath before she bit out, "What are you doing here?"

The smirk deepened. "Little lady, still angry from yesterday?"

"Little man, obsessed with something I forgot about a minute after it happened?"

His smile dropped from his face as he walked with Mimi to the settee, arm-in-arm. She re-arranged herself; he sat next to her. "Mimi is a very busy woman, so I think we should get our discussion underway."

"Sheriff Atkins, these interviews are one-on-one. I'd like you to leave."

"Mimi wants me here to represent her interests."

"Her interests? Excuse me? This is an interview about her missing daughter. She's not under suspicion. You're not a lawyer."

"I'm representing her as a friend."

"That makes no sense." Becker glared at him, ignoring the tickle in her throat. She was going to sneeze again.

Mimi's cultured voice killed the sneeze. "Chief Becker, I asked Paul to be here for moral support. Do you want to conduct this interview or not?"

Becker rubbed her brow. "I..."

The doorbell rang again. They collectively startled. Mimi stayed seated.

Becker said, "Would you like to answer the door, Mrs. Workman? I can wait."

"I'm not expecting anyone else," Mimi said. "Let's get started."

A door slammed in the back of the house and light footsteps fell in the hallway. Mooney peeked around the door frame with a grin on her face, looking at the three of them, eyes settling on Becker. "There you are! I knew you were in town and needed my help. I felt your vibe from the shop."

Becker shook her head. "Mooney, I'm fine. I'm here to interview your mother and can get by on my own. Thank you."

"No, you can't. Paul is in a mood this morning. He told me so himself when he stopped by to check on me. He's going to hijack your interview." She sat cross-legged in the chair next to Becker, across from the settee. "There. We're like hockey players facing off."

Mimi sighed audibly, a hand to her heart. "Monica, you have a business to run. We'll be fine without you."

"Mother, my name is Mooney. Everyone calls me that but you. And thank you for your pretend concern about my shop. I know you'd prefer it dry up. Blow away." She made a hand gesture, like a flying bird. "Chief Becker, could Mother have been the one to shoot up *Apothecary and Amulets*?"

The room was silent. Mimi and Mooney stared at each other. The tension was as thick as a fog over the marshes on a rainy day. Mimi let out another sigh. "Of course I wouldn't hurt your business, unseemly thing it is."

Becker rushed in before the sparring resumed. "Mrs. Workman, let's start the interview." She turned on the recording device. "Can we begin by talking about Michelle in general?"

Mimi responded as if reading from a script. "She was an unruly child, but lovable. By the time she got to high school, she was in full defiant mode. She was impertinent and disruptive." Mimi clasped, unclasped her hands. She'd said her fill, apparently.

"What do you mean by disruptive? Can you give me an idea of her behavior?"

Mimi's face turned red. "She campaigned for a very distasteful man, Gus Fornash, who ran against her father in the mayor's race her sophomore year in high school. Michelle helped him organize door-to-door visits. She even knocked on our door, left a leaflet. I'll never forget or forgive her for it. 'Friends for Fornash', indeed."

Mooney snorted. Becker stifled a laugh. Michelle sounded like her feisty Nonna, impetuous yet steadfast to those she loved. "What was the reason she campaigned for Mr. Fornash?"

"I didn't ask her. It was a slap in William's face. I thought it better ignored."

"Why was Gus 'distasteful'?

Mooney was vibrating on the chair next to Becker.

"The man runs a garage. He's a mechanic."

Mooney spoke, "Mother, just because a person is a blue-collar worker doesn't make him distasteful. As a matter-of-fact, many tradespeople make as much, if not more, then the boujee people in town."

"Don't be vulgar, Monica, talking about money in front of our guests."

"Mother, you're being interviewed for your disappeared daughter. We're not having high tea."

Becker reached over to Mooney and squeezed her arm, willing her to be quiet, then asked, "What happened in the weeks leading up to her disappearance?"

"I can answer that," Sheriff Atkins said.

Becker sighed. What a cluster today was turning out to be. "Sheriff, you and I can talk at a later date. Mrs. Workman, your thoughts?"

"I recall nothing specific."

Mooney said, "I see your aura, Mother. You're fibbing."

Becker wished she had a shot of vodka or bourbon, neither of which she ever threw down the back of her throat. She would make an exception today. "Mooney, please let me handle things, okay?" Becker patted her hand. "Mrs. Workman, Michelle's friend Edward disappeared soon before she went missing. Did she talk to you about it? Did her behavior change?"

"Chief Becker, my daughter and I talked about very little. I made sure she had food when she dignified us with her presence; the maid picked up her bedroom and made her bed. She was a...ghost in the house. Coming and going at will, and not caring whether she was a part of this family."

Becker nodded, although she didn't believe a word of it. Her instincts told her it was the other way around. The family didn't want her. "Nothing changed with Edward's disappearance?"

Mimi let out a small, dignified sigh. "She stopped traipsing around the swamp and spent more time alone in her room. She didn't see Hamilton as much."

"Hamilton was her boyfriend, correct?"

Mimi squirmed in her chair. "I'm not sure that is the appropriate label. Hamilton wanted an exclusive relationship, but it appeared Michelle wasn't as committed. They were on-again-off-again. It's a shame."

"Why?"

"He's such a good boy from a suitable home. You can tell he comes from superior breeding. He grew up in Connecticut and attended a prestigious all-boys school. His manners are impeccable."

Sheriff Atkins interjected, "Hamilton was a good influence in Michelle's life,"

"Excuse me, Sheriff. Can you let Mimi finish?" Becker wanted to spill coffee on his starched white shirt. Only she didn't have any.

"It's alright, Paul," Mimi smiled at him and frowned at Becker. "Hamilton has endured so much yet still has a positive disposition. Sadly, the poor boy lost his parents, both nuclear engineers, a few years back in a horrible car crash. He still talks about them. Wonderful, cultured people." Out of the corner of her eye, Becker saw Moony tense. She rushed on. "Mrs. Workman, when did you realize Michelle was missing?"

Sheriff Atkins said, "Mimi, you don't have to answer that if you don't want to."

"Paul, why wouldn't she answer the question?" Mooney asked.

Beckers' frustration got the best of her. "I think that concludes our interview. Mrs. Workman, thank you for your time."

***

She and Mooney waved goodbye to the sheriff and Mimi as they headed to lunch in his cruiser. They both wore smug smiles on their faces.

"Your headache is getting into my head," Mooney said. "Can you relax? And should we postpone our interview for today?"

Becker rubbed her brow. "I'm fine."

"No, you're not. Physical exercise is what you need. You can burn off that headache and rebalance your chakras. How about a trip into Grimmy Swamp? I want to show you something."

Becker agreed a hike might do her good. She looked down at her uniform. "I've got a t-shirt and jeans in the car, and some boots. I'll need a place to change clothes."

"That's easy. We can go back into the house. I have a key."

Mooney led her to Michelle's old room, where she traded her police uniform for plain clothes. Not surprisingly, Mimi had erased Michelle, replacing her furniture and belongings with a home gym. She contrasted this room to Edward Landon's, still fully furnished, including the feathers he'd collected. She felt a pang of sadness for Michelle.

They went out the back door, through the manicured garden, to an overgrown path; the woods were wild, the bald cypress trees majestic. They had to beat back bushes and small saplings, until the path opened up to an expansive bay, the water a glittering blue. They stopped at the water's edge to watch a bald eagle catch a fish then Mooney led Becker to a smaller trail, through cattails and grass, to an ancient fishing boat sitting on its side. It looked like it was growing out of the marsh.

Mooney hoisted herself up and gave Becker a hand. "Be careful. Some of the deck boards are rotten."

Becker saw rocks lined up on the side of the boat. "Is this Edward's happy place?"

"It was Edward's *and* Michelle's happy place." Mooney smiled. "I followed her one day when she came here. They had lunch. I'd bet they found this as kids, used it over the years to meet, even in high school.

I never asked her, though. Even a little kid knows a secret place when she sees one." Mooney picked up a rock. "I came back later by myself a few times. It's a great place. Very peaceful." She gestured toward the open water. "Grimmy Swamp is on the edge of Bloodstone Bay, over there."

"Besides rocks, did they keep anything on the boat?"

Mooney smiled. "Look at you, all detective-like. I saw a few cans of food, some bottled water...a glass jar with a lid. A note was inside from Edward to Michelle. And before you ask, no, I didn't read it." Mooney's face became serious as her eyes scanned the forest. "We're being watched."

"Do you feel someone?" Becker asked.

"No, I heard a branch snap."

Becker's hand found her Glock tucked in her waistband. The marsh grasses whispered, a hawk whistled, water trickled. She didn't detect any unusual sounds. "Where?"

Mooney turned away, hiding her fingers in front of her, then pointed. "That way."

They crawled out of the boat, Mooney trailing Becker. Mooney pointed to the area the noise came from. They found a spot in the trees, an artificial clearing. Becker sat on a stump, giving her a full view of the boat. She caught a whiff of men's cologne; she recognized it. But from where? Who? It came to her a minute later: the brand Mayor Spinosi wore for special occasions.

Mooney's voice brought her back to the present. "It feels evil here." Mooney shivered.

"It's definitely manmade. Someone used this as a lookout."

"Are we thinking the same thing?"

Becker nodded. "Yes. He spied on us like he spied on Edward and Michelle."

Chapter Eighteen

B ea spent the night with Becker. They went to the Ocean City boardwalk, played a few games, rode a few rides, ate Thrasher's french fries, came home and fell asleep on the couch. Spending time with the young girl was a welcomed distraction; Becker's stomach muscles were sore today from laughing, something she didn't do a lot of these days.

She entered the Silver Hill Police Station, smiling at the memory of Bea's face covered in powdered sugar from the funnel cake she devoured, talking about chickens the whole time.

Becker knocked on the door of the interview room, walked in. A shoebox sat on the table next to Mayor William Workman and across from Sheriff Paul Atkins. Becker bit back a groan at seeing him so soon after Mimi's interview; she wasn't sure she could deal with his ego three days in a row.

She greeted William warmly. "Good morning, Mayor Workman." They shook hands.

"Sheriff, what can I help you with?" She'd be damned if he sat in on another interview.

"Nothing." His smug smile returned, reminding her of yesterday's shit show. "I'm here to help you. I thought Mr. Mayor would want to be updated as well."

Her shoulders relaxed and she sat down. "I'm all ears."

"A Smith and Wesson .38 Special was the gun used to shoot up Mooney's shop, according to the state police forensic people. Unfortunately, there's no match in the system. If we find the gun, we can run a comparison against the casings we found at the scene."

"About what we expected. Anything else?"

"Yes. No prints on the note, but another one of their scientists confirmed the style of writing matched all three of the letters affiliated with your case."

The break-in was none of his business. He stood there, gloating about his knowledge.

"Chief, I don't understand. You received two letters?" Mayor Workman's voice filled with concern, his eyes kind.

She recounted the break-in, graffiti, and letter.

"I'm sorry I've put you in danger. You were right. This is a job for the state police."

Sheriff Atkins said, "I agree."

"With all due respect, sir," she said to Mayor Workman, ignoring Sheriff Atkins, "it's too late for that. He's pissed me off. I'm going to make him pay for the hurt he's caused Mooney. Me. Kevin." She tapped her fingers on the table and caught herself. "Our perp is nasty, stealing dogs, defacing walls, shooting up windows. And we still don't know what he did with or too Michelle. Oh, this is my case, Mr. Mayor. I'm not giving it up

He smiled, his shark teeth gleaming in the dark room. "That's the spirit. I have the same fire in the courtroom." He glanced at Sheriff Atkins. "I'm glad we can put that to bed. Paul, we don't need you any longer."

"I'm not done, Mr. Mayor," the sheriff said. "Chief, there's a bunch of senior citizens...I mean, older adults roaming around in town asking many questions about Michelle and her disappearance. One guy looks like a mobster, slicked back hair, a big gold necklace, swaggering around town. Apparently, he's using Italian swear words to intimidate the locals. You all might ignore that in Celestino Village but down here we take bullying seriously."

Becker ignored the jab. Instead, she almost laughed at the thought of Joey Vito cussing out some grouch in Silver Hill. She worked hard at keeping her face neutral. "I'll take care of it."

Sheriff Atkins stared at her. She stared back. He turned on his heel and left, slamming the door behind him.

William leaned over the table to slide the shoe box to Becker. "He can be difficult, but he's a good cop."

Becker shrugged. "If you say so. Sheriff Atkins aside, how are you doing?"

"Fine. Well, perhaps not fine, but I have big shoulders."

"What's in the box?"

"Some things of Michelle's that I salvaged from her bedroom before Mimi turned it into a home gym. I didn't share in her vision, by the way."

Becker nodded at the rest of his untold story. "I appreciate it, Mr. Mayor."

"Please call me William. Speaking of Mimi, I had a discussion with her about your interview." His face turned hard; his eyes cold. "It was unacceptable that Paul was in attendance. I'm dumbfounded she felt the need to have him there. She called Mayor Spinosi, multiple times, I might add, to ensure Paul was in attendance. I don't understand why, and I had no knowledge of it beforehand. Mimi fully comprehends a second interview is in order, at the police station, with only you in the room."

"Again, thank you."

"My pleasure. We can proceed now."

Becker hid a smile. Listening to him was like reading an encyclopedia out loud; his language was so formal, so proper, his vocabulary so big.

"William, let's start by talking about Michelle, anything you'd like to share. I ask everyone that question, to get to know her as a person."

"I want her to be alive, but I find myself talking about her like she's already gone. Forgive me when I use the past tense." He smoothed his tie, a nervous gesture. "She was a handful, if I can use that term. Unconventional. She started talking in full sentences at age one. By two, she decided she didn't want to talk at all." William's eyes lit up. "Thankfully that only lasted three months. Her uniqueness became more pronounced as she grew older; she was her own person. I loved her panache. I admired her style. Some members of the family viewed it as rebellion; I always thought she was just being Michelle."

"Didn't you get mad at her at times? I understand, for example, she led a campaign against you for the mayor's race."

"No, I wasn't angry. I was proud she took a stand." He glanced down at the interview table fiddling with his wedding ring. "Truth be told, I wanted to be more like her. I love being mayor, and I am well aware of my status as a pillar of this community, but sometimes it would be nice to let loose. Play my trombone up and down the street, like she did. 'Course, I wouldn't be brave enough to have one. People like me stick to the piano, with Chopin as our composer of choice."

Becker gave him a slight smile. "She sounds special. I hope to meet her someday. Okay, hardball question coming up next." He nodded. "Did you arrange for Michelle's arrest for prostitution?"

He met her eyes, blue on brown. "I thought you would ask this question, and if you hadn't, I would have brought the subject up. No, I wasn't behind the arrest. However, at the time I wasn't upset it happened. Let me explain. Michelle's behavior was becoming increasingly unpredictable. One week she would hide in her room, and the next she would disappear in the swamp, or elsewhere. I found her once at the Fornash garage, sleeping on a cot in the back room, for example." His eyes were unfocused, remembering. "One week she would be happy, almost carefree, and the next she would engage in crying jags. I couldn't reach her; she wouldn't tell me what the issue was."

Becker interrupted, "Could it have been mental illness?"

William pulled at his tie again. "I don't believe so. Her actions seemed to be situational, not part of a bigger pattern."

"What do you think contributed to her state of mind?"

"Other than the way she was treated at home?" A pained expression flitted across his face. "It could have been Hamilton. She broke up with him, she got back with him, repeat. But I thought they had a good foundation, based on what I could see. So, it must have been something else; for the life of me I don't know what."

"Then she got arrested for solicitation."

"Yes. What a shock. I'd never repeat this to Mimi, but I thought it might help her...reset? Sounds silly now, but back then I was hopeful it would be a catalyst for positive change."

When Becker was younger, she went through some hard times. She could hear Mama's voice through William's words.

William continued, "Unfortunately, the change wasn't for the good. After the incident, things got worse. She was edgy. Angry. She picked fights with Mimi. Most surprising to me is the way she treated Mooney. They were thick as thieves most of their lives, as close as twins. Suddenly she stopped spending time with her. I often wondered if the reason she spent so much time out of the house was to be free of Mooney."

Becker asked him questions about the week before Michelle went missing, the day of the disappearance, and the aftermath.

"I've often felt we should have looked longer and harder, and involved the state police. Paul had been sheriff for a year or so. I didn't want to usurp his authority. Still, I wonder if we followed the correct protocol, and if we did, would Michelle be home now."

***

Becker was curious about Gus Fornash, hearing his name twice in two days. She drove to the garage he owned, parking next to the open doors. A vintage Volvo sat on a lift in one bay, a new Mercedes parked in the other, with a pair of legs sticking out from underneath the engine.

A grizzled, wiry man in his sixties came out of the shop as she got out of her unmarked police car. Grease and dirt smeared his jeans, his dingy-gray wife-beater ripped. He rubbed his hands on an oil-stained rag. "Help you?"

"I'm Chief Delaney Becker—"

"I know who you are."

The legs under the car moved. Joey Vito's body slid out from underneath. His face lit up with a *Smiling Joey* grin. "Hey, Chief! What brings you by?"

Becker stared at him. "Joey, what are you doing here?"

He got up and walked over to stand next to Gus. "A little work under the hood, so to speak. You?"

"There's a repair shop in Celestino Village."

"Gus and I go way back."

"How far?"

They looked at each other. Joey said, "Um, a coupla decades."

Becker tucked away that tidbit; she'd follow up on the Joey/Gus relationship later. "Mr. Fornash—"

"Gus."

"Okay, Gus. I'm leading the investigation to find Michelle Workman. I stopped by to schedule an interview with you. I understand you two were close."

"The use of the word 'close' is wrong. I know nothing."

"You might have information that could help in the investigation."

Gus looked at the pocked asphalt near his feet and lit a cigarette. "I ain't going into a police station."

"We can talk here."

Gus took a few puffs on his cigarette, then flicked the half-smoked butt into a pile near the door.

"Gus? Can I count on you?"

"Nah. No can do. I have my rights. I'm not talking unless you arrest me."

Becker rubbed her brow. Joey turned on his million dollar *Smiling Joey* face. "Now Gus, these aren't the old days when we had to be, whadda-ya-call-it, antagonistic to the cops. Besides, I can vouch for Becker. She's good people."

Gus spat on the ground near Becker's foot, face pinched, an unmovable force for such a thin man. "Nah, not gonna do it."

Becker sighed and thought through options. There were none. "If you change your mind, call me."

"Wait a minute, Chief." Joey grabbed Gus's arm and led him away from Becker. She saw him gesturing wildly. At one point, Joey said, "...head out of your ass...friend of mine."

They walked back to Becker. Gus said, "Ah, Chief, let's call my answer 'maybe'. Check back in a few days."

Becker drove away, deep in thought. Was Gus "anti-establishment"? Or was he hiding something? How were he and Joey acquainted? Was it mob related? She brooded about it until she reached Nonna's campground where a sign at the entrance read: Parade of Dickies Tomorrow.

Nonna was lying on a new chaise lounge under a bright red umbrella, the sun making her skin glow pink. She was wearing an eggplant-colored jogging suit that was a tad bit small. Tied around her head was a scarf of yellow, blue, and pink elephants, tail on the side, like starlets wore in the 1960s. She was sipping a margarita while playing Sudoku. Becker told her not to get up, and kissed her forehead.

Lester sat on a perch nearby, ringing a little bell, muttering, "Lester bored." When he saw Becker, he yelled, "Cop! Cop! Put the weed away!"

She climbed inside Big Betty to get iced tea, snooping while she poured herself a glass. Nonna had a shiny new microwave. On top of it was what looked like a real diamond tennis bracelet. Other items recently purchased were still in boxes, including a Yeti camping cooler, a chef-inspired knife set, and a name brand computer. Becker went back outside.

"You look weary, Del. Tell your Nonna all about it."

"Only if you tell me about all of your new stuff. Did you win another poker game?"

Nonna was uncharacteristically quiet. She squirmed her sizable butt in the chaise lounge. "None-a-ya business. When I'm ready to spill the beans, I will. Until then, you respect your grandma, okay?"

Becker hated to see her Nonna upset, so she changed topics to Michelle Workman. She told her grandmother about the interviews with the Workman family members, Mooney's shop being shot up, her romp through the swamp, meeting Gus Fornash. She rubbed her brow. "Nothing's been easy about this investigation."

"In other words, it's a shit show. Don't forget your secret weapon...the Gruppo."

"Some secret weapon. I got a complaint from the sheriff in Silver Hill about you all."

"Mr. Testosterone has nothing better to do than pick on the old and feeble?"

"Nonna, none of you are old and feeble. Nice try..."

Nonna smiled. "Thank you for the compliment."

"You called him 'Mr. Testosterone', so I'm assuming you met him."

"Yep, he stopped us on the street. I could tell he's very full of himself. Ego is probably bigger than his—"

"Nonna, please."

"You get my drift, Del. Anway, he puffed his muscles out and told us to leave, so Joey called him a chooch."

Becker laughed. "Sheriff Atkins *is* a jackass! Joey picked the perfect word to describe the man." Becker smiled at the thought of tall and tough Sheriff Paul Atkins being razzed by short and unassuming *Smiling Joey*. "Enough about me. How are you? Are you staying out of trouble?"

Nonna rolled her eyes. "Your Mama sent you, didn't she?" Becker raised her eyebrows but didn't answer. Nonna snorted. "Report back that my new hobby is pole dancing in Ocean City."

Becker growled at her. "Nonna..."

"My favorite song to dance to is that KC and Sunshine one—"

Lester the parrot squawked, "Shake, shake, shake, shake your booty!"

Nonna giggled.

Chapter Nineteen

Angelo *The Angel* Zullo was in town. Becker and Joey planned an "accidental" meeting in front of his house in the hopes Angelo would wander outside. Becker put on her uniform and posed in the mirror, hoping for an intimidating, tough persona. What she saw instead was a bird's nest of unruly brown hair and caramel-colored eyes filled with doubt. She holstered her Glock; that gave her a bit more confidence.

Joey's house was two-stories, twice the size of Mama's cottage. It was probably the most unusual house in the village. Locals and tourists frequently parked in front of it to take pictures. Called the "crazy brick" home, it was a Tudor with red bricks laid in a hodge-podge, asymmetrical fashion, with a stucco and wood beam entrance to the front door. Joey paid a local landscape company to trim the boxwood hedges surrounding the front yard and plant wildflowers inside. It became a wild mess of colors in the summer, which perfectly set off the crazy brick.

Kevin meandered from bush to bush, Becker trailing behind, until Joey yelled, loud enough for the residents three streets away, "Good morning, Chief!" The dog pulled Becker toward a table in the garden, where Joey was sipping tea.

Becker waved. "Hi Joey, what a beautiful day!"

"Would you like a cuppa coffee?" His face was red. He practically screamed, "I bought Italian Cream!"

While Becker sniffed the sweet alyssum, Joey disappeared, then re-appeared with a mug of light brown coffee, and a treat for Kevin. He whispered, "I think I woke him up!"

Becker whispered back, "I think you woke up the entire block!"

He turned on his *Smiling Joey* smile, eyes twinkling.

They made small talk and a few minutes later, the door opened on the side of the house. Angelo appeared. The man was beautiful. His light olive complexion was exotic, his black hair silky and thick. His hands were graceful for such a big man, wrapped around a mug of coffee, a diamond pinky ring winking in the sunshine. He was wearing a thick robe. Becker could see the outline of his biceps and chest through the cloth. She tried not to think about what was underneath it. She stared at him while her mouth went dry; she subconsciously licked her lips.

Angelo said, "Are you single? You're my type."

His voice was as silky as his hair.

Becker licked her lips again telling herself to be professional and all of that. "Um...I'm Chief of Police Delaware, I mean Delaney Becker." She stuck out her hand. Instead of shaking it, he pulled her into a hug. Good Lord, she was going to melt into a gob of Italian gelato if he kept this up.

Wait, she didn't like hugs.

And the man was...

"Are you smelling my hair?"

Angelo laughed; Joey broke the spell. "Angelo, stop it. Chief Becker is off limits."

Becker thought, *I am?*

"Delaney can speak on her own behalf, cousin." He turned, set Becker down, and gave her a warm smile that lit up his mahogany-colored eyes. "I am shipping my convertible Alfa Romeo here. It arrives tomorrow. You would look sexier than you do now, sitting in a candy red car. Will you go for a ride with me?"

She regained her wits by thinking about Mack, lovely Mack, kind Mack, boyfriend Mack. She ignored the question on the table. "It's nice to meet you, Angelo. What brings you to Celestino Village?"

"So that's how you want to play it, huh?" He raised his eyebrows at her. "I'm going to keep asking you to go out with me. For now, though, I'll let you change the subject. I came to your sleepy village to get away from the rat race. I needed a break." He sat down, his robe gaping open. Becker flushed and looked away before she saw anything interesting.

She put on her Chief of Police hat. "Angelo, you are welcome, of course. You are also right; we are a sleepy village. We don't need any trouble. *Capisce?*"

"Yes, Delaney, I understand."

"Everyone calls me Becker."

"I'm not everyone. I'm your next lover."

Her eyes were crossing. She got abruptly to her feet. "I need to get to Silver Hill for an interview. Joey, Angelo, I hope you have a great day."

She and Kevin almost ran back to her apartment.

***

A few hours later, she couldn't help comparing Angelo to Hamilton Parsons. Angelo was handsome in a rugged wrestler sort of way. Hamilton had finer features: a small nose, a slightly receding hairline, a wiry body. He was a sprinter, or a pole vaulter.

Hamilton arrived at the police station early. He chatted with most of the officers in the building. The man had an easy manner and smile, with manners that would impress her Mama. He also had a cup of coffee for Becker, with cream.

"Good morning, Chief! Mooney told me you liked Italian Cream, so I bought a container and left it in her store, in case you visit and prefer coffee to tea."

Becker never told Mooney she liked cream. The woman was amazing, maybe scary. "Hamilton, that is thoughtful and appreciated."

He beamed like a little boy after his first time sleeping in a big boy bed.

They settled into their chairs, and Becker turned on her recording device. He asked her about it. "I take notes but also rely on my interview transcript as a back-up. To get started, tell me whatever you'd like about Michelle. How did you meet her? How did you become friends?"

.

"I met her at Dave's Dive. It's not the most romantic place to meet the girl of your dreams, but that's where I saw her first. I had a flat tire— Wait, let me back up. After I graduated from college and my parents died in a car accident, I decided to explore the US. I was in Maine before I headed down the east coast. My goal was to see the 'real' United States, small towns, the biggest ball of yarn, that type of thing. I came to the Shore to see Chincoteague on account of the book *Misty of Chincoteague*. My mom and I read it together when I was young, and I wanted to see the wild ponies on the island." He took a sip of coffee. "Anyway, my car was towed to the garage next to the bar, you know, the one Gus owns. I walked over to the bar. Michelle was in there, eating a burger while she talked with the bartender. Edward Landon was his name."

"They were friends, from what I understand."

"I think Michelle felt sorry for him. He was so geeky. Weird."

Becker nodded. "You stayed because of Michelle."

"I did. I abandoned the trip across America and settled here." He looked at the table, a wistful smile on his face. "I had never met someone like her. I couldn't imagine driving off and leaving her behind."

"You started dating."

"Yes, we were together for, um...two years or so. We were like two kindred souls. Don't misunderstand me, I'm much more...conventional. Michelle and I were both raised with money, and it shaped me into being someone who fit in. My parents wouldn't allow anything out of the norm. But there's a special bond between us."

"What happened in the months leading up to her disappearance?"

"Chief, I've thought about that almost every day since she went missing. We were great, no issues, no drama, no conflict. That wasn't the case with her family, especially her relationship with her mother. It got so bad at one point Mimi offered Michelle money to leave." His face clouded over. "That's how she solves all of her problems...with the almighty dollar."

"Tell..."

The door opened and slammed against the wall. Sheriff Paul Atkins stood in the doorway, ready for battle. "Chief, come with me immediately. Now."

Becker sensed a power play, not an emergency. "Sheriff, I'm in the middle of an interview, as you can see. It should be wrapped up in approximately ten minutes."

"It can't wait. Postpone the rest of the interview. Your natives have caused a commotion, and you need to take them home."

Becker wanted to groan out loud. She met Hamilton's eyes. "Can we pick this up in another day or two?"

His eyes flashed, whether from irritation or anger, Becker didn't know. "Of course, Chief."

***

She followed Sheriff Atkins' cruiser as he sped through town, flashers on, siren blaring. They made it to Grimmy Swamp in minutes and parked in Edwina Landon's driveway. Cars lined the street, a brand-new BMW blocking part of the road. Becker maneuvered her car around it vowing she'd ticket the stupid thing on the way out until she remembered it wasn't her jurisdiction. Damn.

They practically ran behind Edwina's house. The first thing Becker saw was a snow cone machine. There were multiple drones in the air, circling the marsh. Two dozen people were within eyesight, some with remotes. A little boy was pointing at an osprey, chasing one drone. She rubbed her brow as Nonna hustled up to her, wearing a stretchy black flight attendant uniform, complete with a 1950s pillbox hat.

"Heller, Del!" She eyeballed Sheriff Atkins. "I remember you, handsome. Are you in a better mood today?"

"Nonna," Becker growled, "not now."

"Ma'am, my mood is none of your concern."

"I'm Chief Becker's grandmother, Teresa. I'd love to go out to dinner sometime. I have ways to improve a man's disposition."

Sheriff Atkins stuttered and walked away.

"What's happening here, Nonna?"

"I organized a search party for you!"

"A search party?" she dazedly asked her grandmother.

"Yes! Lunch is being brought in around noon, including beer and wine." Nonna looked so pleased with herself, Becker almost laughed.

"What are we searching for?"

"Well, you mentioned you were in the swamp, that you found a place where Edward and Michelle met. I thought we might find bodies nearby. So, we hired the local drone club to fly over the area to search for them."

"Good Lord, I shared that information with you because you are a good listener, not because I wanted you to arrange...this." Becker gestured at the balloons and a banner that read, *I See Dead People.*

"I did both!"

Becker took a deep, calming breath. What should she do? Send everyone home? Instead, she said, "Thank you, Nonna, for organizing this." Becker saw Edwina, and her stomach dropped. Such a nice person, subjected to this...circus. "Excuse me for a minute."

Becker met Edwina at the refreshment table, filled with pastries, coffee, and what looked like a pitcher of Bloody Mary. "Edwina, I am so sorry. Nonna means well. But all of this isn't exactly respectful of Edward and Michelle."

Edwina's face broke into a smile. "No need to apologize. This is the most fun I've had in years. At first the banner took my breath away not in a good way. But after meeting your Nonna Teresa, I know in my heart that she's not mean spirited. She just wants to help find our lost souls. I'm fine, Chief."

Becker blew out a breath. "I'm glad."

To the side, Sheriff Atkins was barking at Joey Vito. Joey was ignoring him. Nearby, Nonna stood next to Johnny Hudson and Cephas Jones, heads tilted up as they watched a drone carve circles in the air. Mooney tromped out of the marsh with Angelo *The Angel* Zullo, who blew a kiss in Becker's direction.

Nonna started singing Leaving on a Jet Plane; everyone joined in. Becker hummed softly. Professionalism and all of that.

Chapter Twenty

The drone club, mostly young pimple-faced high school kids from Silver Hill High School, met with Becker a few days later at Mooney's shop. It was the biggest place Becker could find in such a short time frame, yet small enough that the Gruppo wouldn't fit. Nonna was not happy at being excluded, so she was throwing her own after-party at Spotted Dicks.

One young kid resembled a blue heron: tall, skinny with big feet and a hawkish nose. He was the current president of the group, and introduced himself as "Birdy". He started the meeting after eating more donuts than Becker thought would fit in his belly.

Birdy said, "To recap the, uh, flyover day at the Landon house. We had twelve drones in the air but lost one when Bill's crashed his into Trevor's." The kid in the corner with big ears turned pink. Must be Bill. "Most of the drones had a camera on board, two had sonar, and one had Ground Penetrating Radar or GPR."

Becker interrupted him. "Can you refresh my memory and explain what both of those are?"

"Sure. Sonar can identify objects underwater with the use of sound waves. For example, bones are denser than, say, the surrounding soil, so they would show up as an anomaly. GPR is really cool. Buzz's mom works at Wallops Island..." A fresh-faced, All-American girl raised her hand; Becker nodded at her. "She's an electrical engineer and messes around with drone equipment in her spare time. Our GPR is still in the test phase, so we sometimes get shit— Excuse me, uh, shoddy results."

"How does GPR work?" Mooney asked.

"It's pretty complicated. Buzz, do you want to take this one?"

Buzz brightened at the chance to talk. "GPR uses electromagnetic signals that bounce off of stuff. That creates a reflection, and when we plug the information into a software program, the screen shows a blip. It reminds me of the EKG monitor. My grandpa was hooked up to one of those after his heart attack."

Mooney nodded. Birdy asked, "Any more questions?"

"No, that's enough science for me."

"Me too," Becker said. "Thanks for the tutorial, Birdy. Can you tell us what you found?"

"I can do better. Here's a printout of all the spots we identified as potential bones." He handed Becker a sheet of paper with thirteen listed coordinates. "We limited our results to anything within a quarter mile from the boat, which includes parts of the Grimmy Swamp and Bloodstone Bay. The first five are in deeper water. You'll need divers. The other eight are in the swamp or forest. Those can be dug by people you or the state cops hand select. I've told the club members not to do anything on their own." Heads nodded around the room.

"Birdy, this is beyond my expectations. Thank you and your club."

"Chief, it was fun flying drones and hanging out with your Gruppo. The old people in our town are boring. They smell. Well, I guess only Old Lady Burk smells."

Becker nodded. "Yes, our seniors are lively. Sometimes too lively. What do I owe the club for your services?"

"Your Nonna took care of it."

"This is a police investigation, Birdy. I need to ensure the results are confidential."

"This might be our first rodeo, Chief, but we're not stupid. I had her sign a contract which prohibits us from sharing confidential police information with a civilian." He pulled a card out of his pocket. "In case you need us again."

The card read: *We see dead people. Call for a quote to find yours.*

***

After Becker told Birdy that their card sounded like they were spirit mediums, and he promised to change it and give her a new card, the club left. Becker prepared for her interview with Mooney while Mooney brewed herbal tea.

"Where would you like to start?" Mooney asked, as she sat on the couch.

Becker had brought the box from William Workman with her, containing Michelle's things. "Can we start with the contents of this box? Your father gave it to me."

They dug through the container. There wasn't much inside: a few rocks and driftwood pieces, one shaped like a bird, a picture of Michelle and Edward, one of her and Hamilton. Toward the bottom of the box was a stuffed bear that had seen better days. Tattered, he was missing an ear.

Mooney smiled picking up the fuzzy animal. "Oh, Katie-Bear! I forgot about her. She was a gift from Edward, years ago, to Michelle. I think he bought her when they were on a field trip to a wildlife preserve or park or something in Virginia. Can I please keep her?"

"I need to check with your father, since it's technically his. How about I loan her to you for now?"

Mooney put Katie-Bear on the couch next to her. "Perfect. Now, what can I answer for you?"

"I've interviewed Mimi, William, and Meghan so far, as you are aware. You and I talked briefly. And I also met with Hamilton, although the conversation was interrupted by Drone Day. I don't need more background on Michelle. I have more specific questions for you."

"Whatever you need, Becker. Today's a good day for you to uncover something important about her. Your aura is bright and strong."

"I'm glad. How about we talk about your relationship with Michelle? I understand you were two peas in a pod."

Mooney's curly brown hair bounced when she nodded. "We were! In a family that saw us as the outcasts, we understood each other. And we had each other's backs."

"Give me an example."

"I covered for her more than a few times when she was with Gus. She got almost...obsessed, I guess, is the best word, with him and his garage. He taught her to build a small engine from scratch, that sort of thing."

"What was their relationship like?"

"Something in between a father-daughter bond and hero worship. I honestly don't know what she saw in him. I never warmed up to him and, as I mentioned before, his aura is brown. Murky."

"What does that mean, aura wise?"

Mooney scratched her forehead. "It could mean a bunch of things: guilt, anger, anxiety. With Gus, though, my guess is he's hiding something."

"Any idea what?"

"No."

"Do you think he would hurt Michelle?"

"Thank you for using the word 'hurt'; you are being kind. I think he could hurt Michelle. He has a temper."

"Who else could hurt her?"

Mooney was silent, pain flitting across her face. "The gods forgive me, but I think Mimi could." Her hand shook as she picked up her cup of tea and sipped. "After Michelle got arrested for prostitution, which was six months before she went missing, Mimi gave her a $5000 check to 'go away'. They had been fighting, horrible screaming matches about Michelle's future: Mimi wanted her to go to college to find a suitable husband. Michelle, of course, thought it an utterly ridiculous idea. She told Mimi she wasn't going anywhere. But she took the check anyway and cashed it."

"Let's change topics. You were at college when she disappeared, correct?"

"No, I actually took the semester off. You might remember I was in pre-law. Already it was clear I would not stick with it."

"How did Mimi react to your change of heart?"

"Two daughters not living up to her expectations. How do you think she reacted?"

"My guess is she tried to talk you out of it."

"*Bully* me is a better way to say it. But I can deflect her aura when I need to keep her out."

Becker nodded. "Back to Michelle. Tell me about the days leading up to her disappearance. Was there anything different about Michelle, or how she acted?"

"She spent more time alone, closed behind her bedroom door, or hanging out by herself in the swamp. It was like she was pulling back from me. It hurt. It seems she was isolating herself from all of us, including Hamilton. I think they broke up but then got back together, maybe even more than once."

"That's interesting. Hamilton portrayed an almost fairytale romance."

Mooney shrugged.

***

Becker met with Molly a few hours later, over a lunch of meatball subs with enough tomato sauce to fill a birdbath, and french fries. Becker had an iced tea. Molly was drinking some green goo that matched her tunic, stretchy pants, and earrings. Franklin was on Becker's shoulder, eating a fry.

"Chief, I have updates on Pete Peters—the officer who arrested Michelle all those years ago for prostitution—Sheriff Paul Atkins, Gus Fornash, and Hamilton Parsons." She handed Becker a piece of paper. "I put some notes down for you. I haven't gotten as far as I wanted, but let me explain." She took a sip of her olive smoothie. "Starting with Pete Peters. He left Silver Hill right soon after Michelle disappeared, which may or may not be suspicious, to join the state police in Pikesville. Internal Affairs. I have a call in to him, no return call yet. As you might imagine, he's clean, nothing in his life to focus on."

The next name on the list was Sheriff Atkins.

"I found little on Sheriff Atkins, either. Not surprising; cops rarely have anything criminal in their backgrounds. I have just two items of interest. First, apparently Michelle and Paul dated when they were in high school. I found a Silver Hill High School yearbook on the internet for a few bucks and bought it." She extracted the book from her pile of papers and handed it to Becker. "Open the book up to page 61."

Michelle and Paul smiled out of the pages, both dressed in formal wear for the Homecoming dance. He was wearing a blue tuxedo. Becker begrudgingly had to admit he wasn't half bad looking, especially when his mouth wasn't spewing sarcasm. Michelle had on a vintage gown, flapper-like, including a headband with a feather and a faux cigarette holder. Not for the first time, Becker admired Michelle's spunk.

"I didn't see that coming. Anything else on the sheriff?"

Molly's face turned serious. "Nothing I can put my hands on, just a hunch." She took her notebook from the pile, thumbing through the pages. "It seems he picks which cases to turn over to the state police. The disappearance of Edward and Michelle wasn't ones he shared. Lesser investigations, if I can use that term, he referred to MSP, like a series of breaking and entering, a shoplifting ring." She scratched her cheek. "Maybe I'm seeing something that's not there, but it just feels off."

Becker told Molly she trusted her instincts, but she wasn't sure what to make of the information. Was it Sheriff Atkins' ego that made him keep the bigger cases? Or was he hiding something? There could be a simple explanation, like a feud with someone in the MSP. He'd shown his colors with her; perhaps he'd pissed off a fellow officer at the state level.

"Up next is Gus Fornash. Fascinating background, and now at the top of my list as a person of interest. I found a fairly long rap sheet on him, from stolen cars to aggravated assault. He ran a chop shop for many years in Philadelphia, my old stomping grounds. And...wait for it, he had ties to the mob."

"Huh. That's why Joey Vito takes his car to his garage."

Molly nodded. "He left Philly about twenty years ago. Do you want to ask me why?"

Becker smiled at her. "Why?"

"Dead body found in his chop-shop, killed execution style. Gus was a suspect, arrested, but then released. I still have contacts at the Philly Police Department and have a call into my one of my colleagues for a copy of the official file. Once I have the file in my hand, I can call a lieutenant from the Organized Crime Unit to get the actual story."

"Wow." Becker picked up a cooling french fry and handed it to Franklin. "I wonder what brought him to sleepy little Silver Hill."

"No idea. Maybe you can ask him if he ever agrees to an interview. I will tell you, based on my research, there's no sign he's doing anything else besides legitimately fixing vehicles now." She slid another few pieces of paper across the deck to Becker. "His police record, in case you want a longer version."

Molly scanned her notes. "Last up is Hamilton Parsons. You told me he's from New Hampshire, correct?"

Becker pulled out her file and scanned the contents. "I don't remember. It's up north... Here it is, it's Connecticut."

"I apologize. No wonder my search came up empty in New Hampshire. Do you have the name of the town?"

"No, but he attended a private all-boys school."

"Okay, I'll search again... He's had few traffic stops here on the shore, but so far, nothing before then."

"Maybe he made up a new identity when he arrived in Maryland," Becker joked.

Chapter Twenty-One

Becker needed a mental boost before her interview with Sheriff Atkins, so of course she chose the best: Nonna.

She pulled her cruiser next to Big Betty and behind the black BMW she saw at Edwina's on drone day. A Mercedes sat a few feet away. More presents from Nonna's boyfriend? Luxury cars? Becker rubbed her brow. It might be time for a serious discussion. This was too much.

As she walked up to Big Betty, the door opened. Nonna came out lugging a platter of baked ziti. Becker met her eyes, and she saw...panic? Then Joey Vito stepped out with a bottle of wine, followed by Angelo Zullo, who carried three glasses.

Becker was momentarily stunned. "What?"

Lester the parrot said, "Cop! Cop! Hide the guns!"

"Angelo," Nonna said, "we need another plate."

Joey smiled. "Well, it's out of the, whadda-ya-call-it, woodpile now!"

Becker recovered. "You're Nonna's boyfriend?"

Joey started whistling *New York, New York*. Lester the parrot joined in.

Nonna wore a too-tight knee length leopard-print dress. Like a toddler, she walked with baby steps, her outfit tight around her knees. Becker was concerned Nonna was going to wobble over; she grabbed her hand and led her to the table. Angelo winked at her while Joey dished out the ziti.

Angelo poured the wine, a lovely pinot noir. Becker watched his arm flex, his pianist fingers delicately gripping the bottle. Oh, he was a fine man.

The hell with the ziti; she wanted him for lunch, dinner, and a midnight snack.

Angelo caught her staring and blew her a kiss. Becker shook her head trying to regain her composure. "Joey, you didn't answer, so I'll ask Nonna. Is Joey your boyfriend?"

"We prefer the term 'companion', but yes, we are dating."

"How did this happen? You haven't been in Celestino Village very long."

"Oh, we've been an item for quite a while. I met Joey when he was on vacation in Florida while I was passing through. The good Lord arranged for us to meet at the Great Wall Chinese Buffet in front of the Moo Goo Gai Pan. I accidentally spilled a bit on his sleeve..." Nonna's face turned red. "Okay, truth time." She looked at Joey. "Jay, I did it on purpose."

Joey grabbed her hand, made a big show of kissing it multiple times. "I know."

"Anyway, the Moo Goo sucked, but I found Joey, so it all worked out."

Becker was still shell-shocked. "Um..."

Nonna said, "Eat some ziti. You'll feel better."

She muttered, "I'd rather have wine."

Angelo winked at her again. Lester the parrot yelled, "Oh, oh, oh, Jay, that's the spot!"

***

She arrived on time at the Silver Hill police station with a belly full of pasta. She caught her reflection in the glass door. Her eyes had the look of a person suffering from a spaghetti coma. She used the fifteen minutes Sheriff Atkins made her wait to banish thoughts of Joey with her Nonna. And Angelo the handsome.

He wore a smirk, and his dress blues, usually reserved for formal occasions. His buttons gleamed, the light bouncing off of his many medals. Becker wondered if he attended an event prior to his meeting with her, or if he was wearing the dress uniform to intimidate her. It really didn't matter. She would not give him the satisfaction of asking, nor was she going to cower in the great man's presence.

"Sheriff, anything we'd like to discuss before I ask you a few questions?"

"Are your geriatrics back in the home?"

"If you're referring to my older adults, yes, they are at Celestino Village, and still talking about how we 'showed up' the folks in Silver Hill. We're farther along in finding Michelle than you ever were."

Sheriff Atkins shrugged his shoulders. "Whatever."

"You'll be interested in knowing the drone club identified a little over a dozen sites to investigate. The state police will be out there tomorrow."

He spoke like he hadn't heard her. "How is your grandmother? I'm surprised she's at the Spotted Dick Resort. It can be...dangerous."

"Why, Sheriff, I'm grateful for your concern for Nonna. But you can attend to other, more important matters like finding the cows missing from the Holloway Farm. Nonna's safe, especially since Joey Vito and his cousin, Angelo Zullo, are frequent visitors."

Sheriff Atkins raised his eyebrows. When his eyes met Becker's, they said *touché*. Everyone knew the Vito family had mob connections.,

"As much as I enjoy small talk with you, let's focus on Michelle. I understand you two were an item in high school."

Sheriff Atkins laughed. "That's your best hard-ball question, Chief?"

She laughed, too. "No, I was extending professional courtesy to another cop by going easy on you. So how about this one: why did you investigate her disappearance yourself? Were you afraid the state police would find something incriminating? Something you wanted to hide?"

The smile on his face withered to a flat line. "That's just bullshit."

"There, there, Sheriff, don't forget we're taping this session. Using vulgar language does not make one sound professional or poised, especially when others are listening to the playback. Can you answer the question, please?"

He tapped his fingers on the table between them. "Michelle and I weren't an item, as you put it, in high school. We had a few dates. Our fourth date or so, she broke up with me."

"That had to be hard on a young guy's ego."

"It actually wasn't. We weren't compatible. She was so...wild and carefree. I was not."

"So, no anger? Residual resentment?"

"None. Did I just piss all over your theory? The one that goes something like: I killed her five years after she dumped me? My heart was broken, and I hated her so I sought...what? Revenge? Well, it doesn't hold water because we remained friendly until her disappearance. Ask around."

"So why did you soft-pedal the search?"

Sheriff Atkins blew out a breath. "I didn't soft-pedal anything. I followed protocols established by the state police. They assisted when I asked."

"Since you did everything right, you won't mind sharing a copy of your file, including timelines, search parties, other actions you took."

"It would be my honor." He gave her a small bow from his chair.

"I'd also like that information for Edward Landon. You and Mimi are close?"

"Nice try to catch me off guard, Chief. Let's see... My relationship with Mimi is only that of a prominent resident, who is also the mayor's wife. I'm her humble civil servant."

"Humble?"

He didn't answer.

"Are you aware she offered Michelle money to leave town?"

"I wasn't aware of that."

Becker couldn't read him. Throughout the interview, he appeared to be telling the truth, and he had no "tells" like nervous ticks, mouth rubbing, adjusting his clothes, or not making eye contact, all of which would show deception.

"Let's talk about Michelle's arrest for solicitation. Did Mimi put you up to it?"

"No," Sheriff Atkins said.

"William?"

"No." He wore a slight smile. He was enjoying himself.

"Then who did?"

"Why do you think the arrest was bogus?"

She rolled her eyes. "Really, Sheriff? You send a fresh-faced recruit—who, by the way, no longer works for you—when were you going to tell me that? —to look for prostitutes in a location where you never have before or since?"

"I needed to toughen the kid up. As you said, Peter Peters was fresh out of the academy, a local kid who needed more exposure. I made up work for him to get it."

He picked off a non-existent piece of lint from of his impeccably pressed coat.

His first tell. What was he hiding?

***

The interview left a gritty taste in her mouth and energy to burn, so she stopped at Gus's garage instead of going home. She groaned spotting Joey and Angelo, especially Angelo, who helped her out of the car and kissed her hand before he dropped it. Could the guy get any sexier?

"Chief, are you following me?" Angelo asked. "No need, you know. I'm ready to give you the ride of your life."

Images their naked bodies flashed in her brain. She stared at him, speechless.

"I mean in my Alfa Romeo."

"Um..." Becker said.

"Angelo," Joey said. "Leave her alone. Chief, are you looking for Gus? If so, he isn't here. He ran to the parts store for a few things."

"Tell him I stopped by?"

"Yeah. And Chief? Me and your Nonna hooking up? I know it was a surprise but are you okay with it? She's a helluva girl. Of course, I didn't know she was your granny when we met. I hope we have your blessing."

Hooking up? Yikes.

Becker's eyes scanned the parking lot, buying her time to think about his request. How to answer? Joey *Smiling Joey* Vito was a good guy, an exemplary citizen. He was also an ex-mobster, the non-violent-money-laundering type, not the murder-for-hire type. Why couldn't Nonna have chosen a retired accountant? Or a doctor? Or nurse? Why did Joey have to be an ex-mafia soldier?

She sighed. "Joey, I'm not ready yet to 'bless' your relationship. Give me some time to let it settle in, okay?"

She left him looking sad and walked across the parking lot to Dave's Dive. It was as forlorn as she remembered. She skirted around empty beer cans, liquor bottles, a pile of red plastic cups in the form of a pyramid. Once inside, the smell of stale cigarettes and fried tater tots competed with the scent of a lemon cleaning product. The floor was gummy and sticky. Becker's shoes made slight sucking sounds as she headed toward the bar.

"An iced tea, please."

The bartender, a man in his fifties with close cropped hair, poured the tea into a surprisingly clean glass. "I've not met you before, Officer. Name's Tom. I own the Low Tide, formerly Dave's Dive. I bought it last month."

"Good to meet you, Tom. I'm Delaney Becker, from Celestino Village."

A voice called out behind her, "She's actually Chief of Police up there."

Angelo sat in a bar chair next to her. His arm was close enough she felt the heat. She moved over a hair, causing him to raise his eyebrows at her.

Tom said, "Ah, here's my partner now."

Becker asked, "Angelo? Your partner?"

"Yep. I'm assuming you know each other?"

Angelo looked her up and down. "Not as much as I'd like to."

Becker hid a grin. "Why would you buy a bar in Silver Hill?"

Angelo answered, "Why not? It gives me a chance to see Cousin Joey. I want to spend more time on the shore. It's beautiful down here, and as good a place as any to get away from the city. Winters in Chicago can be brutal."

Becker admitted it would be nice to have him nearby, then dismissed the thought. She was not getting involved with a mobster. She would avoid him when he visited during the cold months.

"Angelo is going to buy a house in your village," Tom said.

Becker thought her head would explode, the bits and pieces adding to the stickiness already on every surface. Angelo moving to Celestino Village? Down the street? How could she keep her hormones in check? She was the chief of police, for goodness sakes. She needed to stay away from him, his mobster friends...and his arms...and...

"Delaney, I can almost hear your brain. It's in overdrive. Anything you want to talk about?" Angelo's face was inches from hers.

She shook her head avoiding eye contact with Angelo. A picture behind the bar caught her attention. "Tom, can I see that photograph?"

He took it down and handed it to Becker. Gus Fornash and Michelle Workman stood side by side, wearing shooting earmuffs on their heads. Michelle held a target, a cutout of a man, with bullet holes centered on the heart.

Gus Fornash held a Smith and Wesson .38 Special.

Chapter Twenty-Two

A ngelo trailed her marching a direct path across the parking lot to Gus Fornash, who stood in front of his garage with Joey, debating whether Goodyear tires were better or worse than Michelin.

She dug her index finger into Gus's chest. "You killed that guy in your chop shop. You shot up Mooney's store You stole my dog. I'm going to haul you in. Judge Green and I are close." Becker paused at the exaggeration, "He'll sign a warrant for me to handcuff you. I'll stuff you in the car; we'll ride to the station. We'll have an interview, which I'll make very public. Your former life, including the murder in Philadelphia, will spill out all over the internet and be front page news in the *Celestino Press*. Is that what you want?"

Gus backed up a few steps and threw up his hands. "Whoa. Let's settle down here. Get a grip, Sweetheart!"

Joey muttered, "Oh boy."

Becker stood on tiptoes to yell in his face, *"Sweetheart?"*

Angelo picked up Becker from behind like she was a pocket-sized Chihuahua, carrying her ten feet away. He set her down next to Joey. "Gus, apologize for being stupid. Give her a ten-minute interview. Delaney, take a breath."

Gus mumbled an apology while he rubbed his head. Becker mentally shot him in the nuts.

"Fine. I'll talk to you. Office in back."

She trailed him to a grimy, dusty cramped room with an old-style beat-up metal desk. One chair sat in front. She stood in the doorway. "I'd prefer we go to the station."

"Not gonna happen."

"Then give me something to clean off this chair." Becker was being rude but didn't care.

Gus grabbed a clean rag from a pile, handed it to Becker. As she brushed the filth—whatever it was, she didn't want to think of it—off of her chair, he moved stacks of blue-lined paper off the desk, along with a cup of green pens and various fast-food wrappers.

He took his time to sit, then leaned forward, arms on his desk, with a solemn look on his face. " Let's get something straight. I did not shoot up Mooney's place. I know nothing about your dog. Where did those cockamamie ideas come from?"

"You have a .38 Special. The damage was caused by that caliber. I put two and two together, and here we are."

"That's a mile long stretch, Sweet—" He rushed on before she thought of clawing out his eyeballs. "I mean Chief. That's all you got? No judge would have given you paperwork to bring me in with such a flimsy story." He pointed at her. "You played me."

"It worked, didn't it?"

He gave her a slight smile. "You're fiercer than you look."

"I can be, which is one reason I'm leading this investigation. You may have heard through the grapevine the mayors ordered me to find Michelle. Believe me, some days I'd like to walk away. But after the dozens of stories I've heard about her, I'm sort of invested. It's my job to find her, dead or alive. I'm asking you to help me."

The room was silent for a few moments. "I'm not used to helping cops. They've certainly never helped me."

"I get it. But that's big city stuff. Police here are a different breed. We live in our communities. Know our residents. Less corruption, more cooperation."

Gus shook his head, disagreeing with her.

"Besides, we're only talking about Michelle. I'm not here to pry into any of your affairs or trip you up somehow."

He picked up a green pen, rolled it between his fingers. "Fine. But if you cross any line, the interview stops."

"Fair enough, Gus. Tell me about Michelle."

"She started showing up here during high school, I think she was a junior. She'd nose around the cars and trucks, following me like a puppy, asking all sorts of questions. She had an aptitude for engines, understood them more than most full-time mechanics I've hired. I shooed her away at first, but like you, she was persistent." He picked at a callus on his hand. "So, I started teaching her the basics. Eventually, she was as good as me or any other man, I mean mechanic."

"After high school? Did she still come around?"

"Somewhat. She had other things to do, she was spreading her wings. I barely saw her."

"What did she tell you about her family? Her life?"

"Very little. She came here to...escape, I guess, is the right word." Like most people, he looked up to the right to search his brain for memories. "Let's see. Her family wasn't good for her, including her mother. You've met her, right?" Becker nodded. "I don't need to say more about that. She loved her sister Mooney. The other sister Meghan was horrible to her. Nasty. They call it 'gaslighting', you know, when someone says stuff to you and you doubt yourself. Like there's something wrong with you, not them."

Angelo knocked at the door. "Are you both still alive?" He didn't wait for a reply to come in. He plopped down a paper bag and two

Styrofoam cups of iced tea on the desk then eyeballed Becker and Gus. Apparently, he liked what he saw, so he left.

Gus reached into the bag. He pulled out a greasy container of onion rings, asking, "Turkey or ham?" Becker chose turkey. He handed her a wrapped sandwich, opened his. He kept talking around bites of bread and meat. "Her favorite two people on the planet were Mooney and Edward. She saw herself as a big sister to both, even though she was younger than Mooney and the same age as Edward. She was always fretting about their welfare. When Edward went missing, she was so sad. It took her a long time to come around again. When she did, she was different. Stayed alone a lot, quiet."

"What happened to Edward?"

"How the hell should I know?" He stared her down.

"What are your thoughts about Hamilton?" Becker plopped an onion ring in her mouth.

His response was quick. "That asshole?"

Becker stopped chewing, surprised. "Why do you say that? Most everyone I talked to has only positive things to say. He seems like a decent sort."

Gus snorted. "Uh-huh. I don't want to talk about him."

As she nibbled at her sandwich, a poster on the wall caught her attention. It was a map of the wetlands on the shore. She couldn't place it for a minute, then remembered Molly had given her one at the start of the investigation.

"Are you a Swamp Keeper?"

"No, organized groups do little for me. Michelle gave me that." He gestured to the poster, took a bite of his sandwich.

"Tell me about the days before Michelle went missing. Any changes?"

"I already told you I didn't see her much in the later years."

His voice was sharp. Was it defensiveness? Or was he tired of talking with a cop?

He wiped his hands on his napkin. "I saw her a few weeks before she disappeared. Maybe three? Four? She came by occasionally to work on a wreck of a car, a 1976 Ford Pinto. Ugly little piece of shit; the color was a brownish green. The engine was all gummed up and, of course, she had to reinforce the gas tank so it didn't blow up in an accident. Anyway, I was in my office when Hamilton pulled up in his truck. I watched them argue. And before you ask, I didn't hear what it was about."

***

A purple long-stem rose was on the windshield of Becker's police car when she emerged five minutes later. Angelo must have left it; she would bet he knew purple roses symbolized love at first sight. She picked up the rose, smelled it, then set it on the seat next to her while she drove to Celestino Village, retrieved Kevin from Mama's house, and changed out of her uniform. She left it in a small vase when she and Kevin drove to the beach so she could clear her head, or at least pretend to.

She settled in on a blanket. Digging into her bag, she pulled out her painting supplies, a hobby started several years ago to relieve stress. Back then, she tucked canvases in a closet until every time the door opened, one or two tumbled out. She listed a few online for sale to make more room in her apartment. Surprisingly, it grew into a fledgling business. This year, she made more income painting the ocean than she did protecting and serving. She stuffed it all in the bank for a rainy-day.

Becker got lost in an emerging picture of the waves lapping at the shore. It gave her a chance to think about the investigation. She had spent countless hours interviewing Michelle's friends and family: Mimi, William, Meghan, Mooney, Sheriff Atkins, Hamilton, Gus Fornash. Edwina. Was she forgetting anybody? Yes, she needed to talk with Marissa, the fourth sister, who left the area after high school and never looked back.

The interviews all ran together. She felt she knew Michelle, at least beyond the surface, but the facts she learned so far didn't help her solve the case. Heck, she wasn't sure she knew what she was investigating. A missing person? Kidnapping? Run-away? Or was it suicide or murder?

And what about the break-in at her house, the graffiti and note, the destruction of Mooney's shop? Kevin's kidnapping? Someone was trying to scare her off. Who?

She was still waiting for information from Sheriff Atkins. How hard was it to dig up an old file, especially an important one? Why wouldn't he produce it? Was he hiding something?

Gus was somehow involved. How?

She put down her brush to reach for Kevin, who had been laying behind her. She didn't feel his bristly coat, panicked, and jumped to her feet, spraying sand on her work in progress. He was three feet away, digging in the sand.

She took a deep breath and sat back down. He came over to lick her face. She hugged him; her face deep in his wiry hair, his doggy scent in her nose. She put her supplies away; the mood to paint was gone.

***

"William, I have a favor to ask related to the investigation."

"Chief, I am at your disposal."

"I, um, am waiting on Sheriff Atkins to produce reports about Michelle…"

Mayor Workman said, "I'll ask him about the investigation and nudge him at the same time."

"Appreciate it. Also, I had a chance to talk with Gus Fornash. He mentioned Michelle's car. Are you aware of any inventory from it? I'm trying to tie up some loose ends."

"There wasn't much. Mostly detritus." Becker smiled at the word. "I cleaned out the vehicle before I sold it. I am in possession of the contents if you would like to stop by to retrieve it.

Becker detoured to Silver Hill and met William at the doorstep. He handed her a small box.

"While I'm here, can I ask you a quick question?"

"Of course."

"Did you liquidate Michelle's bank account after she left?"

"I left it be…in case she comes home." Pain flitted across his face.

"I understand she had a sizable amount; do you mind telling me how much was in there?"

His eyes sharpened. "No, the balance was less than $500. Where would she get a 'sizable amount'?"

Shit, Becker thought. "Mimi gave her $5000 a few months before she left."

"Whatever for?"

"You need to ask her. Once you have that conversation, let's talk again."

Chapter Twenty-Three

Nonna's BMW, Joey Vito's Mercedes, Angelo's Alfa Romeo, Mack's truck, and Birdy's late model Mercury with a donut tire and *Drones for Hire* sign on the door, lined the road, again. Keisha's and Sheriff Atkins' cruisers were squeezed between the Underwater Rescue Team's boat trailer.

Becker shook her head as she walked into Edwina Landon's backyard. Her grandmother had gone all-out with a taco truck, corn-hole game, photo booth, roulette wheel, a palm reader, who happened to be Mooney, currently under a tent, head low over Joey Vito's hand.

Birdy sauntered over. "Hey Chief, the Drone Club is excited to be a part of today's festivities. As president, let me welcome you to the party!"

She rubbed her brow. "Birdy, I thought we agreed you would not tell Nonna about the results."

He smiled. "I didn't! I only told her the state police were coming, not the locations they would be investigating."

Becker spied Nonna, talking with members of the Underwater Rescue Team, a small group of men and women responsible for the rescue or recovery of people and evidence in bodies of water. Corporal Clarke looked at Nonna the way one would at an unsolvable puzzle. He visibly relaxed when his eyes met Becker's.

She put out her hand, and he shook it. "Chief, good to see you again."

"Corporal. I'm sorry it's under these circumstances."

Nonna butted in, "Nonsense, Del. It's a sad job, these good looking, muscular, manly—"

"Nonna," Becker growled.

"As I was saying, it's a sad job these police officers have to do every day, looking for bones, and sometimes finding them. But today's circumstances are better than most. The crew will have lots of food, and I'll make sure they stay hydrated." She turned back to Corporal Clarke. "John, you'll text me if you find a skeleton? I set up the roulette wheel based on the number of locations. The pot is already at $37."

"Nonna," Becker said more sharply than she meant to, "Corporal Clarke will not be checking in with you. Please tell everyone the roulette wheel is for charity, and you will pull a number at random."

"Del, don't be a killjoy."

"Nonna, no arguments. This is my show, so please let me lead it." She peered over Nonna's shoulder. "Oh, it looks like there's a small fire in the taco truck..."

Nonna hiked up her skirt to run at about the same time Becker identified the pattern on her grandmother's clothes as skulls and bones. She stifled a groan.

"Wow, I wish I had a grandmother like Teresa." Becker gave him a side-eye so he quickly added, "Chief, do you have a minute to discuss our method?"

Becker nodded. Corporal Clarke outlined the process: they would use the shallow boat, similar to a small fishing vessel, to check out the locations underwater with the more sophisticated sonar on board. Divers would go into the water if the sites identified showed promise. After, the divers would trade their wet suits for clothes suitable for digging in the marsh.

Keisha joined them as Corporal Clarke was pointing out the various areas and the sequence in which they would execute the plan. She asked, "What can we do to assist?"

"Because some locations are fairly shallow, I'm going to limit the number of people on our boat. Later today, though, when we're digging, I could use a few extra hands to excavate the marsh mud. Or hopefully soil; it's easier. I'm sure the guys will be tired by then, and glad for the reprieve."

"Count us in," Becker said. She and Keisha headed to the taco truck for a breakfast burrito. She waved at Hamilton and Mack standing beside the roulette wheel.

Nonna met them. "Del, it was a small grill fire. You made it sound like I needed to call 9-1-1." She gave Becker the stink eye. "You were getting rid of me, huh? That Corporal Clarke is a looker. Are you concerned I'm muscling in on your territory?"

Becker looked heavenward for help. No sign came. "Nonna, this is Keisha."

"Ah, the best friend. Aren't you a pretty chocolate brown?"

"And you're a pretty milky white!"

Nonna laughed. "I like her, Del. She's spunky, like you."

They ordered breakfast, declined the $5.00 Bloody Mary. They were sipping coffee when Joey and Angelo walked up. Angelo grabbed Becker's hand to pull her in for a kiss. She moved her head just in time; the kiss landed on her cheek instead of her mouth. Over Angelo's shoulder, Becker met Mack's eyes, narrowed and smoldering, and not in a good way. He turned on his heel toward the edge of the swamp.

She extricated herself from Angelo. "Angelo, you can't do that!"

"Why not? What's wrong with greeting a beautiful woman?"

"How about we're not dating? How about I'm in my uniform and acting in a professional capacity?"

"Cops don't kiss?" He looked at her like wanted to kiss her...everywhere.

"That's not my point and you know it. Besides, I am in a relationship. His name is Mack Brown. He's standing over there."

"I am well aware of your relationship with Mr. Marine Biologist and Art Shop Owner. So? He can give you a sand dollar or a shell. I can give you an ocean where we can frolic and then we can relax in a king-sized bed, followed by...more frolicking. Did I tell you I own an island?"

Of course you do, Becker thought. She excused herself, hurrying across the grass to Mack. She held his hand, both scanning the water, cypress trees and marsh grasses, until he broke the silence. "I'm embarrassed to say I'm jealous of Angelo."

Becker snorted. "You have no reason to be."

"It seems like forever ago I asked you about our relationship and where we were going. You told me you wanted to delay the conversation. Today's not the day to talk about it, of course, but seeing you with Angelo reminded me it's overdue. You've been busy with this investigation, I get that. It's sad you're also too busy for us." He met her eyes. "You have your hands full today. Let me know when you're ready for a serious conversation."

He gave her a kiss on the cheek and walked toward the front of the house. He drove the truck away, tires crunching on the gravel. She contemplated lying down in the fetal position to have a good cry. Despite her intentions, she was successfully ruining their relationship.

She mentally shook off the thoughts and pulled up her big girl pants. She had an investigation to lead.

Sheriff Atkins sidled up to her. "Problems in paradise?"

"If there were, you'd be the last person I'd tell. What can I do for you, Sheriff?"

"I understand you stirred the pot at the Workman house. A family's finances should be their business, not yours."

"An investigation is an investigation. There's no off-limits."

"Uh-huh. Well, if you're so concerned about the money trail, ask Gus Fornash how he bought the new car lift for his garage, days after Michelle disappeared."

Becker hoped she hid the surprise on her face. "I thought you would have asked him during the initial investigation. I guess this is new news?" He scowled at her. "Speaking of which, I'm still waiting for the official files."

He pulled his mirrored glasses down his nose, staring at her. "As I told Mayor Workman, when he asked me on your behalf, I'm working on it." He gave her a cocky salute, turned his back on her, and sauntered to the water's edge.

Over the next few hours, the state police came up empty, spot after spot. The weather, warm for a fall day, drove a few people away. The bugs took care of a few more. And the boredom finished all but Becker, Keisha, and Mooney. Even Edwina took refuge in her house.

Mooney lounged on a huge purple bean-bag pillow on the ground in her tent. Keisha and Becker sat in nearby chairs. Their iced tea glasses were sweating all over the table.

"Father called me about the $5000 Mother gave to Michelle before she disappeared," Mooney said.

"I didn't mean to cause your family additional pain."

"I see your heart, Becker. Of course, you didn't do it to hurt us. You're after the truth." She pushed the hair from her face. "I can't believe Mother tried to bribe Michelle and didn't tell Father. She operates based on her own rules. It doesn't matter who she wounds." She took a sip of the diluted tea. "Father is beside himself. I feel for him. I gave him a piece of rose quartz for emotional healing. He surprised me by slipping it into his pocket. Not to change the subject, but I understand he gave you a box of Michelle's stuff?"

"He did, from her Ford Pinto."

Mooney's brow furrowed. "What?"

"Her car, the one that was abandoned when she disappeared."

"She drove a beat-up jeep."

Becker was confused but put the thought away for later. She retrieved the box from her car, set it on the table to open it. Inside was a spark plug, a tire gauge, a map, a few pens and pencils, a box of tissues, a trombone mouthpiece, and a piece of paper, folded up.

Keisha and Mooney looked over Becker's shoulder as she opened the map. It was smooth from use, and torn around the edges. The map was topographical, showing the terrain of several counties surrounding Silver Hill. Numerous areas had been marked with a star, others with an N. "Mooney, any insights?"

Mooney leaned in closer. "Hmm. Some stars were her favorite marshes or swamps. Of course, here's Grimmy Swamp and Bloodstone Bay, where we are." She moved her finger to a location in Virginia, about an hour from Silver Hill. "This one is Katy Bay." Mooney touched Becker's shoulder. "Do you remember the stuffed bear you found?" Becker nodded. "Michelle named her Katy-Bear after Katy Bay."

She put her nose nearly to the map's surface again. "Let's see. I'm not sure why these are starred." Mooney pointed to a few spots. Are the N locations navigable by boat? I honestly don't know."

Becker carefully folded the map and put it back in the box. She took out the piece of paper, told them it was a note from Edward, and read it out loud.

Michelle,

I'm begging you, please stay away from that garage. It's not safe. I've told you time and time again he's no good. I checked into his background. He's hiding something and I know what it is. You're in danger. We need to talk, please meet at the boat on Tuesday?

Yours,

Edward

Becker, Keisha and Mooney were quiet, lost in thoughts when Corporal Clarke yelled her name. "I think we've found something."

Chapter Twenty-Four

B ecker and Keisha met Corporal Clarke at the water's edge.

"We started digging about an hour ago in multiple locations. I just got a call from one team, indicating they have a spot of interest. Likely bones. Do you want to tag along?"

They pulled on their muck boots and followed the officer to a spot a couple hundred feet from the boat. It was near the lookout Mooney and she had found days before.

Two officers were on their knees, using small spades and brushes to clear dirt. Next to the spot was a large tarp positioned over the ground to collect evidence. On it was a piece of green plastic no bigger than a dime, and a scrap of fabric, its color since drained to gray. The process of excavating bones was painstakingly slow. Shovel a bit of dirt, brush the surface. Shovel a bit more, brush again. Just when she thought the team would call it quits, one officer unearthed a bone fragment. For the next two hours, well into dusk, then darkness, and with the use of portable lights, they found the rest of the body.

The shallow grave was large enough to bury the body in a fetal position. To Becker's untrained eye, the bones were on the larger side. Her guess was the victim was male. Scraps of clothing lay under the corpse. No shoes. The bullet hole in the back of the skull showed it was probably a homicide.

The ME bagged the body and as the procession, not unlike a funeral, walked single file out of the marsh, Corporal Clarke said, "Gene, the lead officer here, has a side hobby. He collects bullets, can identify hundreds of different types. Even does ballistics tests. He's not a certified expert, by any means, but he's helpful if you need some preliminary insights. So, what I am about to say is not official, okay, Chief?"

"This is between us and speculative."

"Exactly. Gene told me the bullet hole was the size of a .38 or .357."

***

Becker hardly slept; shadowy figures carrying guns chased her all night. She woke feeling groggy and disjointed. A cool shower only did so much. On the way to Silver Hill, she held a one-way discussion with herself, a pep talk to stay alert and focused.

She had interviews scheduled with Mimi and Meghan in person, but separately, Marissa Workman by phone, and Officer Pete Peters via Zoom. She was also impatiently waiting for the MSP's report. The autopsy results would take several days—if not weeks—to come back.

Becker's phone rang. It was Cephas Jones.

"Good morning, Cephas Jones. I hope you are well today."

"Chief, I'm doing outstanding. I wanted to talk to you about preparations for the Seahorse Festival in two weeks." They discussed the schedule, volunteers, and help still needed. Becker committed to talking with Nonna to drum up more interest in manning the booth at the entrance. If anyone could prod older adults to put down remotes, abandon re-runs, get out of their chairs, it was Nonna.

"Cephas Jones, do you have a few more minutes to talk? I could use your help."

"Shoot."

"Katy Bay has been mentioned several times during my investigation down here in Silver Hill. You grew up in that area, correct?"

"I did. My kin are all from the Eastern Shore of Virginia, originally brought in as slaves, and then sharecroppers. My father and uncles were in the fishing industry, mostly working in seafood processing. I grew up a stone's throw from Katy Bay. Spent many a day on a fishing boat, or wandering around the marsh. It's beautiful in a rugged sort of way. It reminds me of the Blackwater National Wildlife Refuge, in Dorchester County, Maryland."

"Michelle and her school friends visited there as part of the Swamp Keepers."

"It's a day trip from here."

"I'd love to see it someday."

"I can take you if you like? My cousins own a fishing camp right on the bay. It's not much to look at, the shack itself, but the views are stunning. I owe them a visit, anyway. I try to get down there three or four times a year. What do you think?"

As Becker pulled into the Silver Hill police station, she said, "I think I'd like to be your co-pilot. Let me know what works for them, and I'll fit it in my schedule."

Mimi was waiting for her in the interview room. Becker walked in, met Sheriff Atkins' glare and ignored it. Two coffee mugs were on the table. Mimi sat on a chair covered with a beach blanket. The room, including the table, was spotless. Sheriff Atkins had put his best foot forward for the mayor's wife.

He got up from his chair telling Mimi he would be in his office if she needed him. He didn't dignify Becker with a hello or goodbye.

"Good morning, Mrs. Workman. Thank you for agreeing to see me again."

"I had little choice after you disclosed confidential information to William."

"Ma'am, I didn't intend to upset your family further. I'm simply doing my job by following the facts. I was unaware the money you offered your daughter was a secret. Do you have questions before we start?"

Mimi shifted in her chair as she licked her lips. "Is the body in the swamp Michelle? I can't seem to get a straight answer from anyone."

Becker hid her surprise at the lack of emotion in Mimi's voice and body language. It was as if she was asking about the weather or a new shade of nail polish. "The medical examiner hasn't released the results yet. Unfortunately, there won't be any actual answers until we have his report."

"It's unacceptable that we have to wait. You would think a mayor's daughter would be a priority."

Priority? Since when did Mimi give a shit about finding her daughter, let alone quickly? And why would Mimi think the mayor of a tiny town on the Eastern Shore of Maryland could fast-track a seven-year-old cold case? She resisted the urge to shake her head in disbelief.

"I understand your frustration. Since we can't control what they do, let's focus on what we can accomplish, like this interview. You mentioned I stirred the pot with William. Let's start there. Why did you offer your daughter $5000 to leave?"

"It was for her own good."

"Please elaborate."

Mimi's hands clenched in her lap. "I told you she was like a ghost in our home. That wasn't quite true. She was more like a...wren. Or chickadee. She was nervous, fidgety. She jumped at noises always looking like a little bird ready to fly away. I noticed she lost a few pounds. She looked extremely unattractive so I told her she need to take better care of herself. She turned on me and my concern for her health, typical of her. She told me to, and I quote, 'get out of my face', and if I didn't, she would pack her stuff up and go." Mimi played with her wedding ring, a four-carat square diamond. "I wrote her a check and told her if she wanted to go, I wasn't stopping her."

"So, she left."

"Not right then, but soon after."

"When exactly?"

Mimi was silent. Her hands trembled. Her eyes met Becker's.

"Mrs. Workman? Can you answer the question?"

"They both disappeared about the same time, but Michelle never came home."

"I'm confused. Who else disappeared when Michelle did?"

"Meghan."

"If I have this right, Michelle and Meghan disappeared the same day, then Meghan came home?"

Mimi started crying without a sound. She pulled an embroidered handkerchief from her designer handbag. "This is terrible, having to talk about my family in this negative fashion!" She dabbed at her eyes. "Why do we need have this discussion? It's bringing back so many troubling memories. It was a horrible time in our household. Michelle was creating havoc. Poor Meghan was affected the most. She was exhibiting mood swings, not sleeping. She had bags under her eyes. Her disposition changed. She's always been a good girl, mannerly and polite. Back then, she..."

"She what, Mrs. Workman?"

"I'm not going to talk further about Meghan. I'll say simply: she wasn't herself. It was all Michelle's fault."

"When Michelle left, you were glad she did."

"What an awful thing to say, Chief Becker."

Becker let the silence stretch. "We were talking about your daughters and when they disappeared. You said they went missing the same day. What happened?"

She raised the tissue again to her eyes. "The last time I saw Michelle was a Tuesday. I heard her and Meghan arguing in Michelle's bedroom upstairs."

"What was the argument about?"

"I don't know. But it was ugly. Uncouth. I went upstairs afterward and found my mother's Stiffel lamp in a heap on the floor, shards of glass everywhere. Michelle never did respect anything of value."

Becker interrupted, "How do you know it was Michelle and not Meghan who threw it?"

Mimi glared at her. "A ridiculous question. I've already told you Michelle was unbalanced."

Becker suppressed a sigh. "Both women went missing after the incident?"

"Yes."

"Why did you wait a week to file a report?"

"I didn't want to bother William with girl nonsense. It wasn't until five days later he noticed they weren't at Sunday dinner, a weekly tradition celebrated in proper families."

Becker heard the unspoken insinuation: her upbringing was less than that of the Workmans. She disregarded it. "What did he say?"

Mimi startled. "Oh, he was concerned. I forget his exact words, except he told me we should wait a few days to get worried. So that's what I did."

"That doesn't sound like William."

"I didn't tell him about the argument or that the girls hadn't been home for a few days. He's an important man, Chief Becker. He doesn't need to be bothered about day-to-day minutia. In any event, Meghan came home Thursday, looking splendid." Mimi had a proud-parent smile on her face. "As I recall, she was wearing a Dior dress and her makeup was impeccable."

"And Michelle?"

"Why do you have to be so confrontational, Chief Becker?" She put her handkerchief away, eyes dry. "You know she's still missing."

***

Becker called the number given to her for Marissa Workman and got a message the number had been disconnected. She put Molly on it.

She talked to Peter Peters after Mimi left. He called her cell at the appointed time. After small talk, Becker asked, "Why did you leave the Silver Hill Police Department so soon after arresting Michelle?"

His voice was self-assured. "I have nothing to lose by telling you the truth, so here goes: I was concerned about Sheriff Atkin's methods, his approach, his leadership. I didn't, and still don't, trust the guy. The state police made me a substantial offer. I was happy to jump ship."

"You mentioned his methods. He told me he sent you on various calls and duties to 'toughen you up'."

"Well, that's interesting. The only unusual call he sent me on was to Dave's Dive to look for prostitutes, and he specifically mentioned one with dark brown hair, like Michelle's."

Chapter Twenty-Five

B ecker called an emergency meeting with Keisha, with the promise of wine and chicken parmesan. She had a fraction of her mother's kitchen skills; of the half-dozen dishes she could make, her chicken parm was the best.

They were sitting on Becker's deck. "So, my head is swirling, and not in a good way. I need to bounce things off of you for perspective."

Keisha nodded. "Works for me."

"I feel like my list of suspects is getting bigger, not smaller." Becker flipped through the pages of her notebook. "I haven't ruled out many people, so still under suspicion is: Meghan, Mimi, Sheriff Atkins, Gus Fornash. Hamilton Parsons is not on my list, but maybe he should be. Heck, maybe Kevin did it." Becker caught his eye, and he wagged his tail. "All kidding aside, I can't sleep at night because my thoughts keep turning in on themselves."

"Let's talk about them one by one. What points to Mimi?"

Becker tapped her pen on her notebook. "Michelle embarrassed her. She was someone who didn't fit Mimi's profile of a high-society debutante. She told me Michelle's behavior was disrupting the entire family." Becker paused. "Can you believe she offered Michelle $5000 to leave? Michelle turned her down yet kept the money. I could have cheered when I heard that, but professionalism kept me from doing it." They smiled at each other. "Maybe her being in the house wore Mimi down so Mimi got rid of her another way."

"You've said she's a narcissist. That's a far cry from being a murder-er."

"I agree. It's more likely, if Mimi killed Michelle, it was a crime of passion. When I interviewed her, it was obvious her love was for Meghan, not Michelle, and their fighting was taking a toll on the family." Tap, tap, tap. "It's a stretch. She is lying about something, though. I just can't put my finger on what. The story about Michelle and Meghan missing at the same time feels contrived. But why make up two disappeared daughters?"

"Could Mooney shed some light? Otherwise, you may have to interview Mimi again."

Becker winced. "I hope not. I'd rather have a root canal. It would be less painful." Becker scribbled on the paper. "I'll try Mooney or William, postpone talking to the Queen of Silver Hill."

"Good strategy, Becker."

"Next up is Meghan. She despised her sister. I saw a flash of rage during my interview with her before she tamped it down. She is more capable of hurting someone than, say, Mimi. And, like her mother, she is fiercely protective of the family's reputation." Becker put pen to paper again. "If the story about both girls missing is true, why did Meghan come back and Michelle did not? What was Meghan doing for the week she was gone? Was that time used to kill her sister and dispose of her body?"

"It's plausible, but a whole week?" Keisha asked. They were silent for a moment. "How about your favorite sheriff? What is his motive?"

Becker scowled at her. "Unfavorite sheriff, you mean. Paul Atkins is hiding something, but I haven't figured out what yet. The way he deflects questions reminds me of a boxer in the ring." She rubbed her brow. "Back to motive. Bad blood from high school? Jilted lover? Maybe he wanted to hurt the Workman family, and when his attempt at labeling Michelle a prostitute from a bogus solicitation charge didn't work, he killed her, then he led the investigation himself so no-one would be the wiser."

Keisha nodded. "Hmm, that's a gigantic leap, from wanting her arrested to wanting her dead. Still, he seems to have."

"Agreed, but you've met him. Something isn't right about him."

"Maybe it's his little pin-head. Did you ever notice his head is too small for his body?"

Becker laughed, then stopped. "Keisha, professionalism and all of that."

"Yea, yea. Let's talk about Gus Fornash," Keisha said. "He's at the top of the list. First, he has mob ties. Second, there's the dead body at his shop in Philadelphia. Third, his relationship with Michelle is undefined, and based on what you've told me, it could have been romantic in nature. Another jilted lover? Fourth—"

Becker's phone rang. It was the medical examiner. After pleasantries, he said, "Chief, I have a positive ID on the body we found in Grimmy Swamp. It's Edward Landon."

Becker's heart lodged in her throat as she asked follow-up questions. Edward received close-range gunshot wounds to his head, arm, and leg. A bullet was recovered from near his spinal cord at the base of the brain. The doctor indicated a high likelihood that someone had dragged the body to the burial location.

"Any ballistics results?"

According to the ME, "A .38 Special was used to shoot him; they were able to recover a casing. The gun used in the destruction of property case at *Apothecary and Amulets*, the store owned by Monica Workman, was the same one." He gave her a few more details, and they said their goodbyes.

Keisha had slipped away during the phone call. She re-appeared with two glasses of red wine. "Here. Take a minute."

Becker's hands trembled. She told Keisha the news. "Edwina Landon is going to be devastated."

"She's such a sweet woman. I hate when bad things happen to lovely people."

***

Anger and dread warred within Becker as she drove to Edwina's house with Nonna, who was doing her best to keep Becker distracted from her sorrowful thoughts.

Edwina opened the door with a dazzling smile that withered away when she saw Becker's face.

Edwina led them to her parlor. She sat on the couch, Nonna beside her, and said, "It's Edward, isn't it? The body you found in the swamp." Tears pooled in her eyes, spilling down her face.

Becker sat in the chair next to her. As gently as she could, she told Edwina about her son's death. "I am so sorry for your loss."

Edwina nodded. "I am beyond sad, but so thankful that he's been found." She wiped the moisture from her cheeks. "I would have spent the rest of my life worrying about him. Now I can lay him to rest and have some peace."

Nonna rocked her ample weight toward Edwina. She enveloped her in a hug. "We can plan a memorial service."

Edwina's lips turned up slightly. "I'd like that. But no drones or taco trucks." She turned to Becker, face serious. "I can't help but wonder why anyone would have wanted to kill my son. He was such a good person."

"He was. Everyone said such positive things about him."

"Now what?"

"Without providing specific details, there appears to be a connection between Edward's death and Michelle's disappearance. And Nonna, this is confidential. You can't tell anyone, even Lester the parrot."

"Yes, Ms. Policewoman."

"So, I'll be involved in Edward's investigation. I've got a lead, but that's all I can tell you."

Nonna said, "Del, I'll stay with Edwina. You go get the bad guy."

After saying goodbye, Becker headed to the courthouse for an impromptu visit with Judge Green. He had an hour break between court appearances, and she was hoping for a few minutes to plead her case to his Honor.

"Judge, I apologize for the interruption."

"Chief, always a pleasure to see you. Please sit down; I can tell you're upset about something."

"I received confirmation that the body we found in the swamp is Edward Landon. I'm here to ask for a warrant to search Gus Fornash's garage and house."

"Slow down, Chief. I'm not following. I'm assuming you are tying Mr. Fornash to Edward's death?"

"I am."

"But that's not your case."

Becker and Keisha had anticipated the judge's response last night as they planned strategy; they had discussed likely scenarios and Becker's response. "No, your Honor. However, a firearm connects Michelle Workman's case to Edward Landon's case." She explained the connection.

"So, you've tied a .38 Special to both crime scenes. What does that have to do with Mr. Fornash?"

"I found a picture of Gus Fornash with a .38 Special, the exact bullet caliber."

"You're basing your request on a *photograph*?"

"Well, there's more, your Honor. We found a piece of plastic under Edward's body. It's from a pen at the Fornash Garage. The S and H are visible."

"Slim."

"And he's a former mobster. Someone murdered a man at his workplace in Philadelphia a few years back. They arrested him and later released him." The next sentence was beyond a stretch, it was a reach to the next universe. "He's still the primary suspect."

Judge Green gazed out the window. Becker almost felt his thoughts bounce around the room. "Chief, I'm not supposed to have favorites, so I don't." He rubbed his face. "But I think kindly about you. You've always been professional, and I find your ethics above reproach."

"Thank you, Judge."

"You're asking a lot with so little." She fought the frown spreading on her face. "Against my better judgment, I'll issue your search warrant."

"Thank you again, Judge."

"Don't thank me yet. It will be an extremely limited search warrant for the weapon only. This isn't a fishing expedition, Chief. Keep it simple and take Sheriff Atkins with you."

She gritted her teeth at the mention of Sheriff Atkins. "That will work, Judge. Again, I appreciate your willingness to do this."

She grabbed her paperwork before he could change his mind. She sped to the Silver Hill Police Station, bypassed the cop at the desk and walked into Sheriff Atkins' office, the second visit of the day unplanned and unannounced.

He was typing on his keyboard, eyes on the screen. When he looked up, he grimaced. "I guess they don't teach manners up in Celestino Village. Down here, where people are more genteel, we make appointments in advance."

"Sheriff, can we cut the shit for once? I'm here because of Michelle's disappearance, not because of your charming personality." She handed over the warrant for him to read.

"Huh. The judge doesn't give many of these out. For your sake, I hope we find something. Otherwise, his Honor's going to be pissed off with you big time."

Becker reluctantly agreed, and for the next half hour, they talked through their approach: garage first, as he was likely there working. Then to his home. Becker insisted they drive separately; she had no appetite for small talk with Sheriff Atkins.

They pulled into the parking lot between the garage and the bar. The garage doors were closed, the lights were off. The same car was on the lift from a few days ago. "He's usually open now," Sheriff Atkins said.

The side door was locked, so they continued to the back, to the office. The smell of garbage made her almost gag, although the dumpster was over twenty feet away.

She yelled, "Gus? Are you in there?" She grabbed the handle to his office door, expected it to be locked. It surprised her when it turned.

The putrid smell wasn't in the trash. Gus was in his office chair, legs splayed, eyes open, a bullet hole in his forehead. Flies buzzed around his face, head, and the wall behind him, where blood had been sprayed.

Becker fought the urge to puke.

One arm dangled at his side. The other, on his lap, clutched a .38 Special.

She backed out into Sheriff Atkins, who growled, "What the hell? Watch where you're going, Chief."

She wouldn't let him see her rattled. She took in a big breath, then regretted it as the urge to throw up grabbed her again. "Gus Fornash is inside, dead. Looks like suicide. Call the state police."

"You call the state police. This ain't my crazy train ride or my station."

"You can't help yourself, can you? We've got a dead body and you still have to be an asshole."

He shrugged, opened the door, muttered, "Yep, dead," then got on his radio to request backup. They ran crime scene tape around perimeter of the parking lot, encompassing the garage and Dave's Dive. A small group of people, including Mooney and Hamilton, gathered near the street. In a tiny town, news traveled faster than a pizza delivery guy.

Becker was met with organized chaos as the medical examiner and state police arrived, reminiscent of a beehive. Each person had a role: controlling traffic, supervising the crowd, combing for forensic evidence, interviewing witnesses, and examining the body. She played point, orchestrating the many aspects of a murder scene investigation. An hour later, Mooney yelled her name holding up a to-go Styrofoam cup.

"I felt your aura getting low," Mooney said, as she handed over the coffee. "It's got your favorite cream in it."

Becker smelled hazelnut and cocoa. She took a sip. "Thank you. I was starting to fade. It's been a long day."

Hamilton smiled at her; an "I-empathize-with-you" turn up of his lips. "You've been busy. First Edward, and now this."

"Yes, unfortunately. I apologize we haven't scheduled time for us to finish up our interview. Once I have a handle on today's...activities, I'll reach out to you."

"I'm here when you are ready, Chief."

Becker's name was called. The ME flagged her over, along with Sheriff Atkins. "We're done with the initial examination. I'm probably telling you what you already suspect: our preliminary findings suggest Gus Fornash died of a self-inflicted gun-shot wound. Based on the condition of the body, I'm estimating he committed suicide within the last 24-36 hours."

Chapter Twenty-Six

The face of a dead Gus Fornash was lodged in her mind. She gazed outside of her passenger side window, attempting to replace the memories of his body with views of cornfields. It was sort of working.

She and Cephas Jones were headed to Katy Bay, Virginia. The timing of their trip sucked; she had second interviews to conduct, information to follow up on, but Cephas was a busy man, his schedule packed with God knows what, the man was retired, yet today was the day he could fit her in, so she sat back and tried to enjoy the ride.

"I always forget how flat the shore is until I get out on the road and drive a long distance," Becker said.

Delmarva (DELaware, MARyland and VA) lacked the rugged beauty of the Colorado Rocky Mountains, or the majestic rolling hills of North Carolina, but there were stunning views of the ocean, thick forests of cypress trees, and the simple charm of tilled up soil on hundreds of family farms.

"I love this area," Cephas replied. "These little towns, you know, New Church, Oak Hill, Onancock, that's where my kin are from. Gotta be careful down here, though, and drive the speed limit. They make a killing on fines; I heard they built the new high school from speeding ticket money. That, and cigarette sales."

She glanced over at Cephas, who was wearing a gray short-sleeve polo shirt, black slacks, and tasseled loafers. "Cephas Jones, I believe this is the first time I've ever seen you without a suit on."

"Chief, I believe it is." He gave her a small smile. "Truth is, my kin are dirt poor, and I learned long ago not to 'poke the bear' as my mama used to say. No sense in making them feel like they're less than I am."

"I'd love to know more about your mama. Your family."

"You would have liked her. She was like you, hard on the outside and soft on the inside."

"Don't tell anyone about my soft side."

"It's actually your best side, Chief. Anyway, I had an older brother and sister, God rest their souls. She wanted an entire house full of young-uns; unfortunately for her, she had a few miscarriages so there were only three of us." He focused on a right-hand turn, then continued. "We were poor, yet Mama didn't dwell on it. My dad worked on a fishing boat. She took care of us and the house, and stretched pennies. She also took on sewing for the wealthy folks around the area; she was a genius when sewing new dresses or altering old ones. She even made prom gowns. Once, she sewed a wedding dress from scratch, beads and all."

"Did you get your sense of style from her?"

He nodded his head. "Yes, indeed. And her friends. Black women down here still dress in their best clothes for church, including those fancy hats. She taught me a lot about fashion. For example, I learned at an early age how important a quality pair of shoes are, and how they can make you feel...sure of yourself."

"And your dad? What was he like?

"Hard working. Determined. There's not much employment down here except agriculture, picking tomatoes, that sort of thing, or working in chicken plants. And of course, being a waterman. Dad chose that." He paused at a stop sign. "Those stretched pennies I mentioned earlier, the ones my mama saved? It was enough for my father to buy his first commercial fishing boat when I was in grade school. Eventually, he owned four boats."

"I'm surprised you didn't become a waterman."

"Oh, I worked as a deckhand for a while, then as his bookkeeper after I graduated with a business degree from the local community college. I much preferred office work to being out in the sun, sweaty, burned up by the sun. I guess I never enjoyed the solitude of the water, either, like so many watermen and women do."

They came to a yield sign in the middle of nowhere. A chicken house sat in a cornfield, imploded on itself, the rusty metal roof peeled back, seemingly pointing to the sky. Modest cottages dotted the landscape, most with flaking paint and sagging doors. Raggedy clean clothes hung from drying lines, dogs on chains prowled the dirt yards. The poverty made Becker catch her breath.

"We're almost at my cousin's fishing camp. Wait until you see the view."

A few minutes later, she saw the sparkling water of Katy Bay. Tiny houses, shacks and bungalows sat next to the water, some on stilts in the marsh, others on solid ground, tethered to the ocean with long docks. Red and blue floats the size of a pack of cards littered the water's surface, signaling crab pots below.

"The ocean looks like one of those sparkling dresses the movie stars wear to the Oscars," Cephas said, as he pulled the car into a driveway of crushed oyster shells. Back about fifty feet was a small wooden structure, painted white, surrounded by perennial bushes and flowers. Beyond the house, a pier jutted out into the bay where a bass fishing boat floated, swaying gently in the breeze.

Five men, ranging from roughly age forty to eighty, sat in a half circle on the front porch. One was whittling. They all stood up when Cephas and Becker got to the front porch.

"Chief, this is Cephas *Johnson*. And of course I'm Cephas *Jones*. To avoid confusion when we were kids, we started calling him Cephas and me Cephas Jones. I've been doing it ever since." Cephas Jones introduced her to the rest of the men. "And last but not least, this is my cousin Melvin, only we call him Mel."

Mel shook her hand. "Help me get some tea?"

She trailed him into the house. "Mel, how long have you been in these parts?"

"Why, are you writin' a book?"

Her stomach fell. "No disrespect intended."

She saw a hint of a smile under his mustache and grizzled beard. "No harm, Chief Becker. Just teasin' ya. Any friend of Cephas Jones is a friend of mine, so no worries. Let's see, I'm sixty-six, so I been here for," he took a pause, "...sixty-six years."

They chuckled. "Are you a waterman?"

"Nah. I was a janitor at the high school up in Onancock until I retired a few years back. Loved the kids. Teachers, too. The parents and the bosses, not so much."

She carried plastic cups and a plate of cookies, and Mel toted a pitcher of sweet iced tea to the front porch. Cephas Jones was talking about Michelle. "Chief, I was just telling the guys about your investigation. Remind me why you wanted to see Katy Bay?"

"Michelle Workman, the woman who went missing seven years ago, came down here several times with the Swamp Keepers."

One guy spat on the ground. "They give themselves too much credit. Don't hardly do nothing."

"At least they're doing *something*," Cephas said. "For so many years it was a dumping ground for garbage and God only knows what else."

"True dat, Cephas Jones, true dat. Chief, go on."

"It was also her favorite marshland. She even named a teddy bear after it."

Mel barked out a laugh. "And that's important? Naming a stuffed animal after a bay?"

Becker picked at the skin on her palm, self-consciousness creeping into her brain. "I'm not sure, but it could be. Young girls frequently give things names based on people or places that hold significance for them."

"So, it was meaningful for Michelle. What does that have to do with your investigation?" Mel asked.

"Again, I'm not sure. Maybe nothing. Or maybe she met someone here. Maybe he kidnapped her and brought her to the area, perhaps he murdered her and buried her here. Maybe someone from up north had knowledge of the importance of the place and brought her here to hurt or hide her. Or maybe she ran away..."

One of the men interrupted by muttering, "Or maybe the chief is chasing her tail."

Mel said, "Hank, you need to apologize."

"Actually, please don't. Hank, I take no offense, because you're right. I'm doing my best with a case I didn't want and, frankly, have little to no experience to solve it." She rubbed her brow. "I'm pulling at straws, trying to re-create her life before she went missing. Michelle was so smitten with anything water; I thought why not visit here. We've already searched Grimmy Swamp, which is next to her house in Silver Hill. Since Katy Bay seemed important, I asked Cephas Jones to bring me here. But to your point, Hank, Michelle might not even be on the shore at all." Her shoulders sagged. Becker caught the slump and straightened her spine.

Cephas Jones came to her rescue, the gentleman that he was. "Chief Becker is hard on herself. She's fully capable of figuring this out, but she could use our help. We were going to sit around and shoot the breeze all day, why not do something useful?"

Heads nodded in agreement all around so for the next two hours, over three pitchers of sweet tea, a half bushel of oysters, and Mel's famous crab cakes, they discussed locations where a body could be, and places Michelle may be living. There were dozens, even when the group limited the parameters to areas directly on the bay or surrounding swamp.

Mel and Cephas Johnson volunteered to finish the list. Both were retired and more than a little bored, like members of her Gruppo.

She promised to bring Smith Island cake next visit as compensation for her new investigative team.

***

She hadn't talked to Mack since the day the state police found Edward's body. Gus Fornash's suicide side-tracked her from seeing him until now. Becker texted: *Visit tonight?* Her stomach did little flips until he responded, *Sure. I have a bottle of wine I've been saving. See you around 7:00.*

After a quick shower and trip to Mama's place to drop off Kevin, she got to Mack's a few minutes early. He smiled at her through the kitchen window as he opened a bottle of Amarone della Valpolicella, a robust red with hints of raisin. When she walked into the house, he handed her a glass of wine, eyes full of hurt and disappointment.

They sat on his sofa making small talk. Becker stammered her way through the beginning of an apology before Mack interrupted her. His voice was soft, one you would use with a newborn baby. "I'm in love with you, Delaney."

She almost choked on the sip of wine in her mouth.

He continued, "I'm not ready yet to ask you to marry me because I want to get my finances in order. And," his gaze scanned the room, "this place needs an addition. It's tight for you and me, and when Bea stays, one bathroom won't work. I'm getting a head of myself. What

I'm trying to say is I have serious intentions where we are concerned. Do you feel the same?"

Tension built in the room, awaiting her answer. "I'm trying very hard to be a better partner, the other half of a couple, so to speak." She reached for his hand. "I can see my future tied to yours, but what it looks like exactly, I'm not sure. I need more space and time."

"Take all the time you need. When you decide, I'm here. Until then, it hurts to be in limbo. I'd rather not see you than to see you indecisive about us."

"Mack, that's not what I meant..."

"But that's what you said." He kissed her hand, dropped it, and stood up. "I'm going out to the barn. Let yourself out when you're ready."

She drove home, images of his sad face in the forefront of her mind.

Chapter Twenty-Seven

The morning after the pajama party at Mack's, minus the sleep over, minus pajamas, and minus any sex, she headed to Spotted Dick Resort with Kevin. Nonna and Joey had invited her to breakfast; since Becker needed to pump Joey for information about Gus Fornash, she accepted.

She hoped the Italian "omerta", the code of silence, was relaxed once someone died, and Joey would have enough champagne to make his lips loose.

The campground was a disaster zone. Empty beer cans and liquor bottles littered the resort, deflated balloons hung from trees, banners reading, *Dick's Bingo and Balls* flapped in the breeze. It reminded Becker of a stadium the day after a championship game.

Nonna's spot was clean except for the two huge black trash bags, filled to overcapacity, on the side of Big Betty. As Becker got out of the car, she spotted the new firepit, embers still smoking in the center.

Kevin jumped out of the car. Lester the parrot squawked, "Hairy pig!"

Kevin barked at him. Lester yelled, "Hairy dog! Bad dog!"

Nonna got up slowly from her chair. She gave Becker a hug. After the events of the last few days, Becker was grateful, so she embraced her back, forgetting she didn't really like hugs. Nonna was wearing a polka dot blouse with denim bib overalls that barely contained her bosom, and fuzzy yellow orb earrings that tickled Becker's neck. Nonna's eyes were bloodshot; she wobbled as she sat back down.

Joey was in his signature outfit: bowling shirt, black slacks loafers. His shirt was striped black and blue, with a diamond sewn on the pocket. He raised his Bloody Mary, complete with a spear of olives and pickles, as he gave her one of his toothy grins. He didn't look as worse for wear as Nonna did.

Nonna said, "Heller, Del. I've got a hangover from the party last night, so no loud noises. That means you, too, Kevin. And you, Lester." Lester made kissing noises. "There's a frittata in the oven. It should be ready soon. Go in and get yourself a drink," Nonna said, taking a gulp from her flute.

"What are you drinking?"

"Orange juice. The champagne accidentally jumped in."

Becker opened the RV door to the tune of *Sweet Home, Alabama*. She opted for coffee, fished the cream out of the refrigerator, returned outside, sitting next to Joey. "So, I'm almost afraid of the answer, but I have to ask. What's *Bingo and Balls*?"

"The stupid game that gave me this headache," Nonna said. "Honey buns, you tell her."

"You get in your golf cart—"

"You have a golf cart?"

"Oh yeah, we have an electric six-seater with a mini- fridge under the back seat."

Becker muttered, "Of course you do." Louder, "Where is it?"

"We rented one of those u-store-it places next door. We keep Little Betty in there with our other camping gear. Anyway, as I was saying. You get in the golf cart and drive to sites around Dicks. Find the five campers who are the 'ballers'. They give you a bingo ball, like the kind in those old machines. One site gives out the 'B' balls, one the 'I' balls, you get it. Then you race back to the pavilion to see if you have the winning bingo combination. If not, you can drive back out to get a new ball or two, or you can sit and drink while the results come in, which is what we did, and why your sexy grandma has a big head this morning."

Nonna shook her head and almost fell out of the chair. "Shit."

Becker asked Joey, "Where's your sidekick today?"

"Rehoboth Beach. A few of his goombahs came down for the weekend. They rented this enormous house on the ocean, went marlin fishing yesterday. He asked me to go, but I wanted to be with my best girl, I mean girls." Joey grabbed Nonna's hand and kissed it.

"Good. I enjoy his company, but I'm not in the mood today to fight him off," Becker said.

Joey reached down next to his chair and held up a manila envelope. "He sent you a gift."

Becker hesitated. Should a chief of police accept a present from a mobster? "This doesn't feel right, Joey."

"Ah, take it. Open it. I can always return it to him if you don't want it."

She reached in and pulled out a chunk of citrine with a note: *From Mooney's store. A positive energy stone. Love, Angelo.* She rooted around the envelope, fished out a few sheets of paper scanned the first page.

"This is the official police report from the death at Gus's garage in Philadelphia."

"It is," Joey said. "There's also notes from the FBI about the murder; you probably couldn't get that through your channels."

Becker rubbed her brow. She had conflicting feelings about accepting the stone and report from Angelo. Wouldn't that require some sort of reciprocity? She didn't want to egg him on. Yet, the report could go a long way to help her understand Gus Fornash. His background. Why he committed suicide. What to do?

"Angelo told me to tell you 'No strings attached'. He likes you and genuinely wants to help." Joey sipped again from his mimosa.

Nonna's voice was raspy. "Geez, Del, the damned present is no big deal. It's not like the guy bought you a diamond necklace. Speaking of which, J, a diamond necklace might look really nice hanging on my neck, about here." She pointed to her cleavage.

Lester yelled, "Oh, J, oh, J! A little to the left!"

Kevin barked.

***

Nonna made Becker feel bad about not seeing her mama in several days, so she and Kevin stopped by on the way home. Mama was in the kitchen making pasta from scratch. Homemade marinara sauce bubbled on the stove. Mama gave Kevin a bone, wound an apron around Becker, and put her to work kneading the dough.

"Have you seen the new mixers? The ones that can whip this dough into shape?" Becker asked.

"Bah, what fun is that?" Mama responded. "I enjoy playing with eggs and flour, and it gives me a chance to talk to my lovely daughter. How are you, Cara? How is your investigation going?"

For the next half hour, as the dough set, Becker filled the kitchen with information about Michelle and Edward. Mama listened intently as she stirred the sauce then sat and sipped her lemonade. "You think Mr. Fornash killed Edward and also Michelle?"

"I believe it's entirely possible," Becker said, "but I also think about many other things, Mama! My brain is asking 'what if' questions all day, sometimes into the night. What I'm sure of is the gun that killed Edward and was used to damage Mooney's shop, was the same one Gus used to take his life. So that evidence ties him somehow to Edward's murderer. Michelle is still my black hole. I have a lot of data, but nothing conclusive." She sighed. "To make matters worse, my work in Celestino Village is suffering. I have half a mind to talk to Mayor Spinosi and Mayor Workman about my progress, or lack thereof."

Mama nodded her head. "I can't give you advice on that situation, Cara. You make that decision. I will say, though, it seems you're moving ahead from my perspective. Why else would someone break into your apartment, write unpleasant things on the wall, take Kevin, leave awful letters? Mr. Fornash probably did it. That's why he committed suicide. God rest his soul."

The timer went off, indicating dough-rolling was about to begin. Mama asked, "And how are Mack and Bea?"

Becker pulled her mouth down into a frown. "We're taking a break."

"That's nonsense! Why?"

"Oh Mama, it's complicated."

"Love is simple."

"Not everyone has a storybook romance, free from issues like you and Papa did."

"You think we didn't argue? Have our differences? Disagree on how to run the household? Words over how to raise you girls? I've done my best to help you and Alyssa remember the good times, because that's the right thing to do. But we weren't always 'storybook', as you call it."

Becker sighed. "We just need a little time. This investigation is taking up all of my brain and heart cells. I need to finish it, then I can focus on my relationship with Mack. For now, I'll continue to run all over the shore to find Michelle."

***

Becker sat on the couch, Kevin snuggling at her side, as she read through the paperwork about Gus Fornash and the body found at his shop in Philadelphia. Circumstantial evidence pointed to him as the killer, including fingerprints found at the scene, including the body, a partial footprint that matched one of his work boots, and a heated conversation about money with the deceased, taped by the cops a few days before the murder. Her cell phone rang.

"Chief Becker, it's Edwina Landon."

"Hi, Edwina. I've been thinking of you. How are you getting by?"

"I'm heartbroken...but also grateful you found my boy. Like I told you when you shared the news with me, there is some peace, if I can use that term, in the *knowing*. I can actually grieve, and cherish my memories, instead of being on the edge of my life looking for him."

"Nonna says you're keeping busy."

"She's been stopping to check on me. I guess I am okay. I'm volunteering at the church. The Drone Club has asked me to be their treasurer. Between us, there isn't much to treasure; they have all of $216.52 in the kitty. It will give me something to do, though, so I agreed. The young kids remind me of Edward."

"Good for you."

"Speaking of Edward, I have a box of things you might be interested in seeing, mostly notes between him and Michelle, newspaper clippings, and a journal he used for doodling and scribbling random thoughts. I'm not sure if it will help you find Michelle, but I thought it wouldn't hurt for you to look through it."

Becker thanked her, took Kevin for a short walk then fed him dinner, and settled back down to review the Fornash file.

She couldn't understand why they released him after charging him for the crime...until she came to the last page of the document. The FBI concluded the killer in Philadelphia was right-handed. Gus was a lefty.

Her brain nearly blew up from excitement. She scrambled up from the couch to retrieve her case file, scaring Kevin, who gave her a soft *woof*. She rooted through the paperwork until she found the picture of Gus and Michelle; him holding a handgun in his left hand. Flipping through the unofficial pictures of Gus's suicide scene, she noted the location of the gun and the blood spatter pattern. The pistol was in his *right* hand.

A headache built behind her left eye as she subconsciously petted Kevin's head. Her working theory had been all wrong. She surmised Gus killed himself to avoid prison for the rest of his life because he murdered Edward and was responsible for Michelle's disappearance/death. Obviously, that was *way* off the mark.

Instead, someone murdered Gus Fornash. Becker buried her head in her hands. She felt like she was on the merry-go-round in Ocean City and it wouldn't stop so she could get the hell off.

Chapter Twenty-Eight

O ver coffee the next morning, Becker read the *Celestino Press* online. The medical examiner gave her kudos for her "superior investigative skills" in the Gus Fornash case. "Chief Becker discovered Mr. Fornash did not kill himself. Forensics showed Mr. Fornash's dominant hand was his left, and a right-handed individual murdered him."

Judge Green did not share in the accolades she received from everyone around her, including Franklin, who chirped at her when she walked into the police station. The judge was unhappy he issued a subpoena for an innocent man to root through his place of business and house, looking for the very gun used to kill him. Becker apologized profusely; he hung up on her.

She hid in her office for a while until Molly buzzed her phone. *Can I come in?*

A few minutes later, Molly and Franklin walked in, trailed by Bella the chicken. Molly brought her a steaming cup of coffee and a cupcake slathered with frosting from The Shanty. Franklin scurried on the desk and up Becker's arm. Becker's spirits brightened considerably at the thought of carbs and sugar in her belly.

Bella jumped on her lap, begging for a piece of cupcake. Becker pulled off a small portion and gave it to her. She cooed, took it, and strutted over to her basket. Becker said to Molly, "Close the door for a few minutes behind you? Do you mind if we make small talk? I'm weary today. This investigation is ruining my life."

Molly smiled at her and set down her file. "Sure."

"How are you? What's new in town?"

"Um, let's see...Mack is carrying my knitted blankets and throws in his shop." Becker kept her face neutral as she listened. "Tourists are buying them up by the dozens. With my salary here, and my side hustle, I'm paying my bills and saving a bit. I'm still delivering flowers to Celestino Gardens as well. Your mama has been getting quite a few from an anonymous suitor."

"Really? Any idea who?"

"I'm not supposed to know, but it's a man she's giving private lessons to. I forget his name, but I can find out for you."

Becker nodded as she savored her cupcake. "I'd appreciate it. Mama hasn't had many men friends over the years, and none seriously. I hope he's a good guy."

"Me too... Oh, and I'm dating Guido Tucci."

Becker choked. Molly came around the desk. She pounded Becker on the back as Franklin patted her neck. "Wow."

"We've been in the office by ourselves a lot since you've been in Silver Hill. He's a gentleman at heart, and of course, one of the best cops I've known. He asked me out for coffee then I cooked for him my signature dish, the juiciest meatloaf you've ever had." Molly grinned.

Becker grinned back. "I'm happy for you two."

There was a commotion in the hallway. Franklin glided through the air from Becker to Molly and crawled in her bra. The door flew open, banging on the wall behind it. Johnny Hudson, Joey Vito, Nonna, Arima Patel, and Cephas Jones rushed in, filling her office. The Gruppo was alive and well, shouting at each other. To add to the bedlam, Lester the parrot was screeching, "You're under arrest!"

Molly and Franklin fled. Becker stood up, shouting, "Hey! Inside voices!"

The room went silent; even Lester shut his beak. Becker rubbed her brow. Nonna winked at her while adjusting her Crocodile Dundee hat, which complemented her African safari outfit.

"Gruppo, now is not a good time."

"Heller, Del. I'm glad you didn't single me out. See, I was voted in as a Gruppo member after Drone Day. As the new official spokesperson," Nonna fluffed her hair while Becker groaned, "it's my duty to tell you we have your back. Not your fault you were going after the wrong guy. From what I understand, he was a bad dude anyway."

Becker took a breath and held it, counting to five. Nonna meant well. As she looked around the room, Becker realized that the Gruppo was dressed similarly in long-sleeve shirts and pants tucked into gum boots. "Why are you all wearing rubber boots?"

Cephas Jones sheepishly said, "I accidentally told Johnny about us looking for Michelle in Katy Bay."

"I didn't tell anyone, Chief," Johnny said. "I took it upon myself to run some numbers about the probability of finding her alive or dead, and cross-matched those with locations along the water—"

Joey interrupted him; the man could talk statistics for years without a breath. "I saw Johnny's paperwork in the library at the Gardens when I was visiting. I mentioned it to Arima..."

Arima looked around the room, at everything besides Becker. "I had lunch with your Nonna. She made me spill the beans. Wait, that came out wrong."

"I was pumping you pretty hard," Nonna said. "Not your fault."

Becker stifled a laugh. "And Nonna convinced you all to help her granddaughter? Let me guess...you're planning a trip to Katy Bay."

Five heads nodded; ten eyeballs looked at her with anticipation and excitement.

"Yes!" Nonna cried. "And we took care of everything. You only need to join us. Big Betty is filled up. We're ready to go. We packed a gas grill, hamburgers and hot dogs, potato salad, beer..."

Becker capitulated. What choice did she have? "I'll go home to change and meet you at Mel's fish camp. Do *not* start without me."

"No worries, Del." Nonna blew her a kiss. "We'll sip our beverages until you get there."

***

She drove alone to Virginia using the time for a self-pep talk. This expedition was a good thing. She needed a break from the investigation; she needed to re-group and re-evaluate, but most of all, she needed to leave it be for a few days. Becker thought of a mug she saw recently in a store: *Trust the Timing of Your Life*. It seemed perfect for today.

Mel's camp felt like a family reunion. Birdy's car sat on the side of the driveway behind Big Betty. Plastic red and white checkered tablecloths covered the tables, and soul music spilled out of speakers set up on the porch. Aluminum tubs filled with ice, soda, beer, wine sat underneath a *Good Luck Graduate* banner. Lester the parrot sat on a perch under it, nodding his head to the music. Between the Drone Club, the Gruppo, and Cephas Jones' kin, three dozen people milled around the yard, most with adult beverages in their hands.

Nonna met her in the driveway. Becker asked, "Nonna, what's with the sign?"

"Oh, I didn't want to re-use the *I See Dead People* one, given how that party turned out." She frowned for a minute. "I didn't have enough time to buy a special one for today, so I found this one at the party store. Ignore the 'Graduate' and focus on the lucky part."

Becker caught Johnny Hudson's eye. "Excuse me, Nonna. I'm going to work out a plan with Johnny and Mel."

Ninety minutes later, Becker had organized the group into smaller teams. She paired the locals with a Drone Club member and a Gruppo. While they focused on primary spots north and northeast of Katy Bay, Nonna would supervise the cooks, Becker and Mel would monitor activities, a command central of sorts. They would investigate locations to the south later today, or during the next 'party' if they ran out of time.

Mel produced hand-held radios, one for each team and the home base. Joey walked out to the pier to try one out.

Becker said, "Team one, Joey, do you copy?"

He keyed the mic, his voice yelling through the speaker, "Copy what?"

"It's a saying, Joey, meaning: can you hear me?" Becker said.

Nonna grabbed the hand-held device to add, "Hi lover!"

Lester the parrot squawked, "Do it do it do it!"

"10-45," came back.

"Joey, a 10-45 is a dead animal. You mean 10-4."

"Right-o, Chief."

Over the next few hours, the teams "cleared" dozens of shacks, cottages, lean-to structures, and hunting and fishing camps. The drones flew over thirty-plus sites, equipped with radar to identify anomalies in the topography, including bones. Joey accidentally called in a 10-94, the number for drag racing. Countless interviews with locals produced information about a recent visit of the Swamp Monster to a little boy named Monty, twelve and near-sighted, and little else.

The teams trickled in and the party started with copious amounts of sweet iced tea and beer. Becker even saw a bottle of moonshine passed around, including to her Nonna. Thankfully, Joey was the designated driver, and was sticking to diet soda.

She sat with Cephas Jones during dinner, both of them with a pile of Maryland blue crabs in front of them. He dug a piece of lump crab from the shell, and set it aside for Nonna, who refused to get the "green goo" on her hands Instead, she batted her eyelashes at everyone for the picked morsels. "I interviewed a local today; he mentioned seeing a white girl nearby. Unfortunately, I couldn't get him to tell me when."

Becker leaned toward him; crabs forgotten. "And?"

"Don't get too excited, Chief. It was Old Man Tuggy, known in these parts for not being all there, if you know what I mean. He's a heavy drinker, messes around with wild mushrooms and, if the rumors are correct, in his younger years, cocaine."

"So questionable reliability."

Cephas took a sip of his tea, nodding. "When we walked up, he was sitting in an old broken-down car, playing an air guitar to Smoke on the Water. I knocked lightly on the driver's door. Scared the dickens out of him. He rolled down the window, or what he thought was a window, because there was no glass. I'm telling you, Tuggy's out of it. Anyway, I told him we were looking for Michelle, and described her. He made the sign of the cross then muttered about an ugly white girl, wild horses, bees." Cephas grabbed another crab from the pile. "He rolled up the non-existent window, wouldn't say another word."

Becker sighed. She had to admit today was a bust for the investigation. As she looked around the camp, however, and listened to Lester the parrot squawk, "It's a Small World," she had a flash of love and gratitude for her friends, old and new alike. The search for Michelle would wait another day, while she gave thanks for this one.

Chapter Twenty-Nine

I t was back to the drawing board, again. Becker dug through her file, grasping for threads to pull. Michelle's life was all over her desk: reports, notes, pictures, articles, information off the internet. She listed several items to follow up on, and second interviews to hold. She made appointments for the next day, starting with William, followed by Mooney. If she couldn't get information out of Mimi, she'd go around her. A visit with Meghan was scheduled, as was one with Hamilton.

She pondered how to get the official paperwork from Sheriff Atkins and came up empty. She'd asked him many times with no response. She even used William, his boss, the mayor of Silver Hill, to intervene. He came up empty, too. If William couldn't get the guy to produce documents, who could? She put a question mark in the margin of her page. She'd poke him again under the auspices of another interview.

The Gruppo and field trip to Virginia preempted Molly's visit yesterday. She needed to reschedule with her, to finish up the background checks, still in progress. Unfortunately, she was absent for a few days while her mother had minor surgery.

Last night, while Becker was watching a show about the mob in Youngstown, Ohio, it made her thoughts turn to Gus Fornash and his mafia connections. She impulsively grabbed Kevin's leash. He ran over, eager for his walk and sniff-fest around town. She glanced at her reflection in the window, fluffed up her hair, then berated herself for being vain.

Joey and Angelo saw her coming a block away. Joey yelled, "Good morning, Chief!"

Angelo blew her a kiss as he walked into the house. Happy polka music wafted from an open window, pots of yellow, white, orange and red mums greeted her on the patio. Angelo appeared and set a mug of coffee with cream on the table. Then he threw Kevin a bone treat.

He man-handled her into a hug, picking her off the ground. Lord, the man had a big chest and incredible biceps. Her dangling legs brushed against his thigh muscles. She fought the urge to strip off his clothes right there. Before he settled her on the ground, he sniffed her hair.

"Did you just smell my hair again? Is this a normal thing for you?"

"*Sí*. Your scent is...all Delaney. Earthy with a hint of flowers."

Becker felt her face get hot. "Angelo," she growled, "I'm the chief of police. Professionalism and all of that."

"You're still a beautiful and desirable woman. The uniform is also sexy."

She gave up and tasted her coffee. "Joey, thank you again for making the trip to Virginia. I'm sorry we came up empty."

"Don't be too hard on yourself, Chief. We eliminated dozens of locations where she's *not*. That's something."

"I agree. And Angelo, thank you for my...present. It was helpful. I have a few follow-up questions, if you don't mind."

Angelo said, "I'm an open book."

"Tell me about Gus's mob connections."

They both sat up straighter. Joey stammered, "Ah, Chief, Angelo and I have *alleged* connections with La Costra Nostra! We used to be altar boys, for God's sake!"

Becker grinned. "Joey, this isn't an official visit. And I'll play along. My assumption, of course, is anything you tell me came from rumors and speculation that was learned while playing pool or golf. Or bocce. You have no firsthand knowledge. Our conversation never happened."

Joey gave her a conspiratorial *Smiling Joey* grin. And Angelo *The Angel* Zullo looked, well...heavenly. *Stop it, Becker!* She mentally shook off the attraction she had for him.

"Delaney, you are as smart as you are lovely. What secrets do you want me to spill?" Angelo asked.

"I'll get right to the point: could his previous, um...affiliation have cost him his life? What I mean is, did his history in Philadelphia get him killed?"

"So, you're thinking the mafia was responsible? Not the person who killed Edward? Or Michelle?"

"It could be possible, right?"

Angelo rubbed his face. "With those goons in Philadelphia, anything is possible. But it's not probable. From what I understand through the grapevine—" he winked at her— "the body they found at Gus's place in Philly was a chop-shop guy who started dealing drugs on his own, without permission. The bosses made an example out of him. Gus didn't know about it until *after* the guy was whacked. Gus was angry as hell that the job had happened at his place. Supposedly, he was well compensated for all the trouble it caused, and the word on the street is that he used the funds to buy his garage down here."

She rubbed her brow. "Did he continue any work for his Philadelphia 'friends' in Silver Hill?"

"I can answer that one," Joey said. "No. Presumably when he was falsely charged and imprisoned for, what, Angelo, a year?" Angelo nodded. "The powers to be felt the slate was clean for all of his, um, grief."

Becker took another sip of her cooling coffee. "You saw a lot of people come and go. Anyone stick out as having a beef with him? Any enemies?"

Joey was quiet for a moment as he scratched Kevin's head. "He and Sheriff Atkins were like two, whadda-ya-call-it, hyenas fighting over territory. Also, there's a judge down there who hated his guts. Um, it's a color, I think."

"Judge Green?"

"Yep, that's it. And that boy, Hamilton, was a pain in his side, always hanging around, even after Michelle went missing."

Hmm, Michelle thought. *Judge Green?*

***

When she returned to the office, after a kiss on the cheek from Angelo and a to-go pistachio biscotti from Joey, Sheriff Atkins was waiting for her, talking with Guido like they were hunting buddies. Except that Guido rolled his eyes when Sheriff Atkins looked in her direction. She motioned him into her office.

He followed her, plopped into one of the chairs. "Pretty crappy little station you have here."

"It's nice to see you, too," Becker answered, sweet as pie. She stood on the other side of the desk, a power play. Kevin growled at the sheriff; Becker was silently proud of the mutt. She should have addressed his unacceptable behavior. Instead, she bent down and stroked his head. "To what do I owe the pleasure?"

"This." He threw a file on her desk; it slid to the edge. "You've been hounding me for weeks. I thought I would take a drive up to drop this off, being it's so important you can't find Michelle without it. I also wanted to see how the other half lives. Not very well, if you ask me."

Becker stared at him. "This is an asshole-free zone. Either knock off the digs, or leave."

"Sit down, Chief. I mean no harm." A triumphant smile flit across his face. He knew he was getting to her. She took a breath, thought: Don't let him.

She picked up the file thumbing quickly through it. "You have both Edward's and Michelle's search information in here?"

"Yep."

"Did you think the two cases were related at the time?"

"I presumed they were, how could you not? Two young people disappearing around the same time was implausible, though. I never got traction on what connected them besides their friendship."

Becker nodded. "What do you know about Meghan's disappearance at the same time Michelle went missing?"

He brushed off something on his pants' leg and avoided eye contact. "I didn't know she was missing, too."

"Uh-huh, really? Mimi never mentioned it?"

His eyes bored into hers. "Not that I recall." She met his gaze, held it, staying silent. He broke eye contact. "Look, they are a private bunch, I didn't want to pry."

"You mean you didn't want to cause a fuss with the mayor's wife? Job security and all."

"I mean, Mimi had a nervous breakdown of sorts. She's not an emotionally stable person on her best day. She can be...fragile. I pushed as much as I could. One reason I backed off was because she...cracked, ended up hospitalized right before Thanksgiving that year."

"Did it ever occur to you that Mimi could be the one responsible for Michelle's disappearance? Or her death?"

"I don't get paid enough to suspect the royal family of Silver Hill for anything illegal." He rubbed his face. "Sometimes it's best to let things be."

Becker felt the slow burn of indignation rise out of her chest and into her vocal cords. "That's *so* wrong on many levels. Why become a cop at all if you think it's morally okay to pick how you protect and serve? Who you suspect of a crime or who to interview? What crimes to investigate?" She stood up, finger in his face. "I might have an outdated police station, but I have a team that is on the right side of the law, where law enforcement professionals belong. *Now get out.*"

He rose out of his chair, red-faced. Becker could tell he was working up a retort; Guido walked in saying, softly, "I'll show you to the door."

***

An hour later, Guido knocked on her open door. "Chief, a word?"

Becker motioned him in.

He set a small box on her desk. "Edwina Landon dropped this off earlier today."

"Thanks. She saved me yet another trip to Silver Hill."

He nodded and sat down. "By the way, I knew Sheriff Atkins from playing football in high school. Seeing him again brought some memories back."

She set down her pen. "I'm all ears."

"Well, some background. His father was in the military. I think he retired as a colonel, had a big job. He was one of those macho types who oozed testosterone. Misogynistic. Bigoted against gays, people of color."

"How do you know so much about his father?

"He was an assistant coach for Silver Hill. Every summer, I attended a football camp along with kids all over the shore."

"I did the same thing with band members. It was a great way to meet people from other schools, branch out a bit, have fun."

"Exactly. Except my camp wasn't very enjoyable. Paul Senior is ten times worse than Paul Junior, the sheriff, on the jerk scale. He was also cruel to his own son, belittling him in front of everyone, making him do extra exercises, yelling negative comments to him across the field."

"I should feel sorry for Sheriff Atkins; that's a horrible way to grow up. I'm trying really hard to muster up empathy."

"I know, me too. Here's the reason I'm telling you this: There were rumors Paul was gay, but he hid it because of his father."

"Huh. He dated Michelle for a while. I saw pictures of him in the yearbook at various dances, other events with several young women."

"Well, the gossip could have been just that. Kids sometimes stir up things because they can."

"If it's true, though, I wonder why he didn't leave?"

"Not sure. He told me once he wanted to leave the shore, go to college, and become a forest ranger. He visited Colorado a few times as a kid, fell in love with the mountains, the aspens, the bugling elk."

"I wonder why he didn't go?"

"After seeing him today, I wondered the same thing."

Chapter Thirty

Becker missed a dentist appointment, and if it weren't for Mama, she probably would have forgotten about the Seahorse Festival. Her schedule was no longer her own. The marking of time was simple: another day looking for the disappeared Michelle Workman.

She drove a short way to the festival grounds. Kevin meandered by her side in his official police uniform, trotted out for official events. He was adorable. Her, not so much. Her hair was already an unruly mess, her shirt scratchy, her Glock rubbing her hip. She shook off the cranky mood as she parked the cruiser in a back lot for official vehicles. Then she checked in with her officers, at various locations, and with Cephas Jones, who was organizing the volunteers. Or attempting to. Nonna's voice came from the middle of the pack telling everyone to shut their pie holes so Cephas Jones could talk.

Nonna came into view. Either she didn't get the memo the festival was about seahorses, or she didn't care. She wore a skintight, slinky purple, pink, and light blue mermaid dress, complete with fabric scales. Her long tail stretched on the ground behind her, a ten-foot obstacle for the crowd gathering around to get a better look. She wore a shell necklace and earrings, a tiara perched on her teased lavender hair, bobbing as she sashayed in front of the dunking booth.

Becker silently congratulated her grandmother for her one-of-a kind, over-the-top outfit, then glanced around. She didn't want to be here when Mama arrived.

"Heller, Del! What do you think of my dress?"

"Very colorful. And your hair is purple!"

"I put that temporary stuff in. So did Edwina, only she chickened out, went for red. You can hardly tell there's color in it." She pulled the scales near her boobs. "You have to see this—"

"Whoa, Nonna!"

"Don't be such a prude, Del. Not that I'm showing any goods off, mind you. I wanted to let you in on a little secret." She turned over the fabric; sewn in was a small flask. "I have a few of these inside my outfit. You want a swig?"

She kissed her grandmother's cheek. "I'm good for now. I'll catch up with you later."

"Before you go, there's a young man I want you to meet, now that you're available. You would make beautiful babies with him. I met him at Dick's. He's a nice guy..."

Becker hightailed it out of there. Just what she needed, a new "friend" who hung out at the same dismal campground where her Nonna was living. Kevin pulled at his leash when he saw her Mama at the Celestino Garden's booth, handing out packets of starfish gummy candy to the kids. "Heads up, Delaney. Mack is here with Bea."

Mooney caught her eye across the crowd and waved at her. "Becker, so good to see you and your happy aura today!" She leaned down to Kevin, cooed to him. "I have a tent over by the river for palm readings. Maybe a few tarot card spreads, if anyone asks. Do you want me to keep Kevin for a bit? I could meditate with him between guests."

Meditate with a mutt? "That would be great, Mooney."

She spied Judge Green sitting by himself on a bench under an oak tree. "It's a beautiful day, isn't it, Judge?"

His eyes narrowed. "It is, Chief."

"I'm sorry again for the Gus Fornash situation."

"You mean when you insisted on searching for a gun and found a dead body instead?"

Her face got hot. "Yes, sir."

He gave her a slight smile. "I'm razzing you, Chief. I'm over it. Mistakes happen."

"Thank you, your Honor." Becker was relieved. Judge Green was an important ally. "While we're on the subject, your name came up in the investigation. Someone told me you and Gus Fornash weren't on speaking terms."

He pulled out a cigar. "My wife hates these things. So anytime I can steal a few puffs, I do." He lit the stogie, gestured for her to sit. "One reason I was upset about issuing a search warrant, leading to a dead body was because everyone in town knew we didn't care for each other." He took a puff, blew out the smoke, smelling of spice and leather. "He was dating my niece for a short time, and so naturally I did a background check on him. When he came up dirty, I told my niece. She broke it off. He never forgave me. Truthfully, I couldn't care less." He took another puff. "But in a small town, you have to be concerned about perception, what people think, what gossip they spread, so I was careful in voicing my opinions about the man."

"Do you think he had anything to do with Michelle's disappearance?"

"He certainly could have. My niece was fifteen years his junior, about the same age as Michelle. Perhaps he had a penchant for younger women."

They sat in companionable silence for a few minutes, watching the crowd.

"You have to wonder why he was murdered, though," he said, flicking ashes on the ground.

"Any theories?"

"Mafia related?" He took another puff. "From his past life?"

Becker met his eyes. "Don't ask me how I know, but that's unlikely."

He nodded his head. "Could he have figured out who the killer is? You have stirred up a bee's nest down here; perhaps Gus put two and two together. From all accounts, he wasn't a dummy."

"That's a possibility, Judge."

"Chief, enough work for me today. I want to enjoy the rest of my cigar."

She thanked him, then headed toward the food area for an iced tea. Cephas Jones intercepted her. "All good? Do you need anything?"

"All good. The volunteers are a lively bunch. For now, your Nonna has them under control. She's a pistol, that one."

Becker smiled at him. "She's the best grandmother anyone can ask for. When I was growing up, she was so much fun. Other kids played Chutes and Ladders, you know, the board game. Nonna actually built ours."

"She wants to know when we're returning to Katy Bay."

Becker sighed. "Between us, I was discouraged we didn't find a shred of evidence Michelle was there, or had even been there, except for her field trips with the Swamp Keepers."

"You forgot Tuggy's comments."

"About an unattractive Caucasian woman and bees. Not much of a confirmation of her being there. I'm not sure it's worth it to go back, aside from spending time with your family."

"You have to decide that, Chief. I guess I'm in the camp of 'let no stone go unturned'. By the way, Mel and the guys are still talking about the day we were there. They newly appreciate Italians. I heard Cephas Johnson call Mel a 'Guido' the other day. Made me smile."

"I'll tell you what. Let me get through a few more interviews this week and then we'll see."

Just then, Mack and Bea walked up. "Hi, Mr. Cephas Jones! Hi, Becker!" Bea shook his hand and gave Becker's hand a squeeze. "This festival is wonderful, of course, but I think we need to organize a Roosterfest in Celestino Village. Much more interesting than seahorses."

The twelve-year-old's excitement bubbled over as she talked about a rooster crowing contest, a chick petting zoo, and a poultry judging competition. She was the recognized Chicken Queen of the village; Cephas respected her opinion. While they bantered ideas, Mack pulled Becker aside.

His brown eyes were filled with concern. "How is the investigation going?"

"About the same as when we last spoke." Sadness squeezed Becker's heart at their breakup. "Except I'm guessing you heard about Gus Fornash." Mack nodded. "He was my prime suspect. I'm back to square one and I hate to say it, Mack, but I'm getting weary. This might be unsolvable."

He rubbed her shoulder; she caught herself before she grabbed his hand. She moved away from his touch. *You're no longer a couple, remember? Don't make a blubbering idiot out of yourself.*

"I have faith in you, Delaney. You found Edward and you'll find Michelle. I'm here if you need me." He gave her a kiss on the cheek. She marveled how kind he was, how much he cared for her, even though they were on break.

"So am I, Delaney," said Angelo as he swaggered by with Nonna, Edwina, Joey, a half-dozen people behind them, taking pictures of her mermaid outfit. Nonna told him to "keep your eyes on your own fries" as she poked him in his stomach, His muscles tightened under his tight t-shirt. Becker had a momentary hot flash, Oh, those rock-hard abs.

Becker ignored Angelo and smiled at Edwina, then remembered the box sitting on her desk, unopened, and her smile faltered. *Damn. Need to do that tomorrow.*

Cephas excused himself. Bea said, formally, "Can we talk alone, Becker?"

They walked a few steps from Mack. Bea's face scrunched up; her eyes were watery. "Even though you and Mack are 'on a break', whatever that means, are we still friends?"

Becker leaned down, pulled her into a rare embrace. "Bea, you and I are going to be friends until I get old and frail."

The young girl sniffed into Becker's uniform. "You're wrong. We'll be friends until *I* get old and frail."

"I love you, Bea."

"I love you more, Becker."

***

Mooney talked Becker into letting Kevin stay overnight with her so she could "evaluate his aura and flatulence issues". She drove home alone; it was nearly dusk. She took a country road through the swamp, over wooden bridges and through great cypress trees. She had taken this road dozens of times before; she loved the curvy drive through the marshes and lowland. Her short hair blew around her face as she nodded her head to a funky, upbeat song on the radio.

She drove over the speed limit, not crazy fast, but enough she had to pump the brake to slow down for a turn in the road. Becker stepped on the brake pedal...nothing. She pushed harder. Nothing.

Sweat popped out on her forehead and under her armpits. Her gut dropped to her feet. Her hands shook. Her mouth went dry. She illogically used both feet on the brake pedal.

Nothing. She was going 40 mph. At this rate, she would miss the turn.

Becker aimed for a spot between the trees.

She rasped a one-word prayer: "Help."

The cruiser's front left bumper clipped a tree. The car spun right, metal crunching, glass cracking. Shards hit her in the face and arms. The airbags deployed, smashing Becker's face and shoulders.

The rear end of the car, behind the driver's side, hit another tree with a thud, throwing Becker's shoulder into the door.

The car slid sideways, driver's side down, into a small stream, metal groaning, horn blaring.

It was over in seconds.

Becker blacked out. When she came to, water was seeping into the car. *I'm going to drown. Jesus, what a way to go.*

Stop it, Becker. You will not drown. The stream is shallow, a mere trickle. Breathe.

Her head hurt. Her shoulder hurt. Her foot hurt. The left side of her body was wet. The blood on her forehead trickled down her temple.

The driver's side door pinned her.

Becker fumbled with the console radio. No success.

Minutes passed; she blacked out again. When she regained consciousness, she remembered her cell phone clipped to her belt.

She couldn't reach it.

She used voice activation and told the phone to call Guido Tucci.

No reply. No phone coverage in the swamp.

Chapter Thirty-One

Darkness engulfs the swamp early. Becker did not know the time, but estimated that an hour had passed since the accident.

Thankfully, the horn had died.

Two vehicles drove by, but neither spotted the damage on the side of the road. Nobody knew her mangled car sat twenty feet in.

As the adrenaline in her system drained, she grew sleepy. Her shoulder was on fire. The pain sent her into a sort of stupor. Shock?

Good Lord, she couldn't die here, a stone's throw from the road. She was too young, had too much to do. Her mama needed her. Bea needed her. She wanted children. A picket fence. A chance to visit Italy.

Who would take care of Kevin? Her chest became heavy, a dread-ball growing in her stomach. She couldn't keep out the anxiety; her breaths shortened. Keep it together, Becker. Have faith.

"Saint Christopher, I hope you're listening. You didn't do a very good job of protecting me. I forgive you. Can you please send the calvary now?"

Later, nearly full dark.

She shifted in her seat, causing pain to shoot through her shoulder. Wait! Was that a siren? Getting closer?

It was. "Thank you, Saint Christopher."

She yelled, "Here! Here!" as a car pulled up. Her voice was barely audible, her throat dry, probably from too many Hail Mary's. The bushes rustled outside her vehicle, near the bumper. A few seconds later, Guido Tucci yelled, "Chief! Talk to me! Chief!"

She weakly responded, "Stop yelling! I can hear you."

"Thank God. Hang in there, okay? The fire department and medics are on their way." He was breathless. "Are you hurt?"

"Yes."

"Where? I'll alert the medics."

"Head, shoulder, foot. Left side. Glass cuts on forehead, arms, chest."

"Head?"

"Concussion."

"Keep talking to me. They should be here any moment."

"How did you find me?"

"Mooney called Molly. She said she had a bad feeling, something about hearing a loud murmur. Molly convinced me to take it seriously, whatever 'it' is that Mooney does. I called the Maryland State Police, asked them to work their magic and ping your phone. It was a miracle we got a signal. The swamp is thick here."

Becker started crying. Mooney and her auras and murmuring.

"Chief? You still with me?"

Becker's exhaustion prevented her from caring about crying in front of Guido.

"Still here." She sniffed. Great. Now her nose was running.

"Awe, please don't cry." He sloshed through the mud and water then sat on a rock outside of her door. A faint outline of his expensive shoes gave her comfort. She told him he was going to ruin them.

"Chief, who gives a crap about shoes in a situation like this? Besides, I'm Assistant Chief now. I'll put it on an expense report."

"Your shoes cost more than my monthly budget for uniforms." He laughed.

Sirens blared. The trees lit up with blue and red lights. Guido yelled, "Over here! Over here!"

Tree branches snapped and leaves rustled as people scrambled down the hill. Keisha said, "How is the second-best cop in the state?"

Guido, familiar with their running joke, said, "She was just in an accident, Keisha. I would think today you could let her be first."

Guido relayed her injuries to the medics and firefighters. The first responders, over the next hour, extracted Becker from her vehicle using the Jaws of Life and other tools. They loaded her into the ambulance and let Keisha ride with he. Keisha called Mama and a few others on the way.

At the hospital, the doctors diagnosed her with a concussion, a dislocated shoulder, which they painfully set, a dozen or more cuts from flying windshield glass on all exposed flesh, a sprained ankle, and a fractured toe. She settled in her double occupancy room, without a room-mate, courtesy of Joey Vito's sizable donation to the hospital a half-hour ago.

Voices came from the waiting room, a cacophony of love and concern. She was wilting by the second, but agreed to see her family. Nonna came in first, wearing bright pink scrubs and rainbow Crocs. Mama, Fern, Mack, Joey, and Angelo followed, with Keisha, Guido, then Mayor Spinosi bringing up the rear. Nonna held an enormous arrangement of carnations, Gerbera daisies, sunflowers, with a half-dozen balloons. Fern's, Mack's and Angelo's were more modest. She smiled at her family and sneezed at the flowers.

"I'm here to take your temperature, rectally, of course." Nonna winked at her with red, puffy eyes. She bent down to kiss Becker's cheek. "You shouldn't drive like Mario Andretti. It worries your Nonna! Knock it off!"

Mama ran her fingers through Becker's hair then left a plate of homemade biscotti on the bedside table, Joey stealing one when he thought no-one was watching. The guys set the flowers on available surfaces around the room. Mayor Spinosi told her she was on a mandatory leave; she was too tired to argue. She felt Mack kiss her brow as sleep took her off to a quiet beach where she was painting pelicans flying over Assateague Island.

***

Mama fussed over her for two days until Becker politely asked her to go to her cooking class at Celestino Gardens, and please take Kevin. Plastered to her side since she returned home, he took up a serious role as her watcher and protector.

Mayor Spinosi agreed to promote Guido temporarily to Assistant Chief, and Guido reluctantly took the role. Becker had hounded him for years and was glad he was trying out the position; she was hopeful he would keep it permanently.

Neither man needed to know Molly was on her way with mail, paperwork, and odds and ends to occupy some of Becker's time. It wasn't really "work". Okay, maybe it was...but anything was better than reading Mama's cooking magazines, over and over.

A knock at the door saved her from an article about the many uses for bleu cheese. She was sitting on the couch, sprained ankle propped up on a cushion. It was easier to yell than to hobble to let Molly in. "It's open!"

Franklin rode on Molly's shoulder. When he saw her, he chattered and jumped to her head. His fingers were gentle as he touched the bandage on her forehead then stroked her hair. Molly, wearing an orange and red caftan, chunky jewelry, without shoes, had an over-sized tote bag dangling from one hand. In the other was a dancing lady orchid that matched her outfit. She handed it to Becker.

"It's so good to see you, Franklin! And you, Molly! I'll never look at house arrest the same. It's driving me crazy."

"Chief, it's wonderful to see you, too, although it hurts me to look at your bandages and purple and yellow bruises. Besides dealing with the role of shut-in, how are you?"

"Fine," Becker growled, catching herself getting cranky. She sighed. "My physical injuries are healing. Mentally...I've never been to a therapist, but if I did make an appointment, she'd tell me to let go of my anger. Or channel it."

"You're rarely angry. I'm assuming it's the accident?"

"Yes. The state police confirmed that someone purposely messed with the brakes on my car."

"So, whoever did it knew a bit about cars," Molly said.

Becker shrugged. "You can teach yourself anything on the internet these days."

"True. Do you think it happened at the Seahorse Festival?"

"I do. The official vehicle parking lot was tucked away from the activities."

"The perp took a risk."

"He did. Someone could have walked by at any time, caught him cutting the brake line."

"Let's go there for a minute. Maybe it was a cop."

Becker rubbed her brow. "I can't believe it, but I never thought of that. It could be someone in law enforcement."

"Or a firefighter or one of a dozen other professionals who had cars parked in that lot."

"Would you be willing to research it further?"

"Of course. While we're talking about him—or her, we're not certain it's a man—can I scribble a few notes?" Becker nodded. Molly fished a pad from her tote, pen in hand. "He's a risk taker. Tell me more about him. I'm assuming it is our killer. What does his profile look like, Chief?"

"Hmmm. Let's start with your comment about knowing how to tamper with brakes. That doesn't make him a mechanic, but he or she is smart enough to research it. Also, he writes eloquently; his IQ is above average. He's physically fit; he moved, then buried Edward's body." She rubbed her brow. "Our perp somehow flies under the radar. He breaks into my apartment, kidnaps Kevin, shoots up Mooney's shop, with no witnesses. He kills Gus Fornash and disappears like a ghost." She was quiet for a few minutes. "I'm having a hard time reconciling what I think is the profile with both Mimi and Meghan as suspects. But perhaps there is more than one person involved? They both have the financial means to hire someone."

"That's a new twist."

"When you're an invalid, there's not much to do but think about things. All the time. It gets tiring."

Molly said, "Then don't think about it for a few days. Read a book. Sit in your Mama's garden. Watch a soap opera. I'm assuming they're still on TV?" She and Becker shrugged at the same time.

She reached into her bag and set a small box on the table in front of the sofa. "I thought you would like this, even though it's not on your list and I had to smuggle it out secretly. It's the box of Edward's things that Edwina dropped off."

She pulled out a pile of papers from the bag. "Here's the other stuff you asked for. Oh, and I ran Hamilton's information. Nothing of note, no criminal record. Lived in Connecticut, as you said. I'll leave it with you to review."

"Plenty for me to do now," Becker said. "And Molly? Thank you for taking Mooney's...um, premonition seriously."

Molly blushed. "Well..."

They jumped at the sound of a honk outside the house, long and deep enough to be a foghorn. Her grandmother yelled, "Del! Del! Get off of your sickbed! We're going on an adventure!"

A few minutes later, Nonna, Joey, and Angelo shot in through the door. Nonna had on full body pink camo waders, her curvy body squished in by the neoprene, bosom held up by the suspenders. "Oh, hello, Molly! You wear the best clothes. Can we get together soon to compare notes? Or better yet, go shopping? I need some new outfits."

"I would love to!" Molly said. She and Nonna grinned at each other. Franklin the sugar glider chirped.

"I hate to shoo you away, but we're taking Del away for a few days."

"Nonna, I can't leave now!"

"Why not?" Nonna had her hands on her hips, further pushing out her ample chest. Her eyes flashed. "You can't work and I'm sure your mama is driving you bonkers, fawning over you. Of course, that's very sweet but you don't need sweet. You need to get out of this house and hobble around in the fresh air."

"I—"

"No more arguing. Angelo, pick her up. We're blowing this pop stand."

Becker panicked. She was losing control so she bought time. "Angelo, do not pick me up! Wait! Nonna! How about my clothes? My toiletries? I need a few minutes to pack, at least."

"I've taken care of that for you," Nonna said.

"Oh, Nonna, I love your style, but it's not mine." Becker had visions of a clingy pantsuit or a wild patterned pair of bib overalls. She shivered.

"You don't think I know that? I bought you those silly T-shirts you like, shorts, jeans, a sweatshirt. A dress, in case we go out dancing." She looked at Becker's ankle brace and arm sling. "Well, you can sway side-to-side. You know, slow dance with Angelo. By the way,

Joey wanted to buy you thongs, but I said no. Damn things are like having a pimple in the middle of your butt, rubbing itself raw all day. So...regular panties."

Becker's face flushed. She rubbed it with both hands. "Okay, okay, enough talk about undergarments."

Nonna muttered, "Prude."

Becker ignored her. "Molly, thank you again for stopping by. Apparently, I'm going on vacation for a few days."

Angelo bent down, picked her up from the sofa, then carried her out of the house as if she was a delicate porcelain figurine, his massive arms cradling her like a baby. She got lost in his scent, a blend of spice and earth. His chin touched her hair and if she angled her head just so, their lips would accidentally meet. She sighed then he sniffed; it broke her romantic trance. "Stop smelling my hair!"

"Price of the ride to the car."

"You mean limousine."

"Car, limo, same thing."

He set her down on the seat, taking great care to position her ankle on a pouf pillow in the middle of the floor. He crawled in next to her, close enough for the heat of his body to warm her. She started sweating. His naked arms and legs were right *there,* inches from hers.

She distracted herself by watching Joey pour champagne into flutes. He passed them around. Nonna said, "Here's to day-drinking!"

Angelo clinked her glass to hers, staring into her eyes. "And night calisthenics!"

Oh boy. Becker chugged the bubbly goodness and hiccupped.

Chapter Thirty-Two

They boarded a chartered jet in Ocean City, destination un-known, despite Becker's continued questions. Even Nonna had tight lips for once.

The plane took off and headed west, or perhaps it was north. After a few minutes in the air, she sat back and enjoyed it. She hadn't been on a plane in years and forgot the joy of flying. She took a catnap, woke with a blanket covering her. A new best seller, a murder mystery, sat in front of her. Angelo held a self-help book as he sipped from a snifter.

"What are you drinking?"

His brown eyes met hers. "I'm drinking your beauty in."

She barked out a laugh. "That was cheesy."

He grinned at her. "It was. I guess I need a different self-help book solely for pickup lines. I'm drinking bourbon."

"Let's see...I'm going to guess Blanton's. No, wait, you'd go for the most expensive stuff. Pappy Van Winkles."

"Give the lady a prize, although it's not the twenty-five-year-old bottle. I like the ten-year-old better."

"Does it bother you to use...um, mafia money to buy the best of everything?"

"Very bold question, Delaney, but I'll play along. Hmm, how to answer that? Let's start with the real question you have: how much of a mobster am I? Not much, I can tell you. I drive people around and keep them safe. And I've occasionally had to, ah, persuade someone to change their behavior."

"Beat them up."

"You say potato, I say potado. I'd like to add that I am not a big fan of hurting anyone; I avoid it as much as possible. I prefer to persuade verbally, not physically. And it goes without saying I would *never* hurt you, Delaney. You are special to me, and more importantly, I don't hit women, period." He took a sip of bourbon. "As for my wealth, I have invested wisely. I have an eclectic portfolio that's consistently outperformed the market. I bought up crappy commercial property in Philly years ago, rehabbed it, lease the property to a large insurance company." He shrugged. "So maybe I started with seed money earned while hanging around with other Italian gentleman, but building it has been all me."

Becker wanted to groan out loud. Shit, the man was handsome, smart *and* rich. Yikes.

His voice broke into her thoughts. "Can I ask you for a favor?"

"Depends."

"This one has nothing to do with you and me in bed." She gulped, and he continued, "I'd like us to leave our roles behind for the next few days, Ms. Chief of Police, just have fun. Enjoy each other's company. Can we do that?"

"Yes."

"Okay, let's start now. I have a bottle of your favorite wine, Brunello di Montalcino. It's from a small winery in the heart of Tuscany. I'll take you there someday. They have this gorgeous villa, and a private swimming pool for skinny-dipping."

Becker rolled her eyes.

He uncorked the bottle and poured her a glass. "Since we can't travel to Villa Rosmarino soon, I had a case of Brunello shipped to Joey's house for you." He raised his bourbon glass. "Salute, Delaney."

***

She guessed it was the Great Lakes they were flying over. About a half hour later, the plane landed at a tiny airport taxiing to a nondescript metal building. Water was visible in three directions.

"Welcome to the middle of nowhere, better known as Middle Bass Island!" Nonna burped then giggled. "Oops, too many rum punches!"

"Where's Middle Bass Island, exactly?" Becker asked.

"It's part of the Lake Erie Islands," Angelo answered. "We're about three miles from the mainland. Ohio, that is. I came up four or five times as a kid, loved it, always wanted to come back. Very low-key and peaceful. It's a bit chilly this time of year, but Nonna, Joey, and I thought it would be perfect for your recuperation. I wanted to take you to Paris, but I knew you'd be mad at me. Hard to get upset over a modest trip to Ohio." He smiled at her. "Not much to do here, which is why we picked it. A bar or two, a general store, lots of beaches. We can take my yacht over to Put-in-Bay, a bigger island, for dinner."

Nonna had changed her outfit yet again—the woman wore more costumes in one day than a Vegas performer—a French artist outfit of a short black skirt, black striped shirt, red beret and sunglasses, minus the white painted face. They smiled at each other. "Why are you dressed like a mime?"

"The French landed on Middle Bass Island. They called it *The Island of Flowers* initially because of the beautiful wildflowers. I felt very oh-la-la today."

The pilot came out of the cockpit then opened the door. Nonna (accidentally?) gave him a view of her cleavage as she climbed down the steps. Angelo insisted on carrying Becker to one of the two golf carts waiting on the tarmac. He and Joey loaded suitcases on the back of the

carts, and they were off, Angelo driving the cart down the middle of
the narrow road.

"Are there cars on the island?"

"Yep, a few. I thought golf carts would be more fun."

"What else did you think of?"

"I had the food, wine, other necessities delivered in advance."

"Of course you did." The man was thorough. Probably in bed, too.
Yikes. "Where are we going?"

"To the west end of the island. One of my buddies owns a Victorian
house built in 1881. Apparently, we aren't the only important people
who will be sleeping there. A few presidents and first ladies visited,
including William Howard Taft, Mrs. I-don't-know-her-name-Taft."
He stopped the golf cart to turn left. "There are views from every
window since the grand house sits next to the water, back porch facing
west. I'm told the sunsets from the dock are stunning.

"How many bedrooms?"

His face was serious. "Only one, I'm afraid."

"Angelo, nice try. I see your lips curling up."

He laughed. "No getting over on you, Ms. Detective. Okay, there are
five. Plenty for everyone to have their own space, I'm sad to say."

They zipped along, rarely seeing another human, golf cart, or car. It
was like they were on their own private island. She smelled the water,
the flowers, and was contented to be on Middle Bass for an impromptu
vacation.

The two-story house was stunning, built in the Second Empire style,
with a red roof and bright blue gingerbread trim. The house itself was
a mustard-yellow color. It had a central dormer with double windows,
over a large wrap-around porch. The lake was thirty feet away, with
views of four islands; Angelo shared the names as he pointed to each
one. Becker caught "Rattlesnake"; the rest were a blur. She was too

busy enjoying the sparkling water, the surprise of a jumping fish. He also pointed out Perry's Monument, over 350 feet of it, in the distance.

"I can climb stairs," she growled at him as he carried her up the stairs in the house. He didn't listen. In her bedroom, she unpacked *mostly* appropriate clothing for her, except for the little black dress. Hopefully, they would go to a casual restaurant for dinner instead of some fancy place so she could wear jeans. Wriggling into the damned thing and wearing make-up was not her idea of fun.

Nonna breezed in as she was putting the dress on a hanger.

"Tomorrow we're going to yacht around for a while, then go to Put-in-Bay for dinner at a swanky place. You'll need that little number. Did you see the high heels?" Nonna talked faster than a high-speed train. Becker couldn't get a word in edge wise. "Your boobs are going to look great in that dress. And that's not just a Nonna's pride speaking." She vibrated with excitement. "Oh, I picked up that box you had in front of you at your mama's, and the file. I'll leave them on the dresser for you for later. We're going to JF Walleye's for dinner tonight. Dress casual. It's a fun place, according to Joey."

A half hour later, they arrived at the restaurant. As promised, the food was good; she especially liked the Walleye's Bites. They ate outside at a table next to a pool shaped like a lagoon, complete with an island of plants, and a waterfall. It was a great place to unwind and enjoy mindless chit chatter.

Near the end of the meal, Angelo leaned over to her. "Hellooooo?"

She smelled his spicy cologne. "Hello back to you."

"You seem preoccupied."

"Just a bit. Nonna brought the box of stuff Edwina Landon dropped off. It's from Edward's bedroom. I'm curious what's in it." She glanced at him before adding, "We promised to ditch our roles, but..."

"Well, when we get home, we can grab some amaretto and open it up."

"You don't mind?"

"No, not at all. I like a good mystery, Delaney. I also want to find this guy and choke—I mean, get him behind bars so he doesn't hurt you, or anyone else, again."

An hour later, she and Angelo were sitting next to each other on the couch in the living room. On a long coffee table, they spread out the contents of the box. Then they arranged it into piles. One was pictures, another was letters, a third was keys.

A note from Edwina lay on the table. Becker picked it up first.

Chief Becker,

I pulled together anything that might help you with the investigation. I labeled the pictures if I recognized the location. Edwin previously labeled some. The keys are a mystery. Please return all when you are done.

Sincerely,

Edwina

Becker put the keys and letters aside to focus on the pictures. Edward was a talented photographer, both with landscape and portrait pictures. She and Angelo organized them according to the theme: old boats, buildings, birds, trees, people, unknown. A heron, fish dangling out of his beak, caught her eye.

Many were of him and Michelle.

A few were of buildings, mostly rotten, falling down houses, shacks and fishing camps. Edward had also taken photographs of local historical landmarks, including several in Silver Hill. A picture of a younger Sheriff Atkins, looking off into the distance, piqued her interest.

She broke the silence. "This one of Sheriff Atkins is intriguing."

"I thought the same thing. It might be nothing more than a stolen shot when Edward was taking pictures around town."

"The sheriff is always on high alert. It's hard to believe he would be unaware of someone pointing a camera at him."

He met her eyes. "He was a younger version of himself. Regardless, you look beat. You're still recovering, and need your sleep. Let's look at the notes tomorrow morning, before we head out on the water."

He picked her up and she let him. He buried his nose in her hair smelling it, and she let him. He carried her up the stairs, set her down in front of her door, and kissed her forehead. She let him do that, too.

Chapter Thirty-Three

Nonna and Joey's giggles woke up Becker. They were in the bathroom next to her oblivious their laughter, grunts, noises she didn't want to acknowledge sped through the house like a galloping horse. She pounded on the wall. "Hey, stop it! I can hear you!"

Nonna yelled back, "You're jealous! Get your own man to take a bath with!"

Good Lord.

Becker dressed in a pair of stretchy pants and a bright red sweatshirt with *My Nonna Rocks* in big letters across her chest, smiling as she pulled it over her head. She hobbled past the bathroom as fast as she could, thankfully catching whispers instead of some other love language.

Angelo was on the back porch sitting at a round glass table wearing a wool Irish fisherman sweater. His hair was windblown. When he turned, he gave her a smile that lit his face and made his eyes twinkle. He was...*scrumptious* in whatever he wore, she thought. Her mind wandered to how he would look with nothing on at all. Her face flushed at the image.

He jumped up from his chair, gently grabbing under her elbow to lower her onto the sofa. He kissed her cheek. "Good morning, Delaney! You look rested and...pink? Are you okay?"

"I am. This ankle is getting better but the stairs are a little rough," she fibbed, hiding her embarrassment.

He walked toward the kitchen. "Let me get you a cup of coffee with that Italian Cream you like." Kitchen cabinet doors banged, silverware rattled, the refrigerator door opened, then closed, sounding like he knew his way around a kitchen. He came out a few moments later with two mugs and a plate of almond/cranberry biscotti. "Oh, I was up early with nothing much to do, so I unfolded all the notes in the box and put them into two piles." He slid the stacks of paper in front of her.

"Did you read them?"

"No. I didn't think it was right. I waited for you."

She shuffled through the letters. "Okay, thank you, Angelo. Why don't you work on Edward's pile while I work on Michelle's? Let's skim them first, set aside any that deal with school or 'routine' topics, put the more important ones in their own pile. Then we'll take a deeper dive."

He patted her hand. "Boss, can we drink some coffee first? Nibble biscotti?"

Feet clomped on the steps and through the kitchen. "Looks like we'll be taking a break already."

Nonna and Joey wore matching neon blue bowling shirts, black pants, and gray and blue athletic shoes. Nonna gave her the side-eye. "What are you doing? This looks suspiciously like work, Del. We're on holiday!"

Becker asked, "Do you remember that box you brought? The papers?"

Nonna's shoulders slumped. "Oh. Damn, I didn't think. Wait, just because I snagged it doesn't mean you have to look at what's inside!"

Angelo said, "Now, Teresa, we kidnapped her in the middle of a missing person's investigation..."

She interrupted him. "So? It's Bloody Mary time!"

Angelo frowned. "I made a mistake and forgot to have the mix delivered. I think they carry it at the general store. By the time you get back, Delaney and I will be done with this." Angelo waved a hand over Edward's and Michelle's notes, "And we'll be ready for an adult beverage."

Joey said to Nonna, "Can we check out that private beach we saw on the internet?"

Becker and Angelo raised their eyebrows.

"I'll have you know the private beach is for *lake glass collection*," Nonna said. "Geez...we're not Energizer Bunnies. Joey, let's leave the youngsters to their work." Becker heard on her way out the door, Nonna muttered, "She doesn't get her work ethic from me!"

For the next hour, she dug through Michelle's pile of letters. Most of them were about mundane happenings in a small town. Several spoke of her dream of becoming a small business owner, and she mused about running a tour company that specialized in marsh outings. Another note outlined her desire to manage a garage for women clients, complete with women mechanics, including a spa for customers to use while vehicles were being serviced.

Michelle was a doodler, sketching marsh subjects: birds, water, trees, crabs or crawfish. The scribbles were on notes about family conflict or drama. Did Michelle scribble to relieve tension? Reduce stress? She put those letters aside to evaluate further, along with others she deemed noteworthy.

Angelo silently worked next to her, occasionally chuckling at something he read. Like Becker, he created a second pile of letters that caught his interest. He finished his review, refreshed their coffees, then stood at the window, eyes focused on the water, a slight smile on his face.

"I'm done, Angelo."

He turned toward her shaking his head. "That wasn't easy. I kept thinking who Edward would be today, and it made me sad for Edwina." Becker reached out, squeezed his hand. "He had a great sense of humor. He knew he was nerdy, wasn't above making fun of himself. In one letter, he wrote about a pair of shoes he saw online that looked stylish, yet when he put them on, he felt like Bozo the Clown." They smiled. "He was a kind-hearted young man, would have done anything for Michelle...but he wasn't in love with her. He had a crush on someone else."

"Who?"

"Don't know. Very few of his letters cited people by their names, including the one that he mentioned the romantic interest." He picked up a note from the little pile handing it to Becker. "Here's an example of what I mean. He references someone as 'her' instead of using a first name."

Becker scanned the letter. It referred to a woman in Michelle's life.

Her behavior is escalating. Can't you see it? She can't help herself; it's all about *her*. I'm afraid you're going to get hurt.

She met Angelo's eyes. "Huh."

"Yeah, very cryptic."

"Some of Michelle's notes are written that way."

"I wonder if someone in the Landon or Workman household was a snooper. Or maybe they were cautious because teenagers will be teenagers. You know what I mean?" Becker nodded at him. He added, "I remember this girl in high school who got in trouble for drinking beer because her mom read her diary."

"I could see Mimi doing something like that. And Edward kept both *his* letters and Michelle's. Maybe that was why."

The golf cart pulled up in the driveway, tires crunching on the gravel. Angelo shuffled the papers and handed her one. "We're about to be interrupted. You've not told me much about the investigation, but what I know through Nonna and Gus, is that I've not heard this name before. It might be important." He passed the note to Becker. "This is a note from Edward to Michelle. Look halfway down the page."

You're seeing the judge's son? He stopped by Dave's Dive looking for you. He seems like a good guy. I'd rather you hang out with Jody Green than Hamilton!

Becker caught a reflection of herself in the window behind Angelo. Her eyes were as big as walnuts. "I didn't know Judge Green had a son, nor was I aware he may have dated Michelle. How am I learning about this *now*? I mean, I've been at this for..." She rubbed her brow. "Long enough for *someone* to mention his name."

Nonna yelled from the kitchen, "I demand a work stoppage now! Everyone gets a Bloody Mary!" Doors banged and ice cubes clinked in the glasses. "Angelo, you devil! There was mix in the cupboard all along." Angelo put his hand over his mouth, stifling a chuckle. She continued, "No matter, now we have more to put down our gullets."

Joey appeared a few minutes later with a tray of drinks. Becker pretended to use the restroom so she could secretly text Molly. *Please run a background check on Jody Green, son of Judge Harold Green.* Molly responded with a thumbs-up emoji.

***

After a day on the water in a yacht bigger than Becker's apartment, she changed into her little black dress. She sighed with relief the dress wasn't too small. Nonna had guessed her size spot-on. She combed hair gel on her rowdy curls, dabbed on makeup, something she rarely did, and spritzed on a delicate floral perfume, all products courtesy of her personal shopper, Nonna The mirror showed a softer, more feminine Becker, and she took a moment to smile at her reflection.

She slowly made her way onto the deck, careful not to wobble too much in the modest high-heel shoes. Angelo's eyes followed her across the room. She should have worn her sneakers to spare her broken toe and sprained ankle from further pain, but her vanity got the best of her.

He took her hand in both of his. "You look stunning, Delaney. You're *always* hot, of course, but tonight you look...perfect. Just perfect." He kissed her cheek, lingering, smelling her hair and perfume. She pretended not to notice.

"You clean up well yourself, Angelo." She took in his tailored black suit, starched white shirt, and red striped tie. Mooney would have said his aura was rich, powerful, utterly dangerous. Becker would have added *sexy*.

He handed her a jewelry box. "For you."

She shook her head. "No, I can't take it."

"At least give me the pleasure of watching you open it, then you can decide."

She popped the clasp on the box. A gold Italian horn necklace, studded with small diamonds, sparkled in the light. "It's lovely. And too much."

"No, it's a simple present, Delaney. You would do me an honor to wear the Cornicello for protection from evil and evil spirits. Besides, it's also for good luck. Did you know you shouldn't buy one of these for yourself? It needs to be a gift from someone else."

She impulsively hugged him, arms around his waist, her head nestled in his chest. She breathed in his spicy cologne. "Thank you for caring about me, Angelo. How can I say no? Will you put it on me?"

Nonna squawked like Lester the parrot when she walked in the room and saw Angelo putting the necklace on Becker. "What? I leave you two alone for a minute and you get engaged?"

Becker's head whipped around so fast she thought she pulled a muscle. "Nonna! It's a necklace, not a ring!"

"Well, that's how your grandpa proposed to me."

Angelo said, "I can assure you, Teresa, this is not an engagement gift."

"Uh-huh," Nonna said, "Let's go celebrate the news!"

And celebrate they did. The yacht glided to Put-in-Bay as Angelo poured champagne. On the island, they ate a six-course meal starting with lobster bisque, ending with Steak Diane. Over a slice of chocolate ganache cake, Nonna raised her glass of prosecco to the happy couple, despite Angelo's and Becker's arguments to the contrary.

Becker cornered her in the restroom. "Stop it, Nonna! You're making me feel bad. Do you forget I have a boyfriend? We're on a break."

Nonna replied, "Geez, that broken toe has ruined your sense of humor!"

Her grandmother obviously got the drift; the last toast was to beauty in the world, including Delaney in her dress.

On the return trip, Becker and Angelo stood side-by-side on deck. Twilight turned the water into a golden yellow, the cool wind created small white-caps. She shivered. He took off his coat and draped it around her shoulders, hands lingering on her skin longer than necessary. Mack's face popped into her mind; always the gentleman, always kind. She banished the thought as Angelo told her about the Battle of Lake Erie, during the War of 1812.

Becker was content, something she rarely felt. She leaned towards him, her head on his shoulder. He put his arm around her. "No smelling my hair," she said.

He laughed. "Oh, Delaney, you are something." He looked down at her; she tilted her chin up. "If I'm not allowed to smell your hair, then I'll kiss you instead."

Before her conscience could kick in, his lips, slightly roughened from the wind, were on hers. When his tongue slipped into her mouth to tangle with hers, she lost all thought and gave in to the moment. The kiss was intense, his tongue insistent. His hands gently cupped her face, then rubbed her shoulders. Then they grasped her waist, finally stopping on her ass, pulling her closer.

"Excuse me!" Nonna boomed.

Becker and Angelo jumped apart like two guilty teenagers caught necking at a party. Becker almost fell, her knee giving out from the sudden movement. Angelo scooped her up, and laid her on a couch in the salon. He left to get them an after-dinner cocktail.

"Nonna, what was so important you had to interrupt Angelo and I, um—"

"Oh, Del, the man is gorgeous and rich, but do you want to get mixed up with a gangster? I was trying to save you from making a big mistake. Besides, you were the one to mention Mack, Mr. Hotpants Ocean Scientist, or whatever he is."

"One kiss is not dating."

"If the man kisses like his cousin, you're in big trouble."

She was right.

Chapter Thirty-Four

Since telling him goodbye on the tarmac a few days ago, Becker obsessed about her kiss with Angelo. Despite the piles of paper related to Michelle's disappearance sitting on her desk, needing her attention, she remembered how his lips nibbling hers made her belly all topsy-turvy, and her female parts sizzle. *Knock it off! Focus.* She finished sifting through the letters written by Michelle and Edward, and she listened to her recorded interviews. She reviewed timelines and filled two pages full of follow-up items and holes in her investigation.

Interviews with Meghan and Mimi were later today. Guido was riding shotgun. Becker hated to admit she was afraid to travel to Silver Hill, but she swallowed her pride and asked Guido to accompany her. When he gave her the once-over, she was sure he knew why.

Becker picked up Jody Green's police record from her desk. Thumbing through it, she noted incidences of bar fights, altercations with a homeless man, a guy at a coffee shop, a teenager on a skateboard. An old lady at the Piggly Wiggly. He'd spent time on probation for vandalizing an abandoned store. He took a mandatory anger-management class, and in the years following, his record had been clean.

Molly was hunting him down for an interview with Becker.

Surprisingly, he and Hamilton Parsons had attended the same all boys school in New England. The coincidence of them attending the same school, living in the same place, possibly dating the same woman, had Becker's intuition on high alert. That, coupled with the violence he exhibited as a young man, warranted an interview.

Guido knocked on her door, then walked in carrying a vase of red roses. Her heart melted, anticipating the flowers were from Mack until she remembered they were on a break. "Delivery for you, Chief. And we need to leave in five minutes." Once he left, she pulled the note from the bouquet. *To my almost girlfriend, I miss you. Angelo.* She stuffed the note in her desk drawer, embarrassed to admit she missed him, too.

The trip to Silver Hill was uneventful. They arrived a few minutes before Meghan was due for her interview; Sheriff Atkins met them at the door. "Here to rile up my citizens again? We all know Gus killed Edward and Michelle. Your investigation should have died with him."

"Good morning to you, too, Sheriff. It's always a pleasure to be welcomed warmly by another law enforcement professional." Guido snickered next to her. "And if your theory about Gus is true, then who tampered with my brakes? His ghost?"

His face hardened. Before he could spit out a retort, she and Guido walked down the hall. A few minutes later, the desk officer escorted Meghan to the interview room. Becker did a double-take. Meghan had lost weight. She looked gaunt, her designer dress hung on her, partially askew. Her makeup was too bright, and her bloodshot eyes darted around the room. She looked like an injured bird Becker tended to when she was a young girl.

"Good morning, Meghan. This is Assistant Chief Guido Tucci. He may ask a few questions during our interview. Before we start, I'm going to read the Miranda rights to you. I'll record our session."

Meghan's eyes landed on Guido's shoes. She nodded, pulled out a tissue, dabbed her nose, then began shredding the tissue into small pieces on the table.

Becker dispensed with the required language, then asked, "Are you okay? I don't know you well, but you don't seem like yourself."

She met Becker's eyes. "No, I'm not okay. You've ripped our family apart with your investigation. My parents aren't speaking, and Mama missed her garden club meeting, causing a stir in the community. I'm not sure how much more of this I can stand."

Becker ignored the ridiculousness of a missed flower meeting. "Then help me, Meghan. Let's get to the truth so we can put this all behind us." Meghan plucked another tissue from her purse as tears rolled down her face. Becker said, "I know you and Michelle were fighting in the weeks before she went missing. Tell me why."

"We didn't get along, I told you that already."

"Yes, yet you co-existed for years. Your relationship took a turn." She waited a few seconds, letting the silence expand. "Mimi told me during our last interview that Michelle threw a lamp at you. Why?"

Meghan leaned forward and blurted, "I was the one who threw the lamp."

"Why?"

Her face crumpled. "She was hounding me. I asked her to leave me alone She wouldn't listen. She kept coming at me over and over and over."

"What was she 'hounding' you about?"

She got up from her chair and paced the room, her nervous energy spilling out like water from a pitcher. She muttered to herself as her fingers clasped and unclasped aimlessly.

"Meghan? What was the fight about? A man? Money? Your family?"

Meghan continued to pace, crying, sniffing, muttering. She seemed to age ten years in a few minutes, her posture stooped and deflated. Becker glanced at Guido; he pointed to himself. Becker nodded.

"Meghan," he said softly, "did you kill Edward? Was that the man you fought over?"

She whirled and stuck her finger in Guido's face. "No! That's a lie! I would never hurt that boy. I hardly knew him."

"I'm sorry. I was wrong to suggest you would hurt anyone. You seem like a good person." His voice was low, as if he was calming a skittish kitten. "Tell us what happened."

Meghan stopped in her tracks, staring at him.

"This investigation has been hard on you, and I'm sure it's been hard on your girls. The whole town is gossiping about the Workman family, obliterating your reputation. It's time for it to be over."

She gathered herself, sat down, rigid in the chair. "What I am about to say would probably hurt our family reputation, anyway."

"Our conversation is confidential," Guido said. "Unless you've committed a crime, we don't need to disclose what you say to anyone."

She took in a big breath and let it out, gazing in her lap at her handbag. "Unfortunately, that's the issue. I think I committed a crime. I think I killed her."

Guido and Becker made eye contact, both surprised at the revelation. Becker gestured for him to continue; it was obvious Meghan responded to him. "Okay, Meghan. That took a lot of courage. Did you go after your sister after she threw the lamp?"

"Yes."

"In the bedroom?"

"Yes...I mean no." She put her head in her hands, then rubbed her face with her palms. "I'm confusing myself. It happened in the yard. Well, on the patio..." She started shredding another tissue. "Officer, can I please start at the beginning? Or at least earlier?"

Guido smiled kindly at her. "Of course."

"The argument was about my...reliance on prescription medication. Some might call it 'addiction', but that's for junkies and low-class people. Me, I was taking one or two more pills than my doctor prescribed, but I had it under control. It was not a crisis even though Michelle thought it was."

"Why did Michelle assume you were in trouble?"

"She had been snooping in my room, supposedly to look for a pair of shoes. I find that ridiculous since my taste is more refined than hers, by the way. She found my medication, counted the pills for a few weeks. When she came at me that day, I told her it wasn't any of her business."

"And then you hurt her?"

"No, not that time. But that was one of our worst fights. She threatened to tell Mother. That's when I lost my temper. I grabbed the lamp and threw it at her."

"And then?"

"She left. I composed myself and I hoped she would leave me alone. The next day, she came home pretending nothing happened. We had lemonade on the patio, and after we talked about the weather or some inane subject, I forget, she reached into her backpack and handed me a stack of paper about rehab facilities. She told me other people had noticed my 'unusual behavior' and if I didn't get help, I would be a blight on the family, even worse than her." She sniffed then blew her nose. "I have to admit, I may have been a bit...unbalanced. I didn't mean to, but I threw my empty glass at her, one of mother's Waterford crystal goblets. It hit her on the head. She fell off of her chair and onto the patio with a gash above her temple. It was bleeding. A lot."

Becker and Guido were silent as Meghan took a shaky breath. "I...panicked. I scooped up the papers and left. After driving around for a few hours, holding the steering wheel with one hand and my bottle of pills with the other, I stopped the car somewhere in Big Bear Swamp. I talked myself out of, you know, taking all the pills. Instead, I picked up a pamphlet off the seat about a rehab facility in Baltimore. I was there for a week."

Guido asked, "You mentioned you *think* you murdered Michelle. Did you?"

"I-I-I don't know." She took another tissue out of her handbag and shredded it, letting the pieces drop to the floor. "When I came home, the patio was clean. Even the blood had been scrubbed away. Mother and Father never asked me what happened or where I was." She shuddered, then shrugged with one shoulder. "They reported Michelle missing the day I came home. I assumed one of them disposed of the body, if she was indeed dead. I decided if neither of them was going to talk about it, neither would I."

***

Becker and Guido sent Meghan home. What option did they have? They couldn't arrest her; the statute of limitations for a felony assault charge was three years. They had no proof she killed Michelle; no proof Michelle was even dead. She wasn't a flight risk; she wouldn't dare do anything to embarrass the family. She had a good neighbor persona to maintain. In the end, they lectured her about keeping the conversation confidential, then walked her out of the station.

Now, they sat at the interview table, drank mud-like coffee, and waited for Mimi. Guido looked up from his paper cup, saying, "How do you want to play this?"

"I would like you to take the lead again. I hope she'll defer to you like Meghan did. Mimi does the same with Sheriff Atkins, the so-called 'man in charge'."

He shot her a grin. "That's me."

A few minutes later, the front desk announced her arrival. Guido escorted her back to the room. Mimi was poised and polished in a light-weight baby blue cashmere sweater set with a pair of white linen pants. The veneer of confidence cracked, her voice wobbling. "Chief."

"Good morning, Mrs. Workman. You've met Assistant Chief Tucci. He'll be talking with you today." Mimi shrugged.

Becker read the Miranda rights and Mimi acknowledged them with "I understand," and another shrug.

"Mrs. Workman," Guido said, "we're focusing our discussion today on the days leading up to Michelle's disappearance. You and Meghan have both told us about their fight a week before. Do you know what they were fighting about?"

"I told Chief Becker I didn't."

"Okay. My apologies for asking a question that you've previously answered." He gave her a warm smile. "This has to be painful for you and your family."

Mimi let out a breath of air, and her posture softened. "You seem like an understanding person, Assistant Chief." She launched Becker a dismissive glance. "A *nice* person. But you do not know how my life has been...*disrupted* over this situation. I still can't comprehend why William thought it was necessary to unearth something that happened years ago. The only thing that's for certain now is the neighbors are talking about us, which isn't good for William's re-election bid in a year."

Guido ignored the narcissistic comments. "The Workman family is a pillar of this community. Being under a spotlight is difficult." Mimi gave him a kindred smile, he continued, "Meghan told us why they were arguing..."

Her smile faded as she interrupted him. "Can we please leave the past in the past?"

Chapter Thirty-Five

"I'm afraid I can't honor your request because your daughters' fight led to their disappearances," Guido said.

"I take back what I said." She folded her arms in front of her body. "You don't grasp how horrible this is. And you're *not* a nice person. You want to make my family, especially William, look bad so that your mayor in Celestino Village looks good. Everyone is so jealous of the Workman dynasty."

"I'm just trying to do my job and support Chief Becker in finding your daughter, as your husband requested. To do that, we need to re-visit what happened." Mimi shifted in her chair, sat up straighter, nose in the air, waiting for Guido to continue. "Your daughters were fighting because Michelle wanted Megan to get help with her addiction to painkillers, and Megan refused."

Mimi stood up, hands on hips, voice thin. "She did *not* have an addiction! My family does not do drugs! How...*insulting*! I'm going to contact my attorney and sue you for defamation!"

"Mrs. Workman, defamation is a due course if someone is making *false* statements. Meghan *told* us she had an addiction, and after another argument with Michelle, where she left her sister injured and bleeding, she self-committed to a rehabilitation facility in Baltimore."

Mimi interrupted him. "This is...*outrageous*! Meghan is just covering for Michelle, who didn't deserve to be a Workman! I wished her dead for years!"

Silence bounced off the walls. Becker waited a breath, then said, "So, when you found her in a pool of blood, dying or dead, on your patio, you took matters into your own hands."

Her lips trembled. "I'm not answering any more questions. Call William, tell him I need an attorney."

***

An uncomfortable silence between Becker and William Workman filled the room.

William was the first to speak. "I'm...flabbergasted by what you just told me. My mind is working overtime. I can't believe Meghan would hurt her sister, leave her to die. Worse, that Mimi hated her own daughter, and would cover up a murder. No...manslaughter." He rubbed his face. "Not that it matters what the exact charge is."

"I'm sorry, William," Becker said.

"It's not your fault, Chief. It's mine. I've known for years that Mimi isn't wired right. She created this world where the most important thing to her is looking good in the eyes of others. It's been her life's mission to create this persona of wealth and success in the community." He paused. "Underneath her polish, she lacks love. Empathy. Grace."

"She shows her love in other ways," Becker said. "Her beautiful house. Her volunteer work with the garden club. Her support of you as mayor."

He gave her a faint smile. "Chief, that's kind of you to say, although I'm uncertain you are correct. Regardless. What happens next?"

"We release Mimi, if you agree."

William blew out a breath, his shoulders visibly relaxing. "Why wouldn't you hold her?"

"We're not sure she actually committed a crime. Until she discloses the events of that day, or we find evidence to support Michelle's death, and Mimi's involvement in it, we have nothing to arrest her for. As of right now, the only actual crime committed all those years ago, that we know of, was Meghan's assault of Michelle when she threw the glass at her. Mimi's refusal to confirm or deny leaves us with more questions than answers."

"I don't understand why she's refusing to talk."

Becker shook her head. "Maybe she's covering for someone, probably Meghan. Or perhaps she did it yet is unwilling to face the consequences. We won't get to the truth until she agrees to discuss it."

"What next?"

"Please do your best to get her to talk to you. I may have to charge her in the future if she refuses to cooperate, but for now, take her home. And William, let's keep this situation between you, me, and Guido The town has enough to twitter about."

William touched her arm as he rose to leave. "Thank you, Chief, for your discretion. The way you have handled this investigation is beyond my expectations."

"Some days I don't think I've done much." Becker's phone buzzed in her pocket. "Excuse me, William, I need to take this."

As he was closing the door behind him, Becker said, "Hello, Nonna, what's new?"

"Well, heller, Del! I didn't think I would get you. Thought I would get voice mail."

"Your timing is impeccable. I needed saving."

"Should I ask?"

"No."

"Okay. So, I'll tell you why I called. My schedule is filling up, I don't want to miss the next excursion to Katy Bay. Cephas Jones's kin are like my own, like brothers from another mother. When are we going?"

"I'm not sure. I need to talk to Cephas Jones."

"Well, today is your lucky day! I talked to him for you. He said the day after tomorrow is good. The Drone Club and Gruppo are available. We're hoping you can make it. We'd hate to go without you."

Becker bit back what was ready to spill out of her mouth: *What? It's MY investigation! How about MY schedule?!* Instead, she said, "I can make that work."

"*Fabuloso*! That's Italian for 'fabulous', in case you were unaware. Okay, one other thing: Spotted Dicks is having a cookout this weekend. The Dickies are having a hot dog roast. Can you come?" Nonna giggled and in the background, Becker heard Lester the parrot squawk, "Show me your weenie!"

Becker smiled into the phone. "I would love to attend, Nonna."

"Great! That way, I will get to see you twice in two days! Did I mention it's a costume party? Even though it's not Halloween for a bit, the theme is 'Witches and Weenies'." Before Becker could tell Nonna she changed her mind, she would *not* wear an outfit, Nonna muttered a fast "I love you," and hung up.

A knock on the door interrupted her thoughts about how to get out of the Weenie party. "Come in."

She regretted it when Sheriff Atkins stood in the doorway. "Sheriff, what can I do for you?"

"Can you leave before you piss off *all* of Silver Hill, not just the Workmans? What did you say to those poor people?"

Becker didn't take the bait. She ignored his smirk, hoping she looked relaxed, in control. "I can't disclose anything right now. I promised your mayor I would keep things under wraps until further notice."

His face hardened. "Aren't you a big dog, or maybe I should say 'bitch', keeping secrets?"

"Speaking of a big dog, or maybe I should I say 'mongrel', can you sit for a minute and answer a few questions?"

"Mongrel?" He sneered at her. "I guess I'll play nice, especially since William is still in the building." He lowered himself into a chair, spread his arms and legs wide, taking up enough space for a small family. "Ask away."

She threw her best curve ball at him. "Were you having an affair with Edward Landon? Did you kill him?"

Instead of the anger she had expected, his eyes softened. He looked down at his hands. "No, and no."

Becker hid her surprise at his answer. She had expected he would stonewall her. "He was in love with you."

"Yes."

"Would you tell me the story?"

Sheriff Atkins rubbed his face. "Why should I? You're my favorite nemesis at the moment."

"And you're mine." They shared a rare smile, then caught themselves and turned down their lips again. "You want to tell someone? You've been carrying this around for years. Maybe it's time for you to unburden yourself."

"Maybe. But I wouldn't pick you."

She threw another curveball. "You can either spill or I can arrest you for obstruction of justice."

Hatred flashed in his eyes. She flinched, resisted the urge to grab her gun. He stood over her, menacing. "Becker, you've got balls, I'll give you that. But your lame threats don't work with me. Pack your shit up and leave."

If she could elicit anger, perhaps she could tap into a deeper emotion. She gestured to his chair; he reluctantly sat down. "Look, Sheriff, I don't want to threaten you or anyone else. I just want the truth. I think you do, too. Let's start with you hiding your true self. That's got to be painful."

He sighed, stared at her.

"You're angry all the time. I'm guessing it's because you've bottled up your authenticity. Someone told me you wanted to be a park ranger. That's a far cry from who you are today."

He shook his head. "I forgot I had those dreams. It's been a long time ago."

"You can have them again."

He picked at his fingers. "What are you, my shrink?"

"No, just someone who knows about having to be something you're not, hiding pieces of yourself, living up to expectations."

"Yea, right, the famous Chief Becker hides behind a badge."

"My story is for another day. Today is about you. I'm safe. I don't gossip; unless I hear something that smells like a crime, your history is safe with me."

He stared at a spot on the floor for several heartbeats, then met her eyes. "I realized I was gay in high school, and for reasons you probably can understand, I've never acted on it, then or now." He shrugged his shoulders. "Living in a small town on the Eastern Shore, being a member of law enforcement, and having a father that was homophobic enough to disown his own kid...well, you can imagine the rest."

"I can. We might be three hours from the big cities, but the Eastern Shore is stuck in the 1950s."

"Exactly. Anyway, in high school, I dated a few girls, including Michelle Workman, telling myself I was going through some sort of hormonal phase." He tapped on the table with his fingertips. "I wasn't."

"What happened between you and Edward?"

"We occasionally saw each other at school. One time we met at the old boat in Grimmy Swamp. We had a few beers. Nothing more. I couldn't let it be more."

"But Michelle knew."

"Yes, she saw the chemistry. She occasionally teased me about it. As time passed, though, she got frustrated with the situation. Edward was unhappy, and it affected her. She joked one day that if I came out of the closet, Edward and I could build a house together."

"That scared you."

"Of course it did. I was early into my job as sheriff. I obsessed about people finding out. What would the mayor say? Would the old biddies in town, the godly church-going women, rally to have me removed from my job? I didn't know, didn't want to find out."

Becker took a stab at what happened next. "Then when Edward went missing, you didn't try too hard to find him. You were protecting yourself." Becker's voice trembled.

"I had to. Not that I owe you, of all people, an explanation, but you have no idea how bigoted people are on the shore."

She wanted to slap him. Did he not realize she was the only woman chief in the area?

He continued, "I couldn't risk my father finding out. My mother was ill, fighting leukemia. If he learned I was gay, he would have disowned me. I couldn't do that to my mom; she needed me."

"I'm sorry about your mom; I understand first-hand the narrow-mindedness of some people here. But what you did was *wrong*."

"I can't convince you to believe me, but I regret it."

Becker heard enough, her anger flaring. "Regret? Don't make me laugh. If you regretted the way you handled things back then, you'd be making up for it now. But that's not the case. You've acted like an asshole, not giving me information to help with the investigation, protecting Mimi and others who might have hurt or killed Michelle." He opened his mouth to reply, but she cut him off. "Wait. You killed Michelle. She called you on the carpet over your sham investigation to find Edward, so you silenced her."

He rubbed his face. "I'm not a murderer."

"You're a…what? Kidnapper?"

"No. I merely suggested she should pack up, move before the person who killed Edward went after her."

She looked toward the ceiling for divine intervention, or at least patience. She was going to strangle him. "Did I hear you correctly? *You ran her out of town?*"

He didn't answer. She tapped her fingers on the table and counted using the method Mama taught her: One Mississippi, two Mississippi, three Mississippi. She hit sixty at about the time he began picking at his uniform.

Becker broke the silence. "Is an answer forthcoming?"

He shook his head no.

She leaned toward him. "You leave me no choice but to report your actions to William. You need to resign."

"You've got to be shitting me. Quit? Are you nuts? Besides, you told me this meeting was confidential." His eyes flashed as he stuck his index finger in her face.

That's before I learned you purposely botched Edward's murder investigation and threatened a citizen you were sworn to protect."

"You're so high and mighty, Becker. Like you wouldn't do the same thing if your back was against the wall."

"I'm done talking, Sheriff." She stuck *her* index finger in *his* face, and it felt good. "You can either tell William you're leaving, or I'll make sure your story is on the front page of the *Celestino Press,* and on every social media site known to mankind. I need an answer by the end of today." She walked out the door, slamming it behind her.

Guido was in the hallway, holding two cups of coffee from the diner in town. She wanted to hug him, a rare thing for her. Instead, she gave him a tight smile, and he followed her out of the station.

Chapter Thirty-Six

A ngelo was headed back to the city, no return date, Becker surprisingly sad at the news. She hid it behind her professional chief of police persona while she moved paperwork from one side of her desk to the other, occasionally pitching reports in the trash. Only Kevin knew she was blue, his head on her leg, his eyes watching her every move.

Molly peeped her head in, notebook in-hand, Franklin on her shoulder. "Chief, a word?"

Becker was grateful for the distraction. She motioned her into the room. Franklin scurried across the desk and sat on a pile of discarded forms headed for the shredder. She rubbed his head, taking a minute to enjoy his soft fur before he climbed onto her shoulder.

"I talked to Guido about the investigation," Molly said. Her face had a slight flush at the mention of her boyfriend's name. "I'm awfully confused where we are with things. Should we meet with Keisha to get on the same page? I have a beef roast with veggies in a crock pot cooking, I'm guessing a spicy malbec would pair nicely. I can pick up a bottle on my way home."

Becker shook her head. "It would be helpful to compare notes."

"Great." Molly opened her notebook. "Just a few other things. First, I scheduled Hamilton's interview in Snow Hill on Friday. He seemed a bit put out that your last interview was interrupted, and it's taken you this long to reschedule. He really wants to help."

"Hamilton's about the only one in this damned investigation who wants to be of assistance."

"Agreed. I have a new phone number for Marissa." She slid a piece of paper over to Becker. "Also, with respect to Jody Green: he refuses to talk to you on the phone. He says if you want information, you need to go to Connecticut where he lives. Says he hasn't been on Delmarva for years with no plans of coming back, ever." She tapped the pen on her notebook. "He's creating a huge roadblock with his demands."

"A road trip to New England wasn't in my plans." She told Molly about the Virginia trip scheduled for tomorrow.

"I just have a feeling about this, Chief. I'm not sure what, but he's hiding something, and I think it might have to do with Michelle's disappearance."

"I trust your instincts, you know that."

"Yes, I do, and I thank you for it."

Becker absentmindedly petted Kevin.

"By the way," Molly said, "the drive to his home is about six hours. He said he can meet you this weekend."

Becker took in Molly's serious expression, relented. "Okay, tell him I'll be up on Sunday. Ask if noon works for him. Anything else?"

"I'm good, Chief."

Becker's phone rang; she glanced at the cell screen. "Molly, it's William. I need to take this."

Franklin jumped from Becker's shoulder to Molly's as they left. "William, good morning. How can I help you today?"

"I'm actually outside of your office. I apologize for the lack of notice, but can I stop in?"

Becker assured him it was fine; a minute later, the door to the station opened and closed. He said, "Hello, Bella," as he walked into her office.

He was wearing a black suit, a white starched shirt and a red and yellow striped tie. She wondered if he ever wore casual clothes. She stuck out her hand; he shook it. "What brings you to the village?"

As they sat, he said, "I was attempting to convince your illustrious mayor, Roberto, to join our police forces. You could be Chief of Police for Celestino Village *and* Silver Hill. Share you, so to speak."

She looked blankly at him. "What?"

"It makes sense. You're a superb leader; your character is impeccable. You're honest and communicate well with citizens, politicians, the media, etcetera. It would be a terrific partnership."

"With all due respect, Mr. Mayor, what if I'm not interested?"

William laughed. "That's what Roberto said you would say. But I'd like you to consider it. Roberto said he would, as well. If you decide not to take the joint position, we will initiate a search for Paul Atkins' replacement."

"Let's say it's a 'no' for now. And I am sorry you have to find a new sheriff."

"You did the right thing, Chief, by calling Sheriff Atkins out." He leaned forward in his chair. "He told me he would resign, outlined the reasons for his decision. I was at a loss for words when he confessed to his half-assed—excuse me, I never curse—his shameful handling of both Edward and Michelle's cases. It boggles my mind."

"I didn't ask him about the timing of Michelle's disappearance, how soon it was after he suggested she leave. Did he cause her to run?

"I don't have knowledge of the exact dates but, according to him, Michelle didn't leave right away. Regardless, he refuses to accept responsibility. He said if anyone ran her off, it was Hamilton."

"Why?"

"It's convoluted. Apparently, when Sheriff Atkins failed to convince her to leave, he recruited Hamilton to do so. He led Hamilton to believe Michelle wasn't safe."

Her face scrunched up. "I'm not following...Edward goes missing. Sheriff Atkins doesn't know whether he's missing or dead, his investigation is shoddy, so he never finds out. Yet he tells Hamilton that Michelle needs to leave town to stay safe?"

"Yes. He told Hamilton he suspected Gus Fornash killed Edward, and because Gus had ties to the mafia, Michelle was in danger."

"I need a scorecard."

"Me too, Chief. Bottom line: Paul Atkins lied to protect himself."

They sat in silence for a moment.

William spoke. "Speaking of protecting oneself, Mimi still won't disclose whether she saw Michelle lying on the patio, injured or dead." He smoothed his tie. "I even made Meghan re-enact the scenario with Mimi present, to see if I could garner a response. It didn't go well. Meghan burst into tears. Mimi gave me her trademark scornful glance as she left the patio."

"William, I am so sorry. You don't deserve all of this."

"Chief, it's kind of you to say so. Unfortunately, I've known for years my family is broken, and Mimi is responsible. I fell in love with her long before I understood her many...issues." His face turned pink. "Chief, you're a good listener. However, you don't need to hear about my burdens." He rose from the chair. "I'll continue to work with Mimi to discover the truth."

An hour later, Becker and Kevin were walking past Joey's house when she spotted Angelo. He was shoving a huge yellow mum into the backseat of his Alfa Romero. She waited for him to turn around. When he did, he gave her a huge smile, picked her up and kissed her cheek. Kevin barked, tail wagging.

"Delaney! I am so happy I ran into you!"

"Likewise, Angelo. Now put me down."

"I was going to deliver this mum to the police station, then ask you to dinner tonight."

"Oh, Angelo, I have plans."

He raised his eyebrows. "Don't tell me you and Mack are a thing again. It will break my heart into little pieces."

"Do you steal your sayings from songs? What guy says 'break my heart into little pieces'? Not that it's any of your business, mind you, I'm having dinner with Keisha and Molly."

"Oh, no worries! Bring them! I've already invited your Mama, Joey, Cephas Jones, and a few friends from town. Oh, Edwina Landon is coming. Birdy from the Drone Club. It's my going away party, although I hope to be back soon."

Becker's need for fun, for a break from the investigation, warred with her need to visit with Keisha and Molly to get closer to resolving the damned thing. She hesitated, he noticed.

"I have some news about Gus Fornash and his alleged activities with the mob."

"You're playing dirty, Angelo. I don't like it."

"Whatever works. Wear your little black dress. You'll look marvelous next to me in my black tux. The party is at the Pasta Plazzo, Roman's place, at six-thirty."

"I'm well aware of the restaurant; I've lived here for thirty years." She narrowed her eyes at him, "Fine. I'll come under protest."

"I'll repeat: whatever works."

Chapter Thirty-Seven

Becker arrived a bit late. She'd left a pile of discarded clothes on her bed, the ones she would not wear, in favor of the little black dress. Angelo got his wish granted, dammit. She had to admit, though, she looked sexy and confident, except for the scowl she wore at her own pride. As she walked in the restaurant, Nonna saw her pinched face, told her to get her ass off her shoulders and have a good time.

"Happy to see you, too, Nonna."

"Oh Del, sometimes you have more than your butt around your head. Sometimes you have the weight of the village on top of you."

Nonna was right, so Becker willed herself to relax and enjoy the evening. How could she not with Nonna looking sporty in a captain's uniform (lime green, white was "too boring"), complete with a matching hat? Becker admired the outfit until she spied the breast pockets, adorned with dolphins, their eyes strategically placed over Nonna's...*don't think about it.*

"Okay, I'll shake off the extra baggage."

"You'd be better off shaking your booty in that cute dress. Speaking of cute, here come Angelo and Joey. My man looks good enough to eat."

Joey was wearing a lime green tuxedo coat over a pair of black slacks with a yellow bowtie and orange handkerchief. He looked like a human Skittle; Angelo, standing next to him, looked like a Roman God. She stared at him, caught herself, looked away.

He leaned down and sniffed her hair then kissed her temple. She shivered, pushing him away. "Stop it! I'm here for the scoop on Gus, not to be wined and dined."

"In that case, let's head to the bar. I'll tell you all about it."

As they walked across the restaurant, Mama, Cephas Jones, and a dozen other friends and neighbors greeted them warmly. Fern gave her a once-over, wriggling his eyebrows. Birdy, from the Drone Club, his face the color of a tomato, stuttered, "You look pretty."

She spotted Keisha and Molly at the bar, Guido nearby. She almost stumbled when she realized Keisha was wearing a slinky red dress. Keisha of the jeans and military boots? And Molly was divine in her own version of a little black dress, although hers flowed around her like a cloud. Franklin perched on her shoulder, holding a dandelion. When Becker rubbed his head, he gave it to her; she kissed him in return.

Angelo handed out glasses of Brunello, toasting their loveliness. Keisha said, "Angelo, can you stop with the unicorns and rainbows? We want to hear the scoop on Gus."

He laughed. "No wonder you're Delaney's best friend. Beautiful, purposeful, direct. Maybe I should turn my attention toward you instead of Delaney? I'm not making much headway with her."

Eight pairs of eyes stared at him. No, ten, including Franklin. Angelo shrugged. "Just kidding. Geez." He took a sip of his bourbon. "You all know how this works. I'm passing on information that is probably a rumor, because I'm not involved in mob activities." Becker, Keisha, Molly, and Franklin nodded while Guido smiled. "I had originally heard that Gus's death was unrelated to the mob, specifically the Corelli family, who Gus worked for. But it seems it may have been, um...ordered by a rival family in the area."

"Why?" Becker asked.

"The dead guy they found in Gus's garage was a cousin in the rival family."

Head nods all around. "But why act on it now? The murder in Philly was years ago," Becker said.

Angelo shrugged. "My being here has the mafia's attention. Maybe that opened old wounds?"

Guido asked, "How do you know the mafia is interested in your visit here?"

"Let's just say I've noticed from time to time, a tail. Delaney, do you remember the beefy guy at sitting at the next table next to us at Put-in-Bay? I think he followed us from Delmarva."

Becker's stomach dropped at the prospect of being monitored by the bad guys. Angelo hugged her, whispering, "You've turned white. Don't worry, I always have your back."

Much later, after a mouth-watering dinner of calamari, soft, pillowy ravioli in a mushroom sauce, and tiramisu, Angelo walked Becker home. In front of her building, he said, "Are you going to invite me up?"

"Regrettably, no." She sighed. "I care for you so much, but I can't forget that I am a cop and you're—" she searched for words and came up short— "the farthest thing from that. I can't get involved with you. It's not right."

He took both of her hands in his. "Oh, Delaney, you and your ethics. It's the many things I love about you."

Her head snapped up. "What?"

"I said, I love you."

"You absolutely *cannot* be in love with me."

"Nonetheless, I am."

"Well, shit."

He smiled down at her. "Yes...shit. I should let you get your rest, as you have a field trip tomorrow to Virginia." He stroked the hair near her ear. "Saying thank you for such a lovely evening doesn't feel like enough, but thank you." He kissed her gently on her cheek, nose, lips.

As he walked away, she cupped her hand over her mouth to muffle the words, "Please stay."

***

"Del, are you listening?"

She wasn't; she was thinking about last night, Angelo, their good-bye. Was it possible to miss him already? "I zoned out for a minute, Nonna. What were you saying?"

"You have a moon-pie face."

"A what?"

"You know, like you're happy because you just ate one of those delicious pastry things? A moon pie?"

Becker regretted her decision to ride the chartered bus to Katy Bay with the Gruppo, including Nonna, Joey Vito, Cephas Jones, Arima Patel, and Johnny Hudson, as well as members of the Drone Club, Mooney Workman, invited by Edwina Landon, who was there too. Lester the parrot was on board and, of all people, Mack Brown. Her on-a-break boyfriend had his nose in oceanographic maps; he and Johnny were talking about sites to visit. Nonna had invited him because of his role as a marine biologist. She said it was helpful he knew about "those little fish that eat human bones". Becker didn't dare ask what she was talking about.

"I'm just thinking of the investigation and all the dead ends."

"Uh-huh, I don't believe you. It's Angelo Zullo, do I get a prize for the correct guess? I'm telling you, that boy is not for you."

She shushed her grandmother. Thankfully, they were pulling into Mel's fishing camp. Becker stood to speak to the group. "Everyone, can I have your attention?" The bus was silent. "I have a list of the teams today, and Johnny and Mack—" they nodded to her— "have the assignments. Mel and I will run the communications from here. Nonna has grub duty with Mooney."

"As well as beverage cooling, mixing, distribution," Nonna said. Lester sang, "Ninety-nine bottles of beer on the wall" before Mooney gently touched his wing. He quieted, giving her a soft side-eye.

"To finish, all-hands-on deck, please, to set up camp while I work on final plans. Last, I know we all will have fun today, but let's not forget this is a serious effort. It's the last time we'll be in the Katy Bay area to search for Michelle. I wish us good luck."

For the next half hour, Mel's place was a beehive of activity; everyone pitched in to organize grills, tables, food, wine and beer. Nonna took orders for mimosas carding the youngish-looking Drone Club members. Mooney hung up a banner that read *Bring Michelle Home*, while Joey practiced 10-codes with Arima.

"What's 10-100 again?" Joey asked.

"You need to use the bathroom."

"Oh, I thought it meant 'I need help'."

Arima flipped through a notebook. "I can't find that one. Just say 'mayday' if you get in trouble."

Becker sought out Mooney. "I'd like you to pair up with Cephas Jones."

"He's a lovely soul, if a bit lonely. Last week he visited Silver Hill. I gave him a rough chunk of amethyst. I hope it helped."

"He is a wonderful man...I want him to take you to visit an older gentleman named Tuggy, who may or may not have information about Michelle." Becker chose her next words carefully. "I'm not overly optimistic as Tuggy's brain is mushy from past drug use. However, the last time Cephas Jones visited him, he muttered about a white woman, bees, and wild horses. If he sees you, since you look so much like your sister, perhaps something will break loose."

"I hope so," Mooney said. "I'm sad to say I don't feel Michelle at all. If she was close to Mr. Tuggy's house, I may pick up her vibe there." She touched the green pendant at her throat, then put her hand on Becker's sleeve. "I wore jade today for good luck, but I want you to know, whatever happens with the investigation, it's been an honor to work with you. To call you a friend. I couldn't have asked for a better person to find her."

Becker opened her mouth to respond, but Mooney squeezed her arm. "No putting yourself down. You're giving it your best effort."

Becker thought, *How does she do that?* "Okay, I won't. But I will say it's not over yet. I wore my Italian horn for good luck, too. Now let's get to it, bring Michelle home."

The teams left to Lester the parrot yelling, "Hurry back, now!" while Joey called "10-98" on the walkie talkie.

"Joey, 10-98 is a 'prison break'. Did you mean 10-8, 'in service'?" Becker asked.

"Yep, 10-14."

"You mean 10-4, which is 'yes'. 10-14 is a 'prowler alert'." She rubbed her brow. "Joey, let's use regular language and forget the codes, okay?"

"10-4, Chief!"

The teams reported back after several hours with little in the way of helpful evidence. Cephas Jones returned with Mooney, face drained of color. Cephas guided her into the house, Mel trailing, arms outstretched in case she fell, Becker watched keeping silent as worry lines spread across her face.

"What happened?" Becker asked, as Cephas stepped onto the porch.

"Tuggy took one look at her and asked, 'Where's the gremlin, Marissa?' Then Mooney fainted. I couldn't rouse her, so I carried her back to the car, the little thing that she is. I tried to get Tuggy to say more, but he kept looking at Mooney, saying, 'Marissa, Marissa, Marissa,' over and over."

Becker took a sip of her sweet iced tea, hands shaking.

"Chief, what do you think it means?"

"Mooney's jade for good luck worked. Sort of."

Chapter Thirty-Eight

Becker's sleepless nights caught up with her. Last night, she obsessed over Tuggy's comments to Cephas Jones and Mooney. What did his remarks about a gremlin mean? Why did he mention Michelle's sister Marissa? Had he met her? Did she have something to do with Michelle's disappearance?

Around 3:00a.m. Becker crawled out of bed to make a note to call Marissa again but couldn't get back to sleep, so she surfed the internet. She typed in "gremlin"; images of green beings with big pointy teeth stared back at her from the screen. Scrolling, she passed up a picture of an AMC Gremlin, then went back to it. Her mind made an iffy connection.

Could Tuggy have confused a late model AMC Gremlin for a 1976 Ford Pinto?

The next morning, she fought awkwardness and a slight brain fog as she walked into the Silver Hill police station, the first time since her argument with Sheriff Atkins, and his subsequent resignation. She straightened her spine to her full 5'2" to project her most powerful self. She held her head high. It wasn't her fault their former sheriff was crooked; damned if she would have regrets about ratting the guy out.

Officers stared at her from all corners of the room. Some gave her a half-smile, some gave her a scowl, one muttered "Bitch" under his breath. Beside her, Guido had his mean, protective face in place.

"Stop it," she said. His mustache twitched.

Hamilton was sitting in the interview room when they arrived, look-ing relaxed and at ease in his button-down, sky-blue shirt, khaki pants, and Sperry Topsider shoes, no socks. He shook their hands and then passed each of them a to-go coffee cup from the Sunny Side Up, hers with Italian Cream. His cologne made Becker sneeze.

"Thank you," Becker said.

"Glad to help, Chief. I'm ready with questions you have about Michelle."

"You've met Guido several times. He's been attending the second interviews with me. I'm citing Miranda rights and recording all second interviews. Are you okay with that?" Hamilton said he was, so she dispensed with reading him his rights. "Let's go over a bit of territory we've already discussed to refresh my memory." *A fib*, Becker thought, *I just need to hear consistent stories.* "You and Michelle were close."

"Oh, we were going to get married."

Becker almost swallowed her tongue. "Really? I don't think you mentioned it during our first interview."

"I may not have said so directly, but we had discussed our future; we both knew we wanted to get hitched. We were like two peas in a pod and communicated so well that we got to where we would finish each other's sentences." He chuckled. "We both loved to hike, listen to music, hang out with her family. Well, not her entire family. Mostly Mooney. We even tinkered a bit under the hood together. She was much better than me at it, but it was fun."

"I heard you and Michelle had a big fight right before she went missing," Becker winced at Guido's nasty tone, fabricated so he could play the "bad cop".

"Oh, did you hear this from Gus? And you believed him? I would guess that most mobsters lie, wouldn't you?"

"Probably," said Guido, "but more than one person said you and Michelle didn't always get along, had arguments."

Hamilton shrugged. "What couple doesn't have an occasional disagreement?"

Guido didn't let up. "What did you disagree about?"

"Gus, for one. He was an evil seed. Edward for another. Jody Green, for a third." He caught himself and smiled. "But just a difference of opinion, nothing major."

Guido leaned in toward Hamilton. "Interesting that all the fights were about other men. Are you the jealous type?"

"Not at all. Just protective. How about you, Officer Tucci? Are you the jealous type?"

Becker rushed in before Guido got sucked into some sort of male ego sparring match, although he routinely stayed above such nonsense. But just in case, she asked, "Hamilton, what were you protecting Michelle from?"

"Getting hurt. She had a big heart and was very loyal, sometimes to people who weren't loyal to her."

Guido hammered him. "Speaking of loyalty, why wasn't she faithful to you? You broke up with her several times because of it."

His face flushed. "That's a lie. She broke up with me."

"Oh?"

He recovered quickly. "What I meant to say is we took a few breaks from each other, but it wasn't because of either of us running around. I'll give you an example because I know it will be your next question. I told you I could be protective. Jody Green bothered her, asking her out several times. She said Jody scared her but she could take handle it. I wasn't convinced, so I ran him off, which upset her; we didn't see each other for a few weeks. Then when we did, we both confessed we missed each other terribly. Needless to say, we put the incident behind us."

"Why was Michelle afraid of Jody?"

"He threatened her." He turned to Becker. "Chief, I wanted to tell you during our first interview about my concerns, but you got called away."

She nodded. "What did he say or do?"

"He told her if he couldn't have her, no one else would."

"If he said that, it's concerning." Becker's trip to New England was tomorrow to talk to Jody Green; she would verify Hamilton's story. Or not.

She asked, "What was your relationship with Edward Landon?"

"None, really. He and Michelle were friendly."

She gave him a quizzical look. "Oh, they were more than friendly. They were very close—"

Guido interrupted her. "I heard from several sources they met frequently at an old boat in the swamp to have sex."

He pounded his fist on the table. "Another lie! They just *talked* on the boat."

Guido pounced. "How do you know?"

Silence stretched for a second, then five, then ten. Hamilton shrugged. "I noticed sometimes she and Edward would be gone at the same time. One day I got curious, followed Michelle to make sure she was okay. She is, I mean was, a...naïve soul. Too trusting. Anyway, once I realized Edward wouldn't hurt her, at least not physically, I let them do their thing."

Guido rushed in. "What do you mean by Edward not hurting her physically? Is there another way to assault someone?"

"Yes, sir. Edward was a strange boy. He seemed, at least to me, unbalanced. He crept around taking pictures all day. It was unsettling."

Edward was *unique*. Not strange. But she let the comments pass and changed topics. "Do you own a gun?"

Hamilton's head whipped around from Guido to her. "What?"

She met his eyes and waited him out.

"I don't have one currently, but you must know I've had registered guns before. I believe I owned a Winchester rifle, given to me by my father, and a few pistols."

Becker kicked herself. She hadn't read his entire police report and the background data Molly unearthed. "Where are the guns you used to own?"

"I sold them. Chief, this conversation is making me uncomfortable. I'm thinking I did something wrong, which is untrue. Michelle was the love of my life. We both know Gus is the one who killed Edward, and had something to do with Michelle disappearing."

She backed off. "You've done nothing wrong; as a matter of fact, you've been extremely cooperative." He beamed at the compliment. "Can you expound on your theory that Gus is a murderer?"

He picked at a callus on his left hand. Becker noticed his palms were leathery, worn. He caught himself fiddling with the scab. "I think Gus was romantically interested in Michelle. He killed Edward because he was jealous, then hurt Michelle when she wasn't responsive to him. Or," his eyes were misty, "he killed her."

"If that's the case, why didn't Gus kill you? Why would he go after Edward, a friend, and not you, her boyfriend?"

"He must have figured out he would have a hard time with me. He went for the easy pickings, so to speak."

Becker leaned back in her chair and took a sip of the cooling coffee. "It an interesting theory. But I'm surprised you think Michelle is dead. You've been optimistic during past conversations."

He gazed down at the table for a minute. When he looked up, he had tears in his eyes. "I don't mean to contradict myself. I want her to be alive but if she is, wouldn't she come back to me? Our love was so strong. I mean, is still so strong."

***

Becker and Guido ate brunch at the Sunny Side Up before returning to Celestino Village. She had a fried soft-shell crab sandwich with coleslaw, extra hush puppies. He ordered a small salad with chicken. She admired his choice; her meal was delicious, carb-packed; his was low calorie, nutritional. No wonder he was so fit and trim and she was...not.

She noticed the tail as soon as she pulled the police cruiser away from the curb. Heart beating fast, she told Guido to hold on while she made a quick circle in Silver Hill, putting her cruiser behind the other vehicle. She threw on her flashing lights; the car in front of her pulled to the curb.

She held her hand over her Glock as she walked up to the driver's window. Joey Vito sat inside with Lester the parrot, perched in a cage on the front passenger seat. "Cop! Cop! Throw out the beer bottles!"

She rolled her eyeballs at the parrot and the man. "Joey, why are you following me?"

"Ah, I ain't doing nothing."

"Yes, you are. Do you want me to ask Nonna what is going on?"

"No, no, no...Angelo asked me to get someone to keep an eye on you, so I volunteered myself. You don't need some goombah drooling over you, I mean bothering you. Besides, you're like a daughter to me."

She patted his arm. "I have Guido with me today, so I'm safe. Go to Nonna's. She probably needs help with getting ready for the party tomorrow."

"I was trying to get outta that," he muttered.

"Then go home, weed your garden."

"Much better idea." He drove off. Lester the parrot yelled, "Goodbye, Copper!"

Guido raised an eyebrow as she buckled her seatbelt. "Joey Vito, keeping me out of harm's way."

"He's a good guy."

"Yes, with a sordid past in the mafia. He's my grandmother's boyfriend. His cousin, also a mobster, is interested in me. Remind me, how did I get here?"

Guido smiled at her. "They all care about you. Let them."

She scowled at the windshield. "Speaking of the mob, what do you think of Hamilton's theory that Gus killed Edward, then Michelle?"

"At first blush, it sounds plausible. I think there are too many holes, though. For one, no one's ever mentioned a romantic relationship between Gus and Michelle. I have the sense he was a big brother figure, even a surrogate father, not a lover." He paused while the radio clicked, a greeting from the Maryland State Police officer sitting in an unmarked car on the side of the road. "It also doesn't fit that Gus was jealous of Edward. Again, all accounts are Edward was a sensitive, thoughtful friend, but nothing more."

"Agreed."

"And Chief? There's something...off...about Hamilton. On the surface, he's personable, good-looking, cultured...but maybe too much?"

"Maybe he's trying too hard?"

"Something like that."

She sighed.

Chapter Thirty-Nine

B ecker did *not* want to go to the Witches and Weenies event at the Spotted Dick Campground today. She did *not* want to wear a costume, and she did *not* want to make the pot of meatballs Nonna requested. Of course, she did all three.

Her bib overalls, stuffed with straw, itched as she drove to Dick's. Her face, painted like a scarecrow, was greasy. She looked ridiculous, felt cranky, until she crawled out of the truck to Nonna's beaming face, eyes filled with love and pride.

"Del, you are adorable! Well, more adorable than usual! I'm glad you didn't sew a fake crow onto your shoulder; Lester hates the damned things. He screams 'Nevermore, nevermore,' over and over when he sees one, then hides under the couch pillow. Wouldn't be so bad, I can tune him out, but he throws up, too. Be careful if you sit in there, by the way. A crow flew by the window yesterday." Nonna grabbed the crock pot from the backseat as Becker complimented her on her sexy alien vibe.

"I'm supposed to be an octopus. Well, crap. I'm going to change into my crab outfit. You can't go wrong with a crustacean get-up." Nonna told her to put on her scarecrow hat and mingle while she became a curvy crab.

She scanned the crowd. Joey Vito was either a tree or broccoli, Becker couldn't tell which. Mama favored Julia Childs, and Johnny Hudson was a passable Albert Einstein. Lester the parrot had on a bumblebee hat, bouncing his head to dislodge it. Becker felt sorry for him and took it off. He sang, "If I only had a brain."

Cephas Jones dressed as a 1930s mobster, complete with a fake machinegun slung over his shoulder. He put his hand on her shoulder, leaned down and whispered, "You look like you belong on the Wizard of Oz set," before saying in a normal volume, "Hello, Chief, how are you today?"

"I am well, Cephas Jones. And before this party gets off the ground, can we talk business?" He nodded at her. "Any more information from Tuggy? I've been thinking about it a lot." She had also asked Molly to double down on finding Michelle's Ford Pinto. If they could uncover the registration information, perhaps Becker could pinpoint the dates Michelle owned the car, and put a year to Tuggy's sighting of the car, or Michelle, or both.

"Nothing. Mel has visited a few times to check in on him, take him food; he's done that for years for the older folks who live near him." They smiled at Mel's kindness. "Tuggy doesn't know what Mel is talking about." A shout interrupted their conversation. Joey had thrown a corn hole bag, pushing three in the hole for his team. "We may want to get Mooney to visit again, but the first meeting was disturbing. We should wait until there's no other choice but to jiggle Tuggy's memory."

"Got it. Good advice and thank you."

A car door slammed behind her. She turned to William Workman, dressed in a suit. Cephas teased him. "Are you dressed in costume as the Mayor of Silver Hill?"

William gave them a slight smile. "Spotted Dick's is technically in the town limits of Silver Hill, although they, and I, usually pretend they're not. It's one of their large events, though, so I thought I would stop by to say hello to the permanent residents in the back." He explained several small cabins ringed the west side of the campground. One of his most active campaign volunteers, a truck driver, lived there.

He pulled Becker aside. "Mimi continues to say silent about what happened after Michelle and Meghan argued. She refuses to answer questions related to whether she found Michelle lying on the patio, what she did, if anything. I'm beyond my wit's end trying to get her to talk about it." His jaw tensed and his eyes watered. "I hate to resort to this, but I want you to arrest her for hampering an official investigation."

"William, that's pretty drastic. I still have other leads to pursue."

"Regardless, Chief, she's hiding something She needs to be held accountable for what she did, whatever it was." He paused. "Sadly, it's time for me to accept she's not the woman I thought she was."

Becker rubbed her brow. "I won't go against you, William. Not only do I respect your position as mayor, but I respect you as the person who asked for the investigation. How about this: On Monday, I'll reach out to you. We can talk through how best to notify her, get her through the process with dignity."

"That's more than acceptable." It looked like tears were going to run down his cheeks at any moment. He rubbed his face. Becker guessed he mentally checked himself as he said goodbye. He turned then woodenly walked down the gravel path toward the cabins.

The afternoon slipped pleasantly by. She played corn hole with Mama as her partner. Becker accidentally hit Big Betty with a bag and narrowly missed Nonna's grill with a bocce ball. She ate a hot dog with sauerkraut, onions, mustard, ate more than her fair share of macaroni salad. Stole three cookies from the table, feeding one to Lester. She drank a non-alcoholic beer; she wanted to be fresh tomorrow for her road trip to New England. Unfortunately, the near-beer tasted like crap, so she traded it for a diet soda, which tasted almost as bad.

The crab claws of Nonna's costume kept getting caught on the table and chairs. She knocked over Becker's diet soda, just before one appendage caught fire from the grill. Lester squawked what sounded like "Great Balls of Fire".

Nonna now sat next to Becker clad in bright pink shorts that barely covered her private parts, and a t-shirt with *Drink Up, Witches*. Mama was on her left, her Julia Child's wig slightly askew.

"You're the best-looking woman here today, Del," Nonna said. "How is it you have two boyfriends yet you came by yourself?"

"Oh, leave her alone, Mother." Mama always came to her defense.

"I don't have two boyfriends. I'm on a break with Mack, nothing is going on with Angelo."

Nonna muttered, "Bullshit."

Lester the parrot: "Wash your mouth out with soap, you heathen!"

Becker wanted to ignore them both, but said, "It's complicated, as you know. I'm a cop, Angelo's a criminal."

"Bah, it doesn't have to be difficult. You're two healthy, horny youngsters who have great chemistry. Go for it." Nonna winked at her.

"You told me last week Angelo was trouble, Nonna."

"Mack is her boyfriend," Mama said. "Enough talk of Angelo."

"You're both right." Mama and Becker raised their brows. Nonna agreed with them? Was she sick? Something was up.

"Besides, there's another man your age I want you to consider." There it was. Nonna the matchmaker. "He is attractive, blond hair, suntanned. He's the boy I wanted you to meet, but he didn't show up today. His name is Hamilton and—"

"Hamilton Parsons?"

"I'm not sure of his last name. Oh, are you already involved with him? You have *three* boyfriends?"

Lester the parrot yelled, "Three times a lady!"

"No, his name came up in Michelle's investigation," Becker said. "How do you know Hamilton?"

"He lives here, in a cabin in the back."

"Are you sure? The Hamilton I know lives the high life on a trust fund from his deceased parents."

Nonna crinkled her nose. "The Hamilton I know is a hard-working handyman who services the campers and fifth wheels in the campground. But I've seen him clean up, and he's very handsome. Even wears those Sperry Topsiders, no socks, which is awfully fashionable, don't you think?"

Becker told Nonna she wanted to take a walk to the cabins. Nonna called her a "Nosy Rosy", and told her Hamilton's campground number: fifty-nine. She headed to the permanent section, under a canopy of trees interspersed with lush plantings of columbine, ferns, and hostas. Cabin 59 looked deserted, except for a pot of red geraniums fading from the cool fall temperatures. A twelve-inch tall fairy statue, like the kind Mooney sold at her store, sat to the right of the front door.

An older man sat in a chair on the porch one cabin over. He waved at her. "Howdy, Miss!"

"Hello to you!" He introduced himself as Fred, no last name.

"Haven't seen you around here before, but you look familiar."

"I'm Nonna's, I mean Teresa's, granddaughter. My name is Delaney, but most folks call me Becker."

"Yep, you resemble her. She's a hoot. She talks about Del all the time. That you?"

"It is." She gestured toward the cabin next door. "Hamilton is a friend of mine. I understand he lives there."

"That he does. Nice man. Helped me with my leaking faucet."

"Oh, he helped me with my truck battery." She was getting good at fibbing. *It's nothing to be proud of, Becker.*

"Really? I didn't know he worked on vehicles. You wouldn't know it by the old Impala he drives, told me it was a '74 but I swear it's a '75 model. The color of blue is the right shade for '75."

"Huh. He's not home today?"

"Nope, on Saturdays he goes to Virgina for work. Likes to get his hands dirty crabbing. Brings me some every now and again."

"I love Maryland blue crabs." Fred was such a sweet man. Why couldn't Nonna date him instead of an ex-mobster? "Have you ever had scallops off the boat in Ocean City?

"Only all summer long!"

"Fred, it's been great visiting with you. I need to get back to Nonna. Do me a favor and don't tell Hamilton I stopped by? I'm coming back, ah, sometime this week and I'd like to surprise him.'

"Mum's the word with me. Tell your Nonna I said hi and tell Lester, 'Gooney Goo Goo'. That makes him cackle."

Becker's thoughts raced on the way home as she unstuffed her bib overalls, straw flying out the window of her vehicle. Why was Hamilton living in a campground? Why was he working as a handy man when he inherited a sizable amount of money? Was he leading a double life?

And why did Lester laugh at "Gooney Goo Goo"?

Chapter Forty

B ecker was up and out of her apartment at the ungodly hour of 6:00a.m. even though her meeting with Jody Green was at one, and it was only a four-hour drive.

She was operating on four hours of sleep. She blamed Kevin and his gassiness at first, an easy target; but it was her brain's fault. It wouldn't stop asking questions about Hamilton, well into the wee hours of the morning.

She needed coffee *badly*. After a quick stop at The Shanty for a large hot cup of joe with cream and two biscuits made from scratch, hold the butter, she was on her way north. A few hours later, around eight, she called Molly to tell her about Hamilton's living arrangements. "I couldn't sleep last night, so I pulled out the file you put together. I don't see any obvious holes, but things don't add up. You researched his parents' deaths, correct?"

Molly's voice was low. "Hold on a minute." She came back on thirty seconds later. "Didn't want to bother Guido."

"A sleepover?" Becker heard the smile in her voice.

"Yes, one of many. Say nothing to him, though. He's private about such matters."

"Cross my heart."

"Okay," Molly said. Papers shuffled in the background. "I didn't give you all I had, but yes, his parents died in a car accident. I found a newspaper article. Let me read it to you: 'David and Priscilla Parsons were involved in a one-car accident last night a half-mile from their home, Forsythe Manor. Investigators believe the car was traveling at a high rate of speed and Mr. Parsons failed to yield to a curve in the road. The vehicle veered to the left, striking several trees. Both were pronounced dead on the scene. Further investigation is forthcoming'.”

"Can you send me the address to Forsythe Manor? And while you're at it, look up the address to the all-boys school Hamilton and Jody Green attended?”

"Sure. And Franklin says he misses you but wants to go back to bed.”

"Give him a kiss for me. Talk soon.”

***

Forsythe Manor reminded her of the Biltmore, in Asheville, NC, only on a smaller, shabbier scale. The Grand Dame had been neglected for years. The once-ivory colored brick was black and greenish in spots, the painted trim around the windows peeling, mold growing in the eaves. The roof on one of four towers had caved in, a small tree poking through it; weeds intermingled to create a small jungle. Ivy fully concealed the brick to the right of the door.

Becker parked the truck, then picked her way through grass reaching above her knees. Several windows on the side of the structure were covered with plywood boards. Behind the house, a small, well-kept cottage sat next to a pool filled with water, algae floating on its surface. Someone had cut the grass around the cottage, and the flower beds looked recently tended. A short, slight man stood half-bent-over in the vegetable garden, harvesting tomatoes, laying the fat red fruit in a woven basket on the ground.

"Hello,” Becker called out.

The man startled. His eyes darted around, wide and fearful. "Ma'am, can I help you?"

"I wanted to have a word with you about Forsythe Manor."

"You a historian or photographer?"

"No, a police officer. My name is Delaney Becker." She handed him her police ID.

He took off his gloves to shake her hand. "Oh, a chief! And all the way from Maryland. I'm Thomas Parsons. Come in for a glass of tea."

She followed him into the cozy cottage, filled with antiques and secondhand furniture. "You're a Parsons? Are you related to Hamilton?"

He whirled around, almost spilling the tea he was pouring from the pitcher into a pink Depression glass. "What's he done now?"

"I'm not sure if he's done anything. Would you tell me about him?"

He handed her a glass, then gestured her over to the table, into a chair. "How long do you have?"

"An hour."

"Not sure an hour is long enough, but I can start. We'll leave time for you to tell me what nonsense he's gotten himself into. I'm sure it's the more of the same." Thomas sipped his tea. "Where to begin? You know he went to an all-boys boarding school, right?" She nodded. "You probably don't know why or the details of the school. He tells everyone about his upper crust life, but leaves out the grimy details. The truth is, Brier Hill Academy was for troubled kids, and Hamilton was the worst of the bunch. He was a bully. Why, in the fourth grade he broke a kid's arm. Mom and Dad wanted to believe it was an accident. I knew better. He had a gleam in his eye whenever he told the story."

"It wasn't the first time he hurt someone."

"You're intuitive, Chief. No, it wasn't the first time. I had the bruises to prove it, throughout the years, but my parents wouldn't listen. He could lie as smoothly as anyone I've ever met. Anyway, they sent him to Brier Hill. He seemed to flourish. When he came home, he was...polished. Cultured. Charming. The bully was gone, and the lying became less, eventually stopped. But I found out years later he was hiding behind a mask of sorts."

"What do you mean?"

"My parents wanted a perfect son, so he became one. It wasn't until I learned he was swindling money out of them I realized it was all a sham. It was some sort of sick game for him, I think. He always wanted to win." He shrugged. "A few months before they died, he convinced them to name him as their sole heir. Told them I had a mental illness. He made up many stories so they would believe it. He then walked away with a hefty inheritance, sold off all of their jewelry, valuables, and most of their furniture. As you can see, he let the mansion fall into ruin. He's threatened to run me off, but he has no interest in living in a 'shitty little cottage' as he calls it."

"Did he cause the accident that killed your parents?"

He stared at her. "You're very perceptive. To answer your question, I can't prove it, but I think he was somehow involved. My parents weren't heavy drinkers, yet Dad had a blood alcohol level significantly above the legal limit. And you can guess who was with them for dinner. Hamilton. I often wonder if he told them something that led them to drink too much. Or maybe he kept refilling their wineglasses. I'll never know for sure, but I do know he was gleeful about the money they left him, and his ability to spend it."

They sipped their tea. "You mentioned when he was home, he acted like the perfect son. Did he have any trouble at school?"

"I never heard one way or the other," Thomas answered.

"Would it surprise you to know he's driving a car from the 1970s and living in a cabin at a campground?"

"Not really. I figured he'd exhaust the inheritance earlier rather than later."

"He still projects the image of a wealthy trust fund recipient in public."

"That sounds about right. Chief, your turn. What's Hamilton done now?"

Becker gave him a synopsis of Michelle's disappearance or death, of Edward's death, of Gus's murder. Thomas listened without interrupting. When she finished, she asked, "Is Hamilton capable of killing someone?"

Thomas looked at his glass of iced tea, sweating on the vintage table cloth, for a long time before answering. "I can't believe we're talking about my baby brother. It's so surreal." He met her eyes. "Unfortunately, and sadly, I would say he is. I could see him wiping them all out and declaring himself the winner."

**

Brier Hill Academy was on the way to Jody Green's house. As she motored up the long driveway, Molly called.

"It was surprisingly easy to find information on a 1974 Chevrolet Impala. There aren't too many in Maryland, even less in New Hampshire. I'm almost sure I have a match." She gave Becker the details, and they disconnected.

Becker parked her truck in the lot. A few random vehicles sat on the pavement, including a late model Ford Pinto. She walked up to it, cupped her hands near the window, taking in the interior's neatness. She circled the car and noticed a Katy Bay sticker on the back bumper.

"Cute little car, huh?" a male voice asked behind her.

She looked over her shoulder at a man dressed in janitor clothes. "You must be Darren."

He nodded. "Yup, and you are?"

"Delaney Becker." She extended her hand, and he shook it. "Did Hamilton Parsons give you this car?"

"Whoa, Ms. Becker. You're creeping me out. How did you know my name and about the Pinto?"

She showed him her police ID. "Is there someplace we can talk?"

"Sure. It's nice enough to sit under the trees over there."

She followed him to a grove where they sat on picnic benches across from each other. "I'm a chief of police in a small town on the Eastern Shore of Maryland. It's called Celestino Village."

He smiled. "I've actually visited your town. I go down to Assateague Island to fish for marlin every two or three years. Beautiful area. So, what brings you here?"

"An investigation. Several years ago, a young woman went missing. She was Hamilton's girlfriend."

"I'll be darned. He likes girls?"

"What do you mean?"

"When he was here, he didn't date anyone, man or woman. I always thought he was, I forget the word..."

"Asexual?"

"Yup, that's it."

"Huh. How did you get the Ford Pinto, and he got your Chevy Impala?"

"I'm embarrassed to tell you I lost the Impala to him in a card game, maybe four years ago. He gave me the Pinto, a consolation prize. Said no one was using it, so I might as well have it."

***

Becker's interview with Jody Green was short. He told her Hamilton ran him off when he showed an interest in Michelle. Apparently, Hamilton told him, "I'll kill you and Michelle if you ever return to the Eastern Shore," and Jody believed him.

Chapter Forty-One

Under false pretenses, Mooney brought Hamilton into the Silver Hill police station. She told him merchandise from her store was missing and she wanted to file a report. Would he please come with her?

Becker and Guido sat in the interview room, waiting. They had worked on a script earlier that morning, after a call from Cephas Jones changed everything.

Hamilton didn't hide his surprise. "Chief Becker, Assistant Chief Tucci. What brings you here?"

"Please sit, Hamilton. We have some new information, and we need your help."

"Why the cloak and dagger? Why send Mooney after me?"

Becker shrugged. "I wanted this to be friendly, and I was afraid if I made a big deal of it, you would be less than cooperative. You've been wonderful during this investigation."

"Thanks, Chief, for the compliment." He gave her a big smile. "What do you need from me?"

"Of course I have to Mirandize you." She read the rights, then said, "I went to New Hampshire yesterday."

"It's lovely in New England, isn't it?"

"Very much so. I met Thomas."

Hamilton's face closed up momentarily. "Don't believe half of what he says. Mother and Father disowned him, and he's sour about it."

"He said your inheritance is gone."

"Not true." He wiped his mouth. "I have most of my funds in high yielding stocks and bonds."

Becker caught the tell. Putting a hand over one's mouth indicated deception. It didn't hurt to already know, through a court order, that was indeed the case. He had $489.52 to his name. And he lived in a cabin in a campground.

"Excellent choices. I could use your help with my investments. I understand you're a card shark, too." They shared a conspiratorial smile. "You won a Chevy Impala from Darren."

"I did. It's a sweet ride, a 1974 with an almost-neon-blue paint job. I love driving it when I'm not driving my Mercedes." Another lie. Becker knew it was his only car, and she wasn't about to tell him she had heard about the Impala from his neighbor.

"Nice. Darren speaks highly of you. He still appreciates you gave him the Pinto. It was in the parking lot at the Brier Hill Academy. Did you win that in a poker game, too?"

"Nah, I've won, let's see...a Rolex watch, diamond ring, two tickets to a New England Patriots game, but no other cars."

"So where did you get the Pinto?"

"I don't mind telling you, Chief, I'm one lucky man. I actually found it abandoned on the side of the road, just south of Silver Hill."

Guido said, "You mean Michelle left it and you scooped it up?"

Hamilton's eyes dilated, and he gasped. "What? That was Michelle's car?"

Becker and Guido exchanged glances. Was the guy lying or telling the truth? Becker couldn't tell.

"She worked on it at Gus's place," Guido said, "which made you mad. She spent a lot of time there. I'm surprised you didn't see it."

"Gus and I didn't get along. Why would I hang out there?"

Becker took over again in the Good Cop role. "I believe you, Hamilton." She worked out the next comment in her mind, a fib to put him off balance. "Michelle could be secretive so it doesn't surprise me. She must have hidden the car from you."

"Oh, we were very open with each other. I'm sure she thought it wasn't important for me to know about the car."

Becker looked at her notes, then at her watch, buying time. "I also talked to Jody Green when I was in New England."

"He's an asshole. Not sure why you bothered to meet with him."

"Well, he's the real reason I went to New Hampshire. See, I found a note between Edward and Michelle that mentioned him. Apparently, they were having an affair behind your back."

Hamilton's face turned red; he started shaking his right leg. When he spoke, it was with an eerie calmness. "No, they weren't. Edward was mistaken."

"I thought so, too. She was in love with you. But Edward knew her better than anyone. Why would he make it up?"

"Probably for the attention. He monopolized her time."

Guido leaned closer to Hamilton. "Is that why you killed him?"

Hamilton laughed. "That's ridiculous. Chief Becker, are you going to allow this to continue? I thought I was here to help."

She patted Guido's arm. "He gets excited, which is why he isn't chief and I am. But I'm curious. Guido, why would you think he murdered Edward?"

"Probably jealousy. After all, it was his first girlfriend, and he had to take second fiddle to Edward."

Hamilton rolled his eyes. "Didn't happen."

Becker's phone vibrated, followed by a knock on the door. Showtime.

She got up from her seat, cracked the door.

Michelle Workman stood in the doorway.

She wore a plaid shirt with a missing breast pocket, frayed cuffs, splotches of what looked like grease. Her dark blue work pants had holes in the knees, and she had mud caked on her shoes. She smelled like the marsh, faintly earthly.

Fear filled her eyes.

Becker whispered, "You're safe."

Michelle gave her a nervous smile. Even with her mismatched clothes, hair slightly tousled and tangled, pinched face, she was beautiful. She looked like Mooney, only brighter. Becker couldn't see auras, but Michelle's was surely a sunny, brilliant yellow.

Becker stood aside and let her in. Hamilton pushed back his chair with his legs, stood in one motion, scrambled to his feet, and rushed to greet her. Guido cut him off telling him to sit back down. "Michelle doesn't want you near her, or touching her. Sit and be a good boy or I'll put handcuffs on you."

"Michelle? *Oh my God*, where have you been? I've searched high and low for you."

Her voice was husky and scratchy, like an instrument rarely played. "I'm aware you've been trolling Katy Bay looking for me."

"Why didn't you show yourself? I've been worried about you! My life has been a nightmare, worrying about you living in the swamp."

"Your life has been a nightmare, how about me? I've been *hiding* from you for over five years."

"Oh, darling, you can't mean that. I love you."

"Hamilton, you only love yourself. Stop it." Michelle started trembling.

Becker put a reassuring hand on her arm. She asked, "How did you know Michelle was in the swamp?"

Hamilton couldn't take his eyes off of Michelle. "Because I found a stash of pictures Edward took of Katy Bay under the backseat of the Pinto. I remembered how much Michelle loved the place. I had a

hunch she would be there. No, more than intuition. I followed Gus
Fornash one day, then got stopped by a cop for speeding, couldn't
catch up with Gus. But I knew where he was going, the general direction."

"Wait, back up. You told me you found an abandoned Pinto; you
neglected to mention it was Michelle's vehicle."

"I was protecting her. It's my responsibility to love her, keep her
safe." Michelle blanched; Becker patted her arm.

"So that's why you went to Virginia on the weekends? To hunt for
Michelle?"

He was in a trance, looking at Michelle from head to toe, then back
again. "What?"

Guido shouted, "Hamilton! Answer the chief's question!"

It broke the spell. "Yes, every weekend. I couldn't let go. I want to
marry you, Michelle."

"No, you want to control me," Michelle said. "I'm an obsession with
you."

"I loved no one as much as you."

Michelle turned green. Becker was concerned she was going to vom-
it. She grabbed a trashcan and set it next to the emotionally fragile
woman.

"So much that you killed Edward for me?"

"I told you, Michelle, he wasn't good for you. You wouldn't listen."

"That gave you the right to murder him, murder my friend."

"He needed to be removed from your life."

"Hamilton, you are sick. There's something rotten underneath that
New England veneer. You killed Edward because he found out about
your past, the bullying, the kid you almost killed at Brier Hill Academy,
the way you scammed your parents out of their wealth. He made you
look bad, so you killed him."

He pounded his fist on the table. "Not true!"

Michelle lowered her voice. "I was there. You shot him." She shuddered. "I should have said something. Done something. But I was so afraid. Then you threatened to hurt Mooney. I couldn't let that happen."

"I love Mooney. I would never hurt her. You misunderstood."

"You're a psychopath, Hamilton."

He gave her a pitying glance. "You're mistaken. Your head is in the clouds, like it's always been."

"Wrong. You told me I had to marry you or else Mooney gets in a car wreck. What's there to misunderstand?"

"It was just words."

"Words? *Words*? You already killed my best friend; my sister was next."

"I told you; Edward was a drag on you. He had to go. But Mooney was different."

"No, she wasn't. You would have hurt anyone in your way to possess me. Like Gus. Why would you hurt him? He was like a father to me. He wasn't a threat to you."

He didn't answer.

"Gus kept my location a secret, and you couldn't stand it. He knew more than you. It made you look like a loser."

Hamilton got on his feet, yelling, "*He* was the loser! You should have seen his face right before I shot him! Wasn't such a bad-boy mafia goon then!"

Becker and Guido stood up on either side of Hamilton. She said, "You have the right to remain silent..."

***

After Becker and Guido handed Hamilton over to Keisha for booking at the state police barracks, Becker walked into the adjacent interview room, where Cephas Jones and Mooney were waiting. Mooney jumped to her feet, reminding Becker of a wind-up Jack-in-the-box. "I feel her! Michelle's here! I've been sitting here for hours. I can't wait anymore! I need to see her!"

Becker hugged her. "You know I'm not a hugger, but you need some calming energy." Mooney embraced her hard enough for Becker's breath to whoosh out of her lungs. "Breathe with me, Mooney."

They stood together until Becker felt utterly awkward, then she led Mooney to a chair.

"I can't believe we found her," said Cephas Jones. "It was God's wish, I guess. I was telling Mooney that Mel and I saw Tuggy yesterday. His nephew stopped by while we were at the shack. He heard us ask about Michelle, volunteered he had seen a woman matching that description in a little dinghy on Katy Bay. Mel and his friends jumped in a half-dozen boats, cruised the area; after a few hours, they found Michelle at secluded fish camp in a hidden cove. When she spotted them, she ran. That's when Mel told everyone to leave. He stayed behind, talked to her until she came out, pretty near an hour. It was Mooney's name that did it."

"To think she's been living in a shack on a marsh for all these years." Becker shook her head. "She's amazing."

Mooney said in a low voice, "Why would she run away? Why did she leave me behind? I've already forgiven her, but I wish I understood her reasons for doing it."

"She was protecting you," Becker said. "Hamilton threatened to hurt you. She left to keep you safe."

"Oh." Mooney's brown eyes filled with tears. "Can I please see her now?"

Becker stood up. Mooney followed. "She's fragile, Mooney. She needs us to be easy, okay? Cephas Jones, please tell Mel, your cousins and friends thank you."

He frowned at her. "No can do. Mel is already planning a welcome home party for Michelle. He wanted to call Nonna this morning, but I begged him to wait. He gave me until—" he looked at his watch—"ten minutes from now."

"Call him. Mooney, are you ready? Let's go next door."

Mooney walked into the interview room, instantly locking eyes with her long-lost, beloved sister. The women cried out loud and ran to each other. They hugged murmuring words of loss, of love, of gratitude, while they stroked each other's hair.

Becker and Guido didn't make eye contact, both rubbing the moisture from their eyes. Damned allergies, Becker thought.

Chapter Forty-Two

Nonna went all-out with Michelle's homecoming party at Mel's fish camp. About an hour ago, not one, not two, but three luxury buses spilled out forty-plus people from Silver Hill and Celestino Village, including Kevin and Lester the parrot. A banner reading *Miracles Happen* fluttered in the breeze, above a dozen tables; twice as many chairs littered the yard. Mel's friends were already at the grills, laying down hamburger patties, hotdogs, ribs. Bushels of crabs waited to be steamed.

Becker gazed at the crowd, recognized Judge Green and his son, Jody. They walked over. "It's good to see you both today," Becker said.

"Wouldn't miss it," Judge Green answered. "It's a chance to welcome Michelle home. And, Chief, say thank you for paving the way for my son to return to Delmarva. It's been too long."

"I'm happy you're back, Jody. Will you be staying?"

"I hope so."

"Good. I look forward to seeing you around town." She turned to leave, felt a hand on her arm.

"Can I talk to you for one minute, Chief?" Jody asked. "It's important."

She led him away from the activities. "What's on your mind?"

"Something's been bugging me for several years; now's the time to spill it. You may know Hamilton and I were good friends with Luciano Cavello."

"I was not aware."

"We were. Luciano and I played sports in high school, hung out and listened to music, went to the beach, that sort of thing. There were five or six of us that ran around together. When he left for college, our group fell apart. But that's only part of the story. What I wanted to tell you is Hamilton and I were with Luciano when he died at the campground."

Becker guessed at his next sentence. "You wonder whether it was an accident."

"I do. Hamilton killed Edward and Gus. Could he have murdered Luciano?"

***

A half hour later, Mooney and Michelle arrived. As they got out of Mooney's car, the crowd clapped, cheered, whistled. Michelle waved. In the months following Hamilton's arrest, she had gained weight, lost the haunted look she wore in the past. Today, she had on a long flowing dress, similar to Mooney's, with a blue and cream-colored cabochon around her neck, shimmering in the sun. If Becker remembered correctly, moonstone was for new beginnings. *Good for you*, Becker told Michelle silently.

Michelle opened the back door of the vehicle. A large, wriggly black and white puppy jumped out. His feet were enormous, his legs uncoordinated. When he pounced on Kevin, she held her breath, fearful her baby would get trampled. Kevin, however, tumbled to the side, then pounced back.

Lester the parrot yelled, "No pooping on the lawn!"

The sisters walked up to her. Mooney gently touched her right arm. Michelle reached out, put her hand on Becker's shoulder. Becker felt a...sizzle. "Whoa! How did you do that?"

Mooney giggled. "I felt you from the very beginning, when you were in Silver Hill. Remember?"

Becker nodded.

"I told you I could feel Michelle. I thought if the three of us were together, we'd create some sort of...bond. I was right."

Becker glanced around the fish camp. "Geez, Mooney, don't tell anyone." Mooney giggled again. Becker turned to Michelle. "How are you holding up?"

Mooney had told her Michelle was splitting her time between her shack in Katy Bay and Mooney's shop, sleeping on the couch. She was planning on an addition to Gus's Garage, a modest living room, kitchen, bedroom, bathroom, using sizable life insurance policy Gus had left her. The new build wasn't in compliance with zoning codes; the city council had approved the construction anyway. She was the heroine of Silver Hill. How could they not?

Since her return, Michelle had not talked to William, Meghan, or Mimi, having no interest in seeing them. She had visited Edwina several times, and was learning how to fly drones, courtesy of Birdy, who apparently was a good teacher.

"I've apparently lost my mind in adopting a Great Dane/Dalmatian mix." Her warm gaze landed on the puppy, staring at Lester the parrot, who said, "Here's looking at you, kid."

Michelle laughed at the parrot then continued. "His name is Edward. May he be half the friend Edward Landon was." She handed Becker a small package, the size of a cigar box. "This is for you. I wanted to say thanks."

Becker unwrapped the bundle. A photograph of Katy Bay at sunset, the golden sky reflected in the rippling waters. "It's lovely."

"Mooney told me you are an artist." Becker scowled at Mooney. "Your secret is safe with me. Anyway, I thought the artist in you would love the colors and vibe."

"I do. Thank you, Michelle," Becker said, as she caught sight of William Workman at the corner of her vision. She hoped she didn't screw up today by asking him to come. She held her breath.

"Michelle," he whispered. She slowly turned around; her body stiffened.

Becker stood beside her. "I invited William. Mostly for selfish reasons. You see, my dad died when I was young, I've lived most of my life without him. Forgive me but I wanted more for you." She paused then touched Michelle's arm, feeling that little jolt again. "Also, because William is a wonderful soul; you wouldn't be here today if he didn't insist on us finding you."

When he got within a foot of Michelle, she launched herself at him. He caught her and twirled her around, kissing her face. "I missed you! I am so sorry! I should have treasured your quirkiness and quick wit before but I'll make up for it now!" He held her a few inches away, saying right into her face. "If you want to play the trombone in front of Ladybank Manor, I'll invite the town to listen!"

"Aw, Daddy, I play the banjo now! I taught myself! Now put me down." He did, and they held hands. "What would Mother say about me playing a banjo at the mansion? That's so *gauche*."

His face was somber. "Mimi isn't living at the house anymore. I've ensured she is in a home of her liking, and she may visit from time to time." He sighed. "I can't divorce her; I feel an obligation, and will take care of her, but that doesn't mean I have to be subjected to her...issues, I guess that's as good a word as any."

Michelle touched his cheek. "Always the gentleman, always strong of character. Always doing the right thing."

"While I have you holding my hand, I want to talk to you about us doing the right thing with Meghan."

She growled at him. "I guess I get my persistence from you."

"She's had a tough time, Michelle. I'm convinced she turned to prescription drugs because of our...mess...of a family. I'm grateful to you for pushing her to go to rehabilitation, even if it meant you got knocked in the head with a glass."

"No gratitude necessary, Daddy. It was a turning point for me. Mother had already tried to bribe me to leave. Mooney's wellbeing was threatened by a psychopath who had killed my best friend, and my other sister was on the brink of a drug addiction disaster. When I woke up from the glass incident, I realized the only way out, so to speak, was to leave. Gus and I had already bought my, um...house in Katy Bay with the money Mother gave me. Months before, he helped me plan an exit strategy just in case. He was one of my best friends so I had confided in him about, well...everything." She paused, eyes intent on her father. "What I'm trying to say is everything turns out as it should."

"I love you, Michelle."

"I love you to the moon and back, Daddy."

***

Nonna said to Michelle, "You don't look like a swamp monster."

Becker, sitting within earshot, said, "Nonna!" then shut up when Michelle smiled.

"I understand you were integral to the investigation. Thank you, Teresa."

Nonna sat up in her chair, causing the button between her breasts to pop. Not surprising since the glittery, sleeveless dress, with matching shoes, was for a person much smaller than Nonna. "Shit! I mean, yes, I was very involved. Organized several search parties, that sort of thing. You are welcome." She sipped her vodka spritzer, with a smidge of spritzer, yelling, "Excuse me, partygoers! I have a button emergency! Joey, can you come here?"

He ran over, corn hole tournament temporarily suspended. "Yes, love?"

"Can you tell the bus driver I need my suitcase? I'm going to change into my evening wear."

Becker picked up her glass of Sancerre, shaking her head. A costume change, already.

Joey headed off to the bus as Nonna said, "Where were we?"

"You bring a suitcase to a welcome home party?" Michelle looked at her like a child studies a strange bug.

"Honey, you've been tromping around the marsh for too long. Of course I bring several changes of clothes to a party. You need to go shopping with me..."

Becker excused herself. She walked to the dock and sat down. Kevin followed, sitting next to her. She ran her fingers through his wiry hair.

"Delaney?"

She startled and unconsciously answered, "Yes?"

Angelo sat down, leaned over and smelled her hair.

She smiled. "Stop that."

Last Words about Kathryn

Murder at Bloodstone Bay is book two in the Delaney Becker series. Look for book one, *Murder at Capri Cottage*, to learn how Becker got started solving murder mysteries.

Murder at Cassina Cove, number three in the series, will be published in 2025. And if you're not a series kind of person, you can read the books as standalone.

Stay in touch!

Website: www.kathryndanko.com

Facebook: www.facebook.com/KathrynDankoAuthor

Instagram: www.instagram.com/kathryndankoauthor

BOOK REVIEWS MATTER! Please leave one on on Amazon, Goodreads, or wherever you purchase books on-line, or drop me an email at kathryn@kathryndanko.com.

———

Kathryn has been writing since she was twelve years old, mostly poems tha twere unsophisticated; her Mama loved them anyway. She retired from corporate America in 2022 and began writing full time, traditional mysteries light on gore and heavy on humor.

She's a self-professed Chicken Queen, once caring for fifty in her backyard on the Eastern Shore of Maryland. She currently lives in Ohio in a cottage on Lake Erie with her beloved Yorkshire Terrier named Winner Winner Chicken Dinner, AKA Winnie.

Kathryn graduated from The Ohio State University with a Poultry Science major. She also holds an MBA from Wilmington University.

Made in the USA
Coppell, TX
13 November 2024

40179961R00174